It seemed the fortune cookie predictions from
Destiny House were eerily accurate....

ROMANCE IN AN EXOTIC PLACE

DON'T JUDGE A BOOK BY ITS COVER

BEWARE OF...

DECEPTION BRINGS HEARTACHE

For Zara, Laura and Darcy, three longtime pals,
a fateful gals' night out proved one certainty:
Expect the unexpected!

FORTUNE COOKIE

Three romantic adventures by
Janice Kaiser
M.J. Rodgers
and Margaret St. George

ABOUT THE AUTHORS

Janice Kaiser—A former lawyer and college instructor, prolific author Janice Kaiser now has to her credit over forty novels—translated into twenty languages—and a worldwide following. She turned to writing in 1985 after marrying her husband, Ronn, also a writer. She and Ronn collaborate on women's fiction for MIRA books, and make their home in Northern California, although Janice's fascination with exotic locales has taken her to over forty different countries.

M.J. Rodgers—In the few short years since M.J. Rodgers burst onto the romantic suspense scene, she has crafted more than twenty novels. Several have been nominated for Reviewers' Choice awards by *Romantic Times*, and in 1992, M.J. received a Career Achievement Award for romantic mysteries. Now a full-time writer, M.J. has held positions in numerous corporations and has traveled extensively throughout the world. Though she has lived in Europe, Asia and the Middle East, she now makes her home with her family in the Pacific Northwest.

Margaret St. George—A native of Colorado, the talented Ms. St. George is the author of over thirty novels, in categories ranging from historical, to mystery, to romantic romp. A recent innovative title was *He Said, She Said*, a unique dual-perspective story written in collaboration with her friend and colleague, Jasmine Cresswell. Maggie brings a wealth of life experience to her writing, having served as a flight attendant for United Airlines, as well as the national president of the Romance Writers of America. The winner of numerous awards, Maggie is hard at work on her next project, a story for the upcoming Delta Justice series. Watch for *For the Love of Beau*, a May 1998 publication.

FORTUNE COOKIE

JANICE KAISER
M.J. RODGERS
MARGARET ST. GEORGE

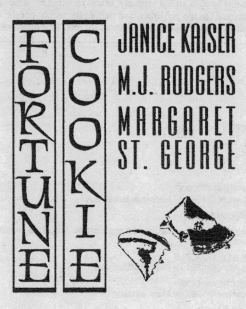

Harlequin Books

TORONTO • NEW YORK • LONDON
AMSTERDAM • PARIS • SYDNEY • HAMBURG
STOCKHOLM • ATHENS • TOKYO • MILAN
MADRID • WARSAW • BUDAPEST • AUCKLAND

FORTUNE COOKIE
Copyright © 1997 by Harlequin Books S.A.

ISBN 0-373-83331-8

The publisher acknowledges the copyright holders of the individual works as follows:

DOUBLE TROUBLE
Copyright © 1997 by Belles-Lettres, Inc.

THE DREAM DOC
Copyright © 1997 by Mary Johnson

DEAR DARCY<g>
Copyright © 1997 by Maggie Osborne

CONTENTS

DOUBLE TROUBLE

Janice Kaiser

Dear Reader,

Several years ago, my best friend gave me a Lucite paperweight that was shaped like a star. It was filled with silver glitter and came with a card that instructed you to make a wish before turning the paperweight over, and the wish would come true. My friend told me she nearly walked away in search of another gift. Then she stopped and thought, "What if it really works?"

At one time or another, we have all made wishes and wondered if they would come true. Nearly everyone wants to know what the future holds—whether it be romance, adventure or mystery. That got me to thinking about fortunes in general, and fortune cookies in particular. What if there was a very special Chinese restaurant that passed out fortune cookies whose fortunes always came true! That is exactly what happens to my heroine in "Double Trouble." The snag is that she gets two very different fortunes in one cookie—and since she is a twin, she can't be sure which fortune is hers.

I hope you enjoy Zara's and Arianna's adventures as much as I enjoyed writing them. And I hope you'll be sure to look for Lina's story in my October Superromance novel, *This Child is Mine*, and Arianna's story in my November Temptation novel, *Double Take*. And the next time you get to a Chinese restaurant, I hope you pull a wonderful fortune that comes true!

Janice Kaiser

PROLOGUE

"IT'S TIME TO SPEAK to the gods of fortune," Madame Wu announced softly. "Are you ladies ready?"

"That's why we came to Destiny House," Zara said, smiling at Madame Wu and then at her two oldest and dearest friends. "Arianna swears the fortune cookies here are very special."

Laura tapped her fingernails on the tablecloth. "I miss Ari. I wish she could have joined us. It figures, doesn't it? I came all the way from the West Coast for this old friends reunion. You came from Colorado. But your sister, who lives here in New York, is the one who has an appointment and can't make dinner." She smiled at Darcy. "I'm glad our other local New Yorker could make it."

"No way I'd miss seeing you two," Darcy said. She looked up at Madame Wu. "Sure, bring on the fortune cookies. Heaven knows I could use a little good fortune."

"I shall return in a moment," Madame Wu

said, smiling enigmatically. "Think good thoughts." Coolly elegant in a floor-length black silk dress, she glided toward another table.

Darcy rolled her eyes. "Oh, brother. Did she really tell us to think good thoughts?"

"Seriously," Zara said in a hushed voice. "Ari swears by this place. She says it's positively uncanny the way the fortunes seem to come true."

Destiny House was deceptive, her twin sister had been right about that. From the outside it looked like another hole-in-the-wall restaurant, one of many in Manhattan's Chinatown. But inside, Destiny House offered sheer elegance. Red-and-gold flecked wallpaper adorned the walls providing an opulent backdrop for ancient-looking porcelain vases and painted screens. The table and chairs were polished cherry wood, and the artwork appeared impressively expensive.

Laura tossed a wave of mink-colored hair over her shoulder. "Is Madame Wu going to try to read our minds?"

"You're kidding," Darcy blinked at them. "You two aren't buying into this, are you?"

Leaning back, Zara smiled affectionately. All four of them, she and Arianna, Darcy and Laura had left Denver and moved out into the world. They were more polished than they had been in high school, but their basic traits hadn't changed much in the last ten years. Laura was still gutsy and determined, Darcy still bright and funny. Zara decided she, too, was the same at heart, still cautious, still taking responsibility for everything around her.

Laura poured another cup of tea from the pot on their table. "Then Ari's fortune must have come true when she was here last. What did it say?"

"Yeah, tell us," Darcy echoed, smiling. "Did Ari's fortune predict that she'd break her engagement a month before the wedding and stick the three of us with bridesmaid's dresses and plane tickets?"

"Good question." Now that she thought about it, Zara wondered why she hadn't asked Ari what her fortune had predicted. And she should have dug a little further into why Ari sounded almost a little spooky when she mentioned Destiny House and Madame Wu, as if she were recommending a psychic instead of a restaurant.

"What if I get a god-awful fortune?" Darcy asked with an exaggerated groan, pulling her napkin through her fingers. "That would be just my luck."

"We're about to find out," Laura said, nodding toward Madame Wu who was coming their way, carrying a silver tray.

Zara smiled and considered the crescent-shaped cookies arranged on Madame Wu's tray. "Let's see, which one to choose..."

"I will decide," Madame Wu said firmly. "I know which cookie for which lady."

"You match us to the fortunes?" Zara inquired, surprised.

"No, miss. Only the gods know which fortune inside each cookie."

Zara didn't dare watch Darcy struggling not to laugh, so she kept her gaze on the tray. But Darcy was right, this was silly. So was the odd tension that even her rational attorney's mind couldn't overcome. She reminded herself that she didn't believe in fortunes any more than she believed in astrology. But she did read her daily horoscope in the newspaper, she recalled uncomfortably.

Madame Wu studied each of them with a penetrating look, then she extended the tray to Darcy. Darcy shook back a mop of brown curls and blinked. "Me first?"

"This one for you," Madame Wu said, pointing to the smallest cookie.

"Ta da!" Darcy cracked open the cookie and withdrew a slender strip of paper.

"What does it say?" Laura asked, leaning toward Darcy, trying to peek.

"Am I supposed to keep it secret?" Darcy asked Madame Wu.

"That is your choice."

"Come on, Darcy," Laura said. "Don't keep us in suspense."

"It's disappointing, actually. It says 'Deception brings heartache.'" She shrugged. "You know me. America's oldest Girl Scout. About as deceptive as a Cabbage Patch doll." She crumpled the thin tissue in her hand.

"Sometimes the meaning is clear right away, sometimes it is not," Madame Wu said quietly.

"Oh! Wait a minute."

"Oh, what?" Zara asked, leaning forward. "I know that expression. You just thought of something."

Darcy placed her fortune on the table and smoothed the slip of paper with her finger, reading it again with a slight frown. "Maybe this does make sense," she admitted slowly, her cheeks turning pink. Then she raised a hand and glared. "No, don't even ask because I won't tell you. It would be too embarassing."

Madame Wu extended the tray to Laura. "Now, you. Take the smaller of the two."

"The itty-bitty one? You're sure?" Laura

teased. At five foot nine, she was six inches taller than Zara and Darcy, and it was a long-standing joke that Laura's height entitled her to the biggest of everything. She accepted the cookie Madame Wu indicated and cracked it open.

A thin slip of paper fluttered out of the cookie and into her tea. "I guess this isn't going to be a good-luck fortune," she said, fishing her fortune out of her cup. "Oh, no."

"What?" Zara and Darcy asked in unison.

"I can't read it. All I can make out are the first two words. 'Beware of...'" Laura looked up at Madame Wu. "What's the rest of my fortune?"

Madame Wu regarded her from bottomless black eyes. "I wouldn't know, miss."

"Maybe it was a warning not to drink ink-flavored tea," Laura said with a laugh, as she pushed her ruined tea aside.

"The last cookie is for you, Miss Hamilton," Madame Wu said, extending the tray.

Zara took the remaining cookie and broke it open and then gasped. "There are *two* fortunes!"

Darcy and Laura looked at each other. "Now, that is weird," Darcy commented.

Laura nodded. "Zara has an identical twin sister," she explained to Madame Wu. "What do the fortunes say?" she asked, turning back to Zara.

"This one must be Ari's. It says 'Never judge a book by its cover.'"

Darcy groaned. "Pretty obvious." She, too, seemed compelled to explain to Madame Wu. "Zara's sister edits celebrity biographies." She leaned toward Zara again. "What does yours say?"

"'You'll find romance in an exotic place.'"

Darcy sighed. "Why couldn't I have gotten a great fortune like that?" she asked.

"Most people consider Aspen an exotic place," Laura suggested. "You might find romance in your own backyard, Zara. Of course, living there, you probably don't consider Aspen too exotic."

"Maybe I've got it wrong," Zara said, placing the two fortunes side by side in front of her. "The book fortune could be mine. Maybe it means I shouldn't underestimate an opponent in a lawsuit, or take a client at his word. I'll let Arianna have the romance," she added with a laugh.

While they waited for Madame Wu to bring the bill, their conversation dwindled for the first time since they'd reunited. Zara was first to break the silence. "Wouldn't it be strange if Ari is right and the fortunes here do come true?" She reread the two fortunes in front of her.

"Well, I for one hope they don't," Darcy said

firmly, glancing at her watch. "Or I'm in for some heartache."

"Let's tell each other in our Christmas cards if our fortunes came true."

"That's going to be hard for me since I don't know what I'm supposed to beware of," Laura said, opening her purse and taking out her wallet.

"Maybe your fortune is one of those things you'll recognize in retrospect." Darcy slid out of the booth and smoothed down a tailored skirt. "I'm not sure if I like this place," she said thoughtfully, looking around. "The food is wonderful and it's a beautiful facility...but there's something, I don't know. I guess it's the big production Madame Wu made out of the fortune cookies. Like our fate really was about to be revealed."

Laura reached over to pat her friend's arm. "Hey, it's all just for fun, right?" She looked to Zara for confirmation.

Zara didn't say anything, but she shared the same uneasiness she sensed from Darcy. There was something almost foreboding about Madame Wu and the fortune cookie experience that made her chest feel tight.

On the other hand...Darcy was the least deceptive person she knew, Ari was not the type to judge a book by its cover, and she had no plans to take an exotic romantic trip. As for Laura, they didn't know her fortune, but most likely it was as improbable as the others.

After they walked out the restaurant doors, Zara glanced over her shoulder and was struck again by Destiny House's deceptive exterior. Oddy disturbed, she tried to identify what was bothering her.

What if fortunes did come true...?

CHAPTER ONE

As Zara let herself into Arianna's upper floor apartment in a brownstone in Murray Hill, she heard her sister talking on the phone in the kitchen.

"No," Arianna said, "it's not that at all. I am interested in your book, but you're asking too much. I can't drop everything I'm doing. If you'll send me the manuscript I'll... Okay, I understand it's very sensitive and you're under pressure, but I'm getting on a plane at Kennedy tomorrow afternoon for Martinique.... Well no, it's not exactly a vacation, I'll be taking my work with me.... All right, tell you what, give me your number and as soon as I get back I'll call you.... You can't give me your phone number, that's...unusual. Then I guess you'll just have to call me in a week."

Zara headed for the bedroom. She dumped her purse and jacket on the bed, and returned to the kitchen. Arianna, wearing a pink silk teddy, was still on the phone. Her feet were bare and she was peering into the refrigerator.

"I'm sorry, Mr....X, but that's the best I can do. Yes, I know it's urgent. The best I can do is try to get in touch with the editor in chief to run this past him. But you really have to give me a week. Okay?" Arianna said as she pulled a bottle of wine from the fridge. Looking up, she pointed to the wine as if to ask if Zara wanted some. She did and so she nodded at Arianna.

"Talk to you in a week," Arianna said, then hung up.

Zara raised her brows. "Mr. X?"

"Yeah. Can you believe it? This guy claims to have written a dynamite exposé on the underworld, but he won't tell me his name." Arianna got a couple of wineglasses down from the cupboard. "And that's not the best part. Mr. X swears he's got a list of cops, judges and prosecutors that are on the Mafia's payroll. He says he's prepared to blow the lid off the system." She poured the wine into the glasses.

"So why did you put him off?"

"For a couple of reasons. First, I'm not sure he's legitimate. And second, it kind of spooked me that he called here. I didn't give him my home number, and when I asked how he got it, he said, 'There are ways, sweetheart.'"

Zara shivered. "I don't think I'd want anything to do with him."

Arianna touched her wineglass to Zara's and they both took a sip.

"Neither would I," Arianna said, "except that if everything checks out, this book could make my career, because *I* would have brought it in."

"How did Mr. X find you, anyway?"

Arianna led the way into the small living room. "He says he saw me on TV when I did that interview on a talk show a while back. And he figures that since I edit celebrity biographies, I must know how to deal with big shots, and once his book is out, he'll be the biggest thing to hit publishing this year."

They plopped down in facing armchairs.

"Is he right?" Zara asked.

"That depends. If he does have genuine inside knowledge of the workings of the top two Mafia families in New York, the book will hit all the bestseller lists and he'll stand to make a mint."

"What are you going to do?" Zara asked.

Arianna sighed. "I don't know. I'm beginning to wonder if it was a mistake to put him off. Maybe I should have agreed to meet with him."

"But you're leaving for Martinique. That trip is paid for. You *have* to go."

Arianna leaned back in her chair and crossed

her legs. Zara could almost see the wheels turning. Her sister was ambitious. She'd gone to college planning to teach after she got her doctorate
in English, but after getting her B.A., she'd
headed to New York to make her fortune, saying
she wouldn't rest until she had her own imprint
at a top publishing house.

While Zara plodded her way through law
school and set up her practice in Aspen, close to
home, Arianna was working her way up through
the ranks at Symington and Sons. Last February,
she'd announced that she was engaged to Mark
Lindsay of the New York Lindsays, one of the
wealthiest banking families on the East Coast.
Then, the next thing Zara knew, Arianna had broken off with Mark only a month before the wedding, because, as she said, "There's something
wrong, I do love Mark, I do. But... Something
is missing."

Nothing Arianna did could surprise her at this
point. Zara contemplated her sister, almost afraid
to ask what she was thinking.

"Arianna? You *are* going, aren't you?"

"I'm not sure. I'll have to think about it." Ar-
ianna sloshed her wine around in the glass.
"Enough about that," she said, brightening.
"How'd you find Destiny House?"

"Oh, it was…different. Madame Wu definitely is a character."

"Isn't she something?" Arianna smiled sort of sadly, as though remembering her last experience at Destiny House. "Sorry to stand you guys up, by the way. I hope Laura and Darcy weren't too upset."

"Only about the fact you were having dinner with Richard Gere while we had to eat with each other. How'd it go, anyway? Did he do anything that would make us wild with jealousy?"

"It was strictly business," Arianna assured her. "Richard was very pleasant and charming, but a gentleman every minute."

"You're so blasé," Zara teased. "We get our share of celebrities in Aspen, too, but I'm not in the habit of having dinner with them."

"I guess it's all a matter of what you're used to."

"Speaking of which, I'm not used to dressing like this. I've got to get out of these clothes," Zara said. "Mind if I change?"

"Make yourself comfortable, by all means."

Zara headed toward the bedroom. Arianna followed. As Zara undressed, Arianna sat on the bed, sipping her wine.

"You haven't told me about your fortune," Arianna said. "What's in store for you?"

"I'm going to have a long, prosperous life," Zara quipped as she rummaged through her suitcase until she found the cotton turtleneck she was looking for, then pulled it over her head.

"Oh, come on, they don't have dumb fortunes like that at the Destiny House."

Zara got her jeans from her suitcase. "Actually, I got two fortunes in one cookie, so I assume fate has intended one for you." She wiggled into her jeans, then sat next to Arianna, folding her slender legs under her. As she did, she admired the way her sister looked in the teddy. The two of them were petite, with strawberry blond hair and blue-green eyes. Being identical twins, they were nearly impossible to tell apart, though Zara had a few brown speckles on her nose that Arianna didn't have, and Arianna had a chicken pox scar on her left temple.

"Wait, you got *two* fortunes and one is for me?" Arianna said.

"Wouldn't you assume that's what it meant?" Zara picked up her purse and pulled out the fortunes, handing them to Arianna. "Maybe they're both for you, now that I think about it. After all, you edit books...and you *are* going to the Caribbean. That qualifies as an exotic place, don't you think?"

Arianna stared at the slips of paper as Zara

retrieved some socks and put them on. Her head bowed. Arianna studied the fortunes. Then she began to sniffle.

"Ari, what's wrong?"

Arianna smiled at her briefly, then looked away, wiping her eyes. "Every once in a while it hits me that I was going to marry Mark tomorrow."

"But you..."

"Yes, I know," Arianna said, "*I* broke the engagement." She looked into Zara's eyes. "I did the right thing. I wasn't meant to marry Mark. He might not have seen it, but I did." She sighed. "Even so, I'm not sure I can handle going on what would have been our honeymoon, but Mark was so insistent. He said it was a shame to let such a dream of a vacation go to waste. It was paid for. He couldn't go so I should. But the only reason I agreed was because I wanted to sound brave and indifferent and wanted him to think that going alone wouldn't bother me one bit."

"I hate to say this, but don't you think that maybe you broke up with Mark without really thinking your decision through? Maybe you really want to marry him, after all."

"No, I *know* what I want, Zara," Arianna said,

sounding defensive. "I don't want to marry Mark, and I don't want to go to Martinique."

"This is the second thing I hate to say, but you're really getting spoiled," Zara said. "First, you have dinner with Richard Gere and come home yawning. Then you complain about having to fly to the Caribbean. What's with you? Next, you'd probably be turning up your nose at the prospect of romance with some tall, dark stranger."

"Actually I would, so there," Arianna said, crinkling her nose. "Trust me, romance is the last thing on my mind. What I'd really like to do is go home to Colorado. Just for a week or so. To take a little vacation from my life."

"Why not come back with me, then?" Zara said.

"No, I've got a better idea. Those fortunes have gotten me to thinking. Why don't *you* go to Martinique in my place? And *I'll* go to Aspen."

"What?"

"I'm serious," Arianna insisted. "Take my ticket and go. Everything's paid for. And I can take a pile of manuscripts and go to your place. I can catch up on my work, recharge my emotional batteries and get the vacation I need. Don't you see, Zara, it's a great idea. The romance fortune can be yours, too!"

"Ari, that's crazy. I have work at home. Besides, I don't have the right clothes with me, or my passport. And anyway, the ticket's in your name."

"You can use my clothes. The suitcase is packed with a sexy trousseau and you know darn well everything will fit! And I'll give you my passport. Nobody in customs would know the difference."

"I can't do that."

"Why not? You need a change of pace, some excitement in your life. And I need a little down-home quiet."

"What about Mr. X?" Zara said.

Arianna frowned. "That's another thing. I'll talk to Jerry about that and, if need be, I can always hop a flight back here. That'd be harder to do from Martinique. But a trip to the Caribbean would be perfect for you. How long since you've really let down your hair?"

It was too long, and Zara knew it. She hated to admit it, but the idea was appealing. She thought about what it might be like to stay at a fabulous resort, maybe meet an exotic Frenchman. Could the romance fortune be hers? No. She was crazy to even consider switching places. "I have appointments next week. A big deposition is scheduled."

Arianna shrugged. "So postpone it. For once in your life, do something impulsive! Besides, it's your turn to get into trouble. Remember the time I switched places with you in high school and went out on a blind date with what's his name?"

Zara laughed. "That was a huge success. What's his name fell madly in love with you, and was hounding me for the rest of the school year."

"See, this is my way of making that up to you," Arianna said.

"Yeah, sure," Zara said, in a skeptical tone of voice. "Then why do I feel this is going to be a double trouble repeat?"

ZARA ARRIVED AT Kennedy International the next afternoon feeling like some kind of criminal. She'd never done anything more dishonest than cutting class in high school. Yet here she was, wearing Arianna's clothes, carrying her passport, and using her name.

The porter carried her bags to the ticket counter. Zara stood in line, feeling more and more nervous about being found out as she got closer to the front of the line. But the check-in went smoothly. The passenger agent scarcely glanced at the passport.

Zara headed off for the gate, her carry-on bag

in one hand, her purse in the other. Having made it past the passenger agent, she felt exhilarated, and was finally into the spirit of her adventure. She was almost looking forward to the mischief...and romance, coming her way—that was if the fortune selected for her by Madame Wu was right!

To be completely, absolutely, positively honest, she'd have to admit she'd been a little jealous when Arianna had found love and romance with Mark. Mark had a MBA from an Ivy League university, came from a monied background and was a very social, people person—everything her sister had claimed she'd wanted. And Zara had thought he was one of the nicest men she'd *ever* met. Why Arianna had dumped him, she still didn't have a clue. The only thing she could think was that the romance had come a little too easy for Ari. Her sister had always thrived on challenge.

A good, loving man like Mark was hard to find—Zara knew from experience. Although she found her work fulfilling, and had many close friends, she ached to have a man in her life. Someone she could really care for.

As she neared the gate she suddenly felt a presence beside her. She glanced over and caught sight of a man in his late forties—a man with a dark, somber face—edging close to her. He was unshaven and wore a rumpled suit without a tie.

When she moved over a bit, he stayed right with her. "I need to talk to you, Miss Hamilton," he said, "but please don't look at me. Just keep walking."

Zara didn't know what to think, but she kept moving. "Who *are* you?" she said. "And what do you want?"

"You said on the phone you were flying out of Kennedy to Martinique. I took a hell of a chance coming here and hanging around, waiting for you to show up, but I had to get this to you." He opened his jacket, showing a fat manila envelope. "You said you'd be working on your vacation, so I thought you might as well read the book. I know you're the right editor for this. I figure if you were able to make Tom Arnold's autobiography a bestseller just think what you can do with something that has real drama. This book has *bestseller* written all over it."

Suddenly Zara understood. "You're Mr. X!" she exclaimed.

"Keep it down, sweetheart. God knows who might be watching."

"Look," she said, "you've made a terrible mistake. I'm not—"

"Please," he said, cutting her off. "You're

Arianna Hamilton, so don't pretend you're not. Remember, I saw you on TV. I'm not asking much. And we can't talk now, not here. Just take this and I'll call you when you get back.''

The next thing Zara knew he was shoving the envelope in her hands.

''But...''

Before she could get another word out, the man turned abruptly and dashed into a nearby men's room. He seemed so paranoid and uptight that she didn't want to go over and stand outside the rest room until he came out so she could explain. The heavy envelope in her hand, Zara wasn't sure what to do next.

She chewed her lip, thinking. Mr. X wanted to get the manuscript to Arianna. She could always mail it to her sister in Aspen. And that way she'd be certain that he didn't change his mind and give the book to another editor. Arianna had been definite about wanting to have a look at it. Yes, that seemed best for all concerned. Zara stuffed the envelope into her carry-on and continued on her way to Gate J where she was boarding the plane to Martinique.

Behind her, she heard a commotion. There were shouts and several men came scurrying out the men's room. People up and down the concourse were turning to see what the yelling was about. Then suddenly the doors flew open again and Mr. X came out, a huge burly man holding each of his arms. Mr. X looked terrified.

The trio made their way back along the concourse, toward the terminal building. Good heavens, she thought, remembering how Arianna had insisted that an adventure would do her good. She wasn't even in the Caribbean yet, and she was already mixed up in something. Maybe something dangerous.

a foul. Then recrossed the bay. They tied their up until 10 o'clock, except Larry. Larry had to help Gabriel the crane. Mr. K looked half red.

The others their way back along the reefs, toward the sea. Good day to you, said though it was a. Good news invited him, an absentee would to her good

CHAPTER TWO

ALEC PERRIN largely ignored the two French-women who'd been watching him since they'd arrived at the Métropole Café ten minutes earlier. They were about forty, six or seven years older than he, and had the unmistakable air of married women looking for a good time. He'd encountered a lot of that in his years in the Caribbean—more than he'd cared to see. There were plenty of single women around, if he was interested, which right then he wasn't. Romance had become more trouble than it was worth.

With the ceiling fan creaking overhead, Alec drew on his beer, glancing around the café, which had seen better days. Through the dusty, faded plantation shutters next to him, Alec caught sight of Emile Fouré, one of the village's two gendarmes, approaching the Métropole. The officer looked to be on an important errand judging by his purposeful walk. He made his way to the entrance of the café and peered around the semidarkened interior. Emile spotted Alec and strode to his table.

"Here you are! I've been looking for you all over," he said.

"What's up?" Alec said.

Emile, looking very official in his uniform, his kepi sitting smartly on his head, pulled up a chair next to Alec and leaned forward, lowering his voice in a confidential manner. "You've had an urgent call from the police in New York," he said, speaking softly.

Emile clearly regarded a message from a fellow policeman to be of paramount importance. Alec wasn't so sure. Since leaving the NYPD, he'd had no contact with anyone with a badge— at least not with any American with a badge.

"Concerning what?"

Emile shrugged. Alec had discovered early on that Emile took himself quite seriously where his official duties were concerned.

"You must call them back. You can use the telephone in the station, if you like," he said, his expression dour.

They left the café together. Alec noticed disappointment register on the faces of the two Frenchwomen. He smiled, his ego having gotten a little boost. Emile picked up on the byplay.

"One day you'll take advantage of your powers with women," he said. "It is a crime that you don't."

"Emile, mon ami," he said, slapping his friend on the back, "after a while holiday romances become pointless and unfulfilling."

"Are you saying you're ready to settle down?"

"I don't know, Emile. Maybe I'm just getting old."

It wasn't far to the gendarmerie. Any walk in the hot tropical sun was too far, though. Emile led him to the only private office in the station, pointing ceremoniously to the phone. Then, before leaving, Emile handed him the slip of paper with the information he'd need to make the call. Alec was surprised to see Lou Sheridan's name and extension written in Emile's careful block printing.

He dialed and, getting a switchboard operator, waited to be transferred. Alec knew Lou Sheridan, but not well. They'd worked together briefly on the White Collar Crime Task Force during his final year on the force. The last he'd heard, Sheridan was working the organized crime detail.

"Alec," Lou said, coming on the line, "how are all the palm trees and hula girls treating you?"

"I don't pay much attention to the palm trees

and the hula girls are in Hawaii, Lou. What's up? Yours is the last voice I'd expect to hear.''

"We've got a situation," he said. "I thought maybe you could help us with it...if you're available.''

Alec couldn't imagine any sort of situation in the NYPD that would require his help, but he was curious. "Yeah, I'm listening.''

"We've got a woman on a plane, headed your way, and she's carrying extremely sensitive information concerning the mob. It's a book manuscript, and what's in it could be very embarrassing to a number of people.''

"Yeah, go on.''

"Well, what we need is nothing real fancy. We'd like to have that manuscript.''

Alec paused before responding. "Are you saying you want me to steal it?''

"I don't know if I'd put it that crudely. We thought you might persuade her to cooperate.''

"I see. Who is the woman? And what's her connection to the mob?''

"Her name's Arianna Hamilton. She's in publishing. It'd be nice if you could figure out her angle in this, as well.''

"Then she's not engaged in any criminal activities?''

"We don't think so.''

Alec considered that. "If that's the case, it ought to be easy enough to just ask for the manuscript. She'll probably be glad to cooperate…in fact, I don't see why you didn't contact the local gendarmes and have them talk to her."

"No, no. That's the last thing we want." Lou lowered his voice theatrically. "In fact, the reason we need you is because we have to keep our involvement out of it. This is one of those semi-official operations, if you know what I mean. But don't worry, we intend to pay you. Handsomely."

Suddenly Alec understood. The NYPD was not in the business of subsidizing ex-cops. So if Lou Sheridan was offering serious money for a job that sounded simple—and he wanted to keep it hush-hush to boot—then there was a catch. "Somehow I feel I'm only getting part of the story, Lou. I don't like getting involved in things blind. You should have known that. Besides, if this concerns the mob, there's bound to be some of them lurking in the bushes somewhere."

"Possibly."

"I don't think I'm interested. But thanks for thinking of me."

"Hold on, Alec. The girl's all you have to worry about. Get the manuscript and you've earned a fast five grand. Then go sailing off on your boat."

Alec Perrin thought again. "That's too easy, Lou. I may be a fool, but not that big a fool. You want my help, you've got to level with me."

There was a long pause, then Sheridan groaned. "All right, but I'm counting on you to be discreet, understand?"

"Right, Lou."

"Okay, here's the story. There's this Mafia consigliere, a guy named Sal Corsi, who had a falling out with the top bananas of the Pantano family, right? He wants to get even with them and feather his own nest at the same time. And since he's got the goods on everybody, that won't be hard. He's prepared to spill his guts but he wants big bucks for his story, not just a spot in the witness protection program. Bottom line is, he writes this exposé, figuring it's going to make him big bucks. Any way, this afternoon he hands the manuscript to the Hamilton girl at JFK. We find out later she gets on a plane for Martinique. I ask around about who we know down there and whose name comes up but yours. And so here we are, talking."

"Yeah, Lou, but why are you so hot to get the manuscript? What's the harm if it gets published?"

"There's two things," Sheridan said. "First, we know the mob's hot to get their hands on it. So hot that Sal Corsi got whacked out at JFK. Right in the parking lot. I had some people out there, and when we saw some guys dragging Corsi off we moved in. They shot him on the spot rather than let us get hold of him. They got away, but before he died Corsi told us that he passed the manuscript to the girl. There's gotta be stuff in there that would finger a lot of people. Second thing is, Sal Corsi not only had the goods on the mob, he had the details on our antiorganized crime operation. He knew everybody we had undercover, all our mob informants, everything."

"How did he get that?"

"The S.O.B. must have got to one of our people and bribed him."

"But didn't tell his bosses what he'd learned?"

"Naw, he was already going his own way. He's had everybody by the balls, believe me. If his exposé is published, it sets us back five years and a ton of bucks."

"How do you know all this, Lou?"

"Because Corsi came to us awhile back, wanting to deal, but like I said, he wanted big bucks and we couldn't meet his terms. So he went underground. Not the smartest thing he could have done because his buddies eventually got him."

"And now the girl has his legacy."

"Exactly," Sheridan said. "We get the manuscript before the boys in the Mafia, then our people are safe, and we've got the goods on the mob, to boot. They're thinking the same thing, only vice versa."

"Does the mob know this Hamilton woman has the manuscript?"

"This we don't know. Maybe Corsi told them before he was aced, but maybe not. Maybe they saw something, maybe they didn't."

"Sounds like you've got yourself a problem, Lou."

Sheridan chuckled. "I was hoping my money would make it your problem, Alec."

He drummed his fingers on Emile Fouré's desk as he considered the situation. "Tell you what," he said, "I'll help you with your little problem, but I'll need two grand as a retainer for my time and another eight if I produce the manuscript."

"Ten thousand?"

"You're the one who's desperate, Lou. I'm not."

ZARA DIDN'T THINK she was paranoid, but she'd had a funny feeling ever since she'd started reading that damned manuscript. Mr. X had been right…his exposé was dynamite. She'd opened the envelope out of curiosity, wondering if he'd written anything Arianna would want to acquire, and she had found herself mesmerized. Zara didn't know a thing about the Mafia except what she'd seen in films, and she didn't practice criminal law, but she was good at deciding whether or not something was phony. The book exposé had a ring of authenticity. She could believe that a lot of people would want to get their hands on it.

Which brought her back to the little scene at the airport. Who had taken Mr. X away, the mob or the police? And what had happened to him? God knew, he'd looked scared to death when he was being carted off. Worse, from her standpoint, if it was the Mafia, had they seen Mr. X turn the manuscript over to her?

There was no way to know for sure, which was why she was so darn nervous. Changing planes in Miami, she was certain she had been watched. She'd see a suspicious character, then he would be gone. And when the plane had stopped in Haiti in the middle of the night, and they'd made everyone get off the aircraft, Zara had nervously taken the manuscript with her in her carry-on. In the airport she'd been careful to stay with the main group. None of her fellow passengers seemed suspicious. As far as she could tell, they were typical vacationers.

But then she'd spotted a man with rough features in the lounge area. Despite the heat, he wore a dark blue sport coat and no tie. He didn't seem like a businessman, and he didn't have the demeanor of a tourist. She didn't like the way he kept looking at her. At first she tried to tell herself that she was tired and she'd gotten spooked after reading the manuscript. But in her heart of hearts she didn't believe it. Something was going on.

While reboarding the plane, she noticed the man was seated several rows ahead of her. When she caught his eye, he looked away, adding to her anxiety.

The flight to Martinique seemed interminable, but by the time the plane landed at Le Lamentin airport, it was nearly dawn. Zara was exhausted. Arianna and Mark had planned to spend their wedding night in Miami, but Zara had no need to lay over so had taken the airline's offer to book her through on the first connecting flight. She would arrive at the hotel about ten hours early, which hadn't seemed like a problem until now, when she wanted to go to bed.

As the passengers were struggling with their

carry-on luggage, Zara lost track of the man. Nor did she spot him during the disembarkation process. She wondered where he'd gone, then decided she'd be lucky if she never saw him again.

For some reason, the customs officer, a handsome young man who spoke English with a musical accent, decided to search her luggage thoroughly. Judging by his amiable chatter, he didn't suspect her of smuggling, but had decided that looking at her lingerie would be a fun way to start the morning shift. Either that, or he was deliberately detaining her. Zara was relieved when he finally sent her on her way, though she was a bit unnerved to see that by then the other passengers were gone and the terminal building was practically deserted.

The hotel, Maison des Caraïbes, which Arianna had described as a quaint former plantation house, was supposed to send a car, but of course they weren't expecting her then since she'd arrived earlier than planned. Zara called the hotel, hoping to arrange a pickup, but their driver wasn't available. They suggested she take a taxi.

Stepping out of the small terminal building, she had her first look at Martinique. Now that the sun was up, she was able to see the lush green mountains beyond the plain where the airport was located. It was early enough that the air was still pleasantly cool, though humid.

Despite the fact that she was bone tired, the exotic beauty of the island did give her a lift. Zara hadn't traveled nearly as much as Arianna, her biggest trip having been a vacation in Hawaii after she'd passed the bar exam. This was her first time in the Caribbean and already she was liking it.

She'd only gone a few steps when once again she spotted the man from the plane. Telling herself to remain calm, she stuck her head back in the door of the terminal building and looked around for someone she might ask for help. The only people still there were a couple of women behind the ticket counter in the far corner. Outside there were two elderly men sitting on a baggage cart, smoking and talking. When the man from the plane started in her direction, she panicked. Certain he was after her, she rushed over to where the porters were sitting.

"Where can I find the police?" she asked.

They answered her in French which she had trouble making out. "Police?" she asked in a louder voice. This time they pointed to a place around the building. As she hurried off, the guy from the plane started after her, walking briskly and looking as though he meant business.

Jogging around the corner of the building she saw a sign that said Police. But when she peered in the small office, she saw that it was empty and the door was locked. Looking around, she spotted a taxi stand with a lone, beat-up old cab just as her nemesis was coming around the corner.

"Taxi!" she shouted, running as fast as she could toward the vehicle. "Taxi!"

ALEC PERRIN HAD BEEN drumming his fingers on the steering wheel, wondering how long his friend in customs would keep her. No one had come out of the place for over ten minutes. There couldn't be anyone else left. Then, suddenly, he heard shouting. Checking his rearview mirror, he saw a small redhead running toward the taxi, suitcase in hand. Behind her was a big lug, who seemed to be chasing her.

Alec jumped out of the cab and went around to the curbside just as the woman came running up, looking positively terrified. Her pursuer spotted him, stopped in his tracks and turned, heading back toward the terminal building. The redhead dropped her suitcase at Alec's feet and all but threw herself in his arms.

"Oh, thank God!" she said breathlessly. "That man is chasing me!" She grabbed his arm, took a couple of anxious breaths, then looked back to see her pursuer in retreat. The relief on her face was obvious.

"Thank heavens, he's leaving."

"What happened?" he asked. "Who was that?"

Her eyes rounded. "You speak English."

Alec peered into huge blue-green eyes, delightfully surprised by what he saw. Funny, but in talking to Lou, he hadn't thought much about what Arianna Hamilton might look like. Now that he saw her, he wondered if perhaps Emile wasn't right, after all. It had been a while since he'd met a woman who made him want to think in terms of romance. "Well, yes, most Americans do. What's going on?"

"The man who was after me was on my plane," she said, still breathing hard, but trying to calm herself. "I noticed him watching me. I think...well, I'm sure he was up to no good."

"He seems to be gone now," Alec said, glancing toward the building.

"Yes, but I don't know what would've happened if you hadn't been here. I tried the police office. The whole terminal building is practically deserted."

"There's another plane due in three hours. The place will be a beehive of activity again then." He smiled reassuringly as he studied her. She did

seem genuinely alarmed. Lou was probably right
about her being an innocent bystander. The real
question was whether the man chasing her was
some overzealous admirer or some henchman
sent by the mob. He'd bet on the latter. And if
he was right, did Arianna Hamilton know what
she was mixed up in?

"Well, thank goodness you were in the right
place at the right time. Now if you can just take
me to my hotel, everything should be fine," she
said. "It's the Maison des Caraïbes."

"I'm afraid there's a slight problem with
that," he said. "I'm not a taxi driver. I borrowed
the cab from a friend so I could pick up my clients...I operate a charter boat, a sailing yacht.
But it looks like I've been stood up. They were
supposed to be on this flight. You didn't see a
middle-aged couple inside, Americans who—"

"No, I'm sure there's no one else left, except
for that...*man*." She cast a wary glance toward
the terminal. "Please, just get me out of here. I'll
be glad to pay you whatever you think is fair."

Alec glanced at her suitcase, managing to notice her shapely little figure in the process. She
was very pretty, her features delicate and refined.
It wouldn't be easy to keep his mind on the job.

"I really shouldn't, since it's against the law
here to chauffeur anyone without the proper li-

cense. But I guess I can't very well leave a fellow American in the lurch." He picked up her suitcase, opened the rear door of the taxi and put her bag inside. "Maybe if you ride in front with me, the police will believe you're my sister if I get stopped."

She managed a wry smile at his lame excuse.

"Then again, maybe not," he said, grinning.

Opening the passenger door, he helped her in, catching a light whiff of her perfume in the process. A ripple of excitement went through him. Even so, he noticed that she kept hold of both her carry-on bag and her purse, making him wonder if she had the manuscript in one or the other. At this point only one thing was certain—it would be a real pleasure finding out.

CHAPTER THREE

ZARA BEGAN TO RELAX as they entered the narrow two-lane road that went by the airport. For the first time since she'd started reading Mr. X's manuscript she felt safe. And all because of this man—her champion. She turned to look at him, aware only then how very attractive he was. He wore a blue muscle shirt, bleached-out khaki shorts and sandals. He was in his early thirties, tall and good-looking in a rugged, unpretentious way. Best of all, he had a relaxed, confident manner that inspired trust.

"My name is Alec Perrin, by the way," he said, turning to her.

"I'm Zara Hamilton."

"Pardon?"

"I said my name is Zara Hamilton. I was introducing myself."

"Zara?" He turned to look at her. "But your last name *is* Hamilton?"

"Right." She chuckled. "Is there something wrong?"

He returned his attention to the road. "No, no. Not at all. Nice name."

She was amused. People were often confused by her unusual first name. More than one person had asked her to spell it.

"So, what brings you to Martinique?" Alec asked.

"Just a vacation," she said, wishing that were true. But after getting the manuscript, and seeing the man on the plane, she wasn't so sure anymore.

"Where are you from, if you don't mind me asking?"

"Colorado."

"Really?"

"Really."

He seemed to consider that as he glanced in his rearview mirror. "Well, you must be one of those rich Colorado ranchers then, because you're staying at the nicest hotel on the island. It's very exclusive."

"Sorry to disappoint you. I'm just a working girl who managed to get a free ticket and lodging."

"Lucky you."

She sighed. "We'll see. Considering the way this trip has started, I'm reserving judgment."

Alec glanced in the rearview mirror again. "I

don't want to throw any more cold water on your holiday, but if I'm not mistaken your friend is following us. There's a blue Renault about a hundred meters behind us."

Zara looked back and saw the car behind them. "Oh, no."

"He must be an avid admirer," he said.

She thought of the manuscript...the Mafia...the hits and deals and contracts to kill people, and shivered. "I wish that's all it was."

He gave her an inquiring look. "Are you in some sort of trouble?"

She paused for a heartbeat before she answered. "It's beginning to look that way."

"Anything I can do?"

"Thanks, but I'll manage."

"Hmm. Well, if you change your mind, let me know. I know the local authorities pretty well. And I was a cop in a previous life, if that makes a difference."

She blinked. "You were a cop?"

"NYPD."

Zara glanced anxiously out the back window. The blue car was still there. "I have a sister who lives in New York," she said.

"I see."

The road ahead twisted into the lush green

mountainside. They drove for a while before he spoke again.

"So, if you're just a plain old working girl, what do you do? If you don't mind me asking."

"I'm a lawyer," she replied, finding it hard to make small talk while that terrible man was behind them.

"No kidding."

She turned to check the back window again. Alec noticed.

"He's gone," she said.

"No, he's there, a couple of curves behind us."

She sighed, feeling sick.

"I wish you'd let me help."

He was so calm and confident that it gave her heart. True, she didn't know the man from Adam, but he'd already come to her rescue once. And if he'd been a cop, he might be able to give her some good advice. Lord knew, practicing law in Aspen hadn't prepared her for dealing with the Mafia. "Okay. Since you're the expert, what do you think I should do about the man following me?"

"Are you convinced you're in danger?"

Zara thought of the fear in Mr. X's eyes as he'd been carted off and realized that it couldn't have been the authorities who arrested him. If it had been—and he'd told them about her—then they'd have sent an FBI man or a cop to ask for the book. And the thug who'd chased her was no cop. "Yes. I'm sure of it."

"Once you're at the hotel, I suggest that you have a word with the management. They can watch for the guy and if he comes around they can have the police escort him off the island. The French are pretty good at keeping order."

"I wish I were as confident as you."

"If you want me to speak with the manager, I'd be glad to. And the police, too."

"I'd be grateful for anything you could do."

"It's a deal, then. You need a guardian angel and I'm available."

She sighed. "I don't know how I'll ever repay you."

He looked over at her and smiled. "Dinner with me tonight would be a good start."

She hadn't been ready for that. Back in Aspen she was used to being totally self-sufficient—handling her own problems, not to mention those of her clients. But she was thousands of miles from home now and the idea of help sounded awfully good. Still, she didn't want to give in too easily. "How about if I take that invitation under advisement, Alec. I've been flying for hours and I'm dead tired."

"Sure. Whatever feels right," he said.

Zara wondered if he said that knowing she was beginning to feel good about him. Everything was happening so quickly—first the danger, now the sudden appearance of a champion, and a handsome, appealing champion, at that. It was awfully good timing. Maybe fate would wind up being on her side after all.

Soon they'd crossed over the mountain and followed the road south down the leeward side of the island. Fort-de-France, the capital, was farther north. Her hotel was near the southern tip of the island, not far from the village of Sainte-Anne. The road they were following traced a cove called the Cul-de-Sac du Marin where Alec told her he kept his boat.

"We're practically neighbors then," she said, looking out at the sparkling blue sea beyond the point of rocks.

"Though from different sides of the tracks," he said.

Zara hoped he didn't think she was some sort of snob, just because the Maison des Caraïbes was expensive. But before she could explain that this wasn't really her style, they came to the gated entrance of the hotel. Alec was right, it looked very exclusive. She liked it that he didn't seem the least bit embarrassed about driving the old taxi right up to the main entrance. She turned back a final time, checking to see if the blue Renault was still behind them.

"He stopped a quarter of a mile back," Alec told her.

"I guess he knows where I'm staying now."

"If he's there when I come out, I'll stop and have a word with him."

"Do you think that's wise?" she asked.

"I'll be fine," Alec said. "At the moment I'm more concerned about you. But I'm sure you'll feel better after I speak to the manager."

They pulled up in front of the main building. A porter in white livery came out the door and down the steps. Zara put her hand on Alec's arm. "You've been so very kind," she said. "I really appreciate your help."

"No problem. That's what friends are for."

"You know, Alec, I think I would like to have dinner with you. But how about if you join me here? My meals are already paid for and you can be my guest. It's the least I can do after you've saved me."

"I'd be honored."

The porter opened the door and she climbed out. Alec came around the vehicle, taking her carry-on bag from her while the porter dealt with the suitcase. They went up the steps and into the reception area. A desk clerk in a white jacket greeted her. She presented Arianna's passport.

"Ah, Miss Hamilton," the man said. "Welcome. I'm to advise you that there's a gentleman waiting for you in the library, across the lobby, through that door."

Zara blinked. "Who is he?"

"He didn't give his name, Miss Hamilton," the clerk said. Zara and Alec exchanged looks.

"Want me to go with you?" he asked.

Zara drew a ragged breath. "Please, if you don't mind."

She picked up her carry-on bag that Alec had put down and walked across the room, the heels of her sandals clicking on the tile floor. As she neared the door she slowed, then tentatively stuck her head in the room. Mark Lindsay was sitting in an armchair, reading.

"Oh, my God," she gasped.

Mark glanced up from his paper. Seeing her, he jumped to his feet.

"Arianna, sweetheart," he said. "I know this is a surprise, but…" His voice trailed off as he noticed Alec.

She gulped. "Mark…"

A deep frown creased Mark's face. "Who's the guy?"

"Oh," she said, laughing nervously, "this is

Alec Perrin, a…uh…friend who gave me a ride from the airport.''

Mark turned bright red. Zara rolled her eyes. She glanced at Alec, who looked both perplexed and a bit disconcerted. Mark came toward them. Stopping, he looked Alec up and down.

''I can see it was a terrible mistake coming here,'' he said, his voice low with a quiet rage. But there was hurt in it as well.

''Mark,'' she said, ''I need to talk to you. Privately.''

He started to refuse, then, searching her eyes, gave her a quizzical look, as though sensing something was amiss. She turned to Alec.

''I'd be really grateful if you'd speak to the manager for me, Alec. But before you leave, I need to talk to you, too.''

The men exchanged disdainful looks and headed off in opposite directions. Zara groaned. Why did everything have to go wrong, just when she thought the situation was improving?

Sighing, she followed Mark and sat on the chair adjoining his. He was still red in the face.

''Mark,'' she whispered, leaning toward him, ''it's me, Zara.''

He blinked, leaning back in surprise. ''What?''

''Arianna gave me her ticket. She didn't want

to come, so I borrowed her passport and came in her place."

Mark was dumbstruck.

"Look," she said, pointing to her temple, "no chicken pox scar."

"Oh, my God."

"I know it's a shock, but I'm traveling as Arianna and, since I'm using her passport and ticket, it's difficult to say anything."

Mark sat shaking his head with disbelief. "There was something about you that gave me pause, but I was so emotional I..." He obviously was embarrassed. "Wouldn't you know it," he said. "I come all the way down here just to take a last shot at changing Arianna's mind and who do I find, but you." He glanced toward the door. "Considering the guy, I guess I should be glad you *are* Zara."

"I'm not so sure I'm glad."

"What do you mean?"

"Mark, I don't even know where to begin. It's complicated."

"Let's start with Arianna. I assume she's at home?"

"No, she's at my place in Aspen."

"Then the two of you switched places," Mark said.

"Not exactly. I'm getting a free trip to paradise and Ari's getting away from it all. She thought she could get some work done while she deals with her heartache.''

Mark stroked his chin, his soft brown eyes coming to life. ''Real heartache, or are you just saying that to make me feel better?''

She gazed at him thoughtfully. ''Don't tell her I said this, but Arianna isn't completely sure she did the right thing.''

''Really?'' He broke into a grin. ''She said that?''

''No, but she didn't have to. I know Ari as well as I know myself. We've always thought right along with each other, even when we end up reaching different conclusions. I won't make you any promises, Mark, but I will tell you this— my sister is still trying to decide how she feels about you.''

''That's all I need to hear,'' he said. ''I'm going to Aspen.''

''Wait a minute,'' she said. ''Not so fast.''

''Do you think it's a bad idea?''

''No, it might even be a good idea. But if you're going, you ought to be prepared. The better you understand her feelings, the better off you'll be.''

Mark shook his head. ''Why didn't I talk to

you a long time ago, Zara? Okay, shoot. Give it to me straight and don't worry about sparing my feelings."

"All right. You're a great guy, Mark, but I think you've been too nice. Ari told me you're the most caring, considerate, thoughtful man she's ever known, but...my sister is very independent and I think sometimes she felt a bit suffocated."

She paused, then continued. "I'm not suggesting she wants a man who acts indifferent to her or anything like that. But if you want to get her to the altar, you ought to make her work a little. She needs someone who will keep her on her toes, not cater to her every whim. Ari loves a challenge. If you keep that in mind, you'll have the key to her heart."

Mark sat there, apparently considering what he'd heard. Zara sensed that a light had gone off in his head—especially after a little smile touched the corners of his mouth. He shook his head.

"How is it a person can be so blind and then suddenly see everything?" he said. "You know, I already knew that in my bones."

"Arianna has a killer instinct," Zara said. "She doesn't want a man who'll stifle her, but she does want one who'll give her a run for her money."

Mark nodded. "You know, maybe I'm fortunate I came all the way down here to find you instead of her. I'm sure I'd have said all the wrong things." He grinned. "I owe you, Zara."

"Well, if you want to do me a big favor, I've got a burden I'd like to unload."

"What?"

Zara opened her carry-on bag and removed Mr. X's manuscript. "This was given to me yesterday at JFK by some mobster who thought I was Arianna. It's a tell-all book that's got the Mafia in an uproar. If you'd like to put it in my sister's hands, then I won't have to worry about it anymore."

Mark Lindsay smiled. "This may be just what I need as an excuse to see her."

"Well, before you get too excited, you should know there are people who'd kill to make sure this doesn't fall into the wrong hands. I mean literally kill. I'd almost rather Arianna didn't get it, but I also know she wouldn't want me making that decision for her. So I'll leave it up to you to make sure she's all right."

"It's really that serious?"

Zara gave him a brief account of what had happened since her encounter with Mr. X in

New York. When she'd finished, Mark seemed concerned.

"Of course I'll take it off your hands," he said, "but I'm not so sure I want Arianna having it."

"That's between the two of you. I just want to be done with it." She put the envelope in his hands.

Mark glanced toward the door. "Judging by the look on your friend Alec Perrin's face earlier, my presence isn't especially appreciated."

Zara blushed. "He's been wonderful. He literally saved me at the airport. But I don't really know him."

Mark leaned over and patted her hand, smiling. "I have a feeling you two will be getting better acquainted, Zara."

He got up and so did she. Then he gave her a kiss on the cheek and said goodbye. "Enjoy my honeymoon, okay?"

Zara blushed again and watched as he headed for the door. "Be careful, Mark."

He waved over his shoulder. "Count on it."

Zara closed her carry-on bag and went back into the lobby just as Alec was emerging from the manager's office. He looked grim. She didn't know if it was because of his conversation or because of Mark's unexpected appearance.

"I've alerted the hotel to be on the lookout for your buddy," he said. "They assure me their security is excellent. They'll have people checking your bungalow during the night."

"Great," she said.

"The manager is also going to call the police and ask them to pick the guy up. If he can't justify his presence on Martinique, they'll hustle him off the island."

She gave a grateful sigh. "Terrific."

Alec smiled faintly then glanced toward the door to the library. "Where's your boyfriend, by the way, *Arianna?*"

"Mark isn't my boyfriend, and I'm not Arianna," she said, lowering her voice.

"Funny, I distinctly heard him call you that."

Zara glanced over at the clerk, who was acting oblivious, though she couldn't be sure. She didn't want to take a chance, so she said, "Let's go for a walk, Alec."

She took him by the arm and they headed for the door. After descending the steps, they took one of the paths that meandered through the lush grounds. "I have an identical twin," she said. "Arianna. Remember, I said I had a sister in New York. She's an editor, and Mark was her fiancé. This was where they'd planned to spend their honeymoon until Arianna called off the wedding.

Everything was paid for, and Mark gave her the tickets, but she didn't want to come so she gave them to me. That's why I'm traveling on her passport."

"Oh."

"You see," she said, "I've sort of ended up in my sister's soup. The guy following me thinks I'm Arianna, too. It's a case of mistaken identity."

"And what about Mark?"

"When he realized he had the wrong twin, he left."

"So all that's left is to convince the guy outside the gate that you're really Zara and your troubles will be over," he said.

"Well...it's a little more complicated than that."

Alec gave her a questioning look, and she almost told him the whole story. Then she decided that the less said about the manuscript, the better.

"Let's just say it's a problem concerning Arianna's work," she said. "Something I know nothing about and have no desire to get involved in."

They'd done a loop and were heading back toward the main building.

"Does that mean that you can relax now and enjoy yourself?" Alec said.

"I'd like to think so."

"I look forward to this evening," he said.

"Me, too. But I'm going to have a long nap between now and then."

"I'll leave you to your beauty rest," he said. "Not that you need it, from what I can see."

"Oh, you do know how to flatter, Mr. Perrin."

"Diplomacy is as important to my work as seamanship and cooking. The first order of business is to please the client. You want them coming back for more."

Zara smiled, half convinced that he intended the double entendre. They were coming back to the main building. Stopping next to the taxi Alec had borrowed, he took her hand.

"Once again, thank you for everything, Alec," she said.

He surprised her by pulling her fingers to his lips and kissing them. It was a gesture very unlike what she'd expect from a New York cop, and it gave her a thrill. The gesture was sweet, yet arousing.

"Be careful," he said.

"You, too."

"Don't go wandering off the grounds."

She shook her head. "And don't you confront that awful man. Let the police take care of him."

"See you this evening," he said, giving her a bemused smile, then climbing into the taxi.

Zara went up the stairs, and stood on the veranda watching Alec. Their gazes met and they exchanged little waves. She waited until he drove out the gate and disappeared up the road before she returned to the lobby. Sighing, she thought again of the fortune cookies at Madame Wu's. Maybe the book fortune did belong to Arianna. After all, the manuscript would soon be in her hands, where it belonged. And since she was the twin in the exotic place, maybe the romance fortune was meant for her. Thinking of Alec Perrin, and the way he'd come to her rescue, Zara hoped so. She really did.

CHAPTER FOUR

BY THE TIME Alec Perrin made it back to the road, the guy in the blue Renault was nowhere in sight. The gendarmes wouldn't have had time to arrest him yet, so that meant he was probably lying low. His guess was the guy wouldn't be giving up easily. Alec didn't want to get into any pitched battles with some Mafia wise guy—that wasn't what he'd signed on for.

The solution, of course, was simple. All he had to do was walk away, tell Lou Sheridan to forget it. But an hour with Zara Hamilton and his game plan had changed dramatically. This was no longer about a manuscript, it was about her—if he could just be sure who she was.

Initially the twin story had sounded preposterous. And the business with the fiancé had been bizarre, too. But he tended to believe her. The man wouldn't have left the hotel quite so quietly if she'd really been Arianna. Also, Zara had mentioned having a sister in New York before the twin business had even come up.

Still, she hadn't mentioned anything about the manuscript. There was no doubt in his mind that she had it—she'd admitted that her problem had to do with her sister's work, and she'd said that her sister was a book editor. His best guess was that she knew what the manuscript was about, and how potentially explosive the exposé could be. Lawyers weren't dummies. Undoubtedly she didn't want to talk about it until she was certain he could be trusted. Which meant that his next job was to gain her trust.

In the meantime, he'd have another talk with Lou. Maybe his friend could shed some light on this twin business.

Alec also decided to swing by the gendarmerie and chat with Emile. He wanted to know if the manager at the hotel had followed through with his promise to alert the police about the man who'd been tailing them. The French could be territorial and Emile wouldn't be pleased to learn that some mobster from New York was paying their island a visit. The best way to deal with him was to let the French gendarmes handle it.

Alec entered the police station and found Emile Fouré behind his desk.

"I was just thinking about you," Emile said. "I understand you ran into a little problem with the woman."

"The woman was fine, mon ami," Alec replied. "It's the attention she's getting that concerns me."

"We're looking for him. I've already checked with passport control to see who he is. Also, I have a call in to the car rental agency. We'll have him soon."

"It would be nice if you sent him packing."

"It will be arranged. No problem."

Alec wanted to be as optimistic, but he also knew that mobsters were not without resources. Thanking Emile for what he'd done so far, Alec explained that he would go to the post office and put in a call to New York, then return to see if any new information had surfaced.

"Good," the gendarme said. "By the time you get back I may know who the gangster is."

Alec gave his friend a casual salute and left the station. He went up the street to the post office. Fortunately, he was able to get through to Lou without a problem.

"An identical twin?" Sheridan said after Alec explained what had happened. "You've got to be kidding. Nobody would buy that story."

"I think it may be true, Lou. You better check it out."

"I'll look into it. But any news about the manuscript? She did admit she has it, right?"

"Not exactly. She hasn't said so in so many words and I obviously can't ask her about it. But she must have it, Lou. My hunch is she knows exactly what's going on, but has decided not to discuss it."

"So, what's your plan?"

"I'm taking things slow and easy. If a woman feels like you're after something, she backs off fast. You must have discovered that in your bachelor days, Lou."

"Hey, Perrin, what are we talking about here, the book or your love life?"

"Hey, old buddy, I'm just enlightening you about the ways of women."

"Thanks, but I'll settle for the manuscript. Just get it, will ya, please?"

"I'll do my best. But you might as well know I've got competition." He told him about the swarthy hood who was after Zara.

"Why am I not surprised?" Sheridan grumbled.

"By the way, I take it my money's been wired."

"It should be in your bank account."

"Great. Well, I'll let you go. I've got to figure out my next move."

"You do that, and don't forget to bring home the bacon."

"Lou, I've said it before. Your wish is my command."

WHEN ZARA WOKE UP from her nap, her first thought was of Alec Perrin. He had been in her dreams, too. Amazingly, he had been both sexually arousing, and a warm, comforting presence. That was very unusual for her because she normally didn't respond to any man that quickly. She'd never had a vacation romance. She did not go in for flings. Either she dated a man for months before she got seriously involved with him, or she told him to get lost. But something about Alec—and the circumstances—was making her react differently.

In fact, she probably wouldn't have been thinking in terms of romance even now if it had not been for that darned fortune cookie. What did that say about her? That she was desperate? Or lonely? Or that Alec was by far the most attractive man she'd ever met?

She did want to share her life with someone eventually. But it had to be with the right man. What could she possibly have in common with a former cop from New York? Their backgrounds couldn't have been more different. Still, they must have *some* common ground between them.

Zara had to laugh. Well, they did both speak

English. That was enough for him to rescue her, and to ask her out to dinner. If there were greater possibilities, she'd find out soon enough. Meanwhile she'd just have to wait and see.

Zara got out of the huge canopy bed and peered out the plantation shutters at the setting sun. The grounds were magnificent. The Maison des Caraïbes was everything her sister had told her, and more.

When she'd informed the staff that she was expecting a guest for dinner, she was told that the men had to dress for dinner. Arianna had packed evening clothes, but somehow Zara couldn't picture Alec showing up in a dinner jacket.

She had her bath, and afterward put on a pale yellow silk slip dress. It was dressy enough for elegant dining, but wasn't formal. Usually she never wore anything that blatantly sexual, but what the heck? She felt different being here, more alive, more sensuous than she'd felt in the longest time. So, why not dress to match her mood?

Heading toward the main building, she admired the rich oranges and reds and violets of the sunset. She'd always loved this time of day. It was even more magical in a tropical setting.

A number of the guests had gathered in the

lounge to have a cocktail before dinner. Most of the men were in dinner jackets. *Nobody* was dressed casually. That worried her a bit. Had she put Alec in an awkward position by asking him to dine here? She hoped not.

There was still no sign of him, so she wandered out onto the huge veranda with the colonnade running the width of the building. The porter got to his feet and she motioned for him to sit. She looked out over the sweeping circular drive.

As she stared out at the brillant sunset, a car came through the gate, its amber headlights dim and flickering. The wheeze of its engine sounded familiar. Sure enough, it was the taxi Alec had driven that morning. It chugged to a stop in front of the door.

Zara went down the steps and peered in the open passenger window. Alec was shaved and dressed, but not in formal attire. He was in white trousers and a navy blue polo shirt, looking terrific, but unfortunately not suitable for the hotel dining room.

"I looked everywhere for a dinner jacket," he said, "but I couldn't even borrow one. My friends move in different circles, I guess."

"It doesn't matter," she said. "You look good."

"No, there's no point in me embarrassing you. Either go on to dinner without me, or, if you don't mind slumming, you can come with me. I can't offer elegance, but I can offer the best food in the Caribbean."

"Best in the Caribbean, huh? That's a tall claim. Where is this place?"

"Wherever I am," he replied. "I'm referring to my own cooking."

"You weren't kidding about being a cook, then."

"I'm a chef, my dear. And a very good one, if I do say so."

She chuckled. "You certainly don't lack for modesty."

"I have to entice you some way."

Zara glanced back at the brightly lit building and listened for a moment to the social murmur of voices inside. She really had no desire to sit among all those diamond necklaces and gold watches and dinner jackets and pretend to belong. So she opened the taxi door and got in. Alec responded with a grin. She could see his delight by the sparkle in his eyes. She also was very aware of the rich spicy tang of his cologne and felt drawn to him.

"I'm probably naive," she said, "but I'll call your bluff. Where do you cook?"

"Unfortunately, a kitchen is required and the galley on my boat has limited facilities. But as luck would have it, I've managed to borrow the house of two friends for the evening. Paul and Marie Louise have an excellent kitchen. A chef's kitchen if ever there was one."

"And they don't mind you dropping in with a friend for dinner?"

"They're in Paris at the moment, but we're very close, so I have a key and free use of the kitchen."

This seemed a little too convenient, and Zara knew it, but deep down she didn't care. She found herself wanting to go along. When she turned to Alec, she could tell that he knew what she'd been thinking.

"Is that okay?" he asked.

"Is there a reason why it shouldn't be?"

"Not as far as I'm concerned."

"I'm far too trusting," she said.

"Well, I'm known to be a gentleman."

"By whom?" she teased.

"My mother's always considered me reasonably well behaved," he said with a sly smile.

Zara rolled her eyes. "If that's the best you can do, I'm in big trouble."

He started the engine. "I can see I'd better get out of here before you change your mind."

She laughed.

"You look lovely, by the way," he said as he drove through the gate.

She blushed. "Thanks, but they're my sister's clothes. To be honest, I'm more the sweater and jeans type. But it's fun to dress up a little now and then."

"The crowd at the hotel is definitely out of my league," he admitted with a rakish grin.

"Then maybe you're as glad as I am that we didn't eat at the hotel tonight."

"All I care about is the pleasure of your company," he said.

Zara had to smile. He actually sounded sincere.

As they drove along a dark and deserted road, Zara shivered, suddenly recalling the man from the plane. "By the way, when you left this morning, did you see the man who followed us?" she asked.

"No, he'd gone. The police have identified him, though."

"Who is he?"

"His name's Benny Bandini. Unfortunately the local authorities haven't been able to locate him. Apparently he's gone into hiding."

A chill went down Zara's spine. "Oh, Lord."

"But he won't be able to keep his head down

for long. It's not easy to get lost on an island. Other than Manhattan, that is."

"Do you really believe that, or are you just trying to put my mind at ease?" Zara asked.

"I want you to relax and have a good time."

"That's what I thought."

Alec reached over and took her hand. "As long as you're with me, you'll be fine. Trust me."

She wondered about that. "Whenever somebody says, 'trust me,' my first instinct is to do the opposite."

"Well, don't trust me, then," he said raising his eyebrows. "But you can still have a good time."

Zara laughed. Alec couldn't know how much she wanted to do exactly that. "I'll give it a try," she said, gently disengaging her hand from his.

As they drove she leaned back and tried to enjoy the soft tropical air. Putting Benny Bandini out of her mind wasn't easy even with Alec Perrin to distract her—and he was distracting! No question about that.

"You know, Alec," she said, "I hardly know a thing about you, except that you were once a policeman in New York. Why'd you quit?"

"I got shot once too often and finally went on disability."

She gulped. "How many times were you shot?"

"Twice. The second time, I decided I'd had enough. I'd done my bit to save the world."

"How did you end up in Martinique?"

"I actually came to the Caribbean with the idea of starting a restaurant, but it's a tricky business and you really have to know the market. It would have been a gamble even in New York and I'd lived there all my life. So instead, I signed on as a cook and crewman on a sailing yacht, and eventually ended up buying a boat of my own."

"Sounds like an idyllic life," she said.

"It can be lonely, even when I've got a charter party."

"How is it you never married?"

"I did marry," he said. "Then got divorced. Being a cop and being married are a difficult combination. It became obvious I'd have to give up one or the other. The joke was I ended up giving up both."

"It was too late to save your marriage?"

"Much too late," he said. "By then my ex-wife, Toni, was having an affair with the attorney representing me in the disability action."

"Oh my. So, now you hate lawyers and don't trust women," she said.

"Something like that," he said with a grin.

"I'm surprised you'd give me a ride, let alone want to take me out to dinner."

"Hair of the dog," he said.

They fell silent. Alec Perrin, she realized, had a touch of sadness about him. But she liked that because it made him more real.

"Tell me about your life, Zara," he said.

"It's quiet. I practice law in Aspen. I own a little Victorian house in town. I ski. I have a nice circle of friends. Never been married or engaged."

"That's surprising! The rest I can imagine. What kind of law do you practice?"

"A little of everything. Commercial law, real estate, family law, wills and trusts."

"No criminal law?"

"No. But I've done several divorces."

"That's almost as bad," Alec said with a laugh.

"I get to do some good stuff, too," she said. "I've got a case now, for example, that's really interesting. A friend of mine who's single wants to have a baby but she's sterile. She went to a fertility clinic in Denver for an embryo transplant. I looked over the contract and suggested some clauses to protect her interests." Zara smiled when she thought how happy Lina Prescott was at the prospect of becoming a mother. "The law can prevent problems as well cause fights."

"Perhaps so," he said, "but take my advice and stay away from the husbands of your clients."

She chuckled. "Little danger of that, I assure you."

"You know," he said, "I don't doubt that for a minute."

"Why, because I have an honest face?"

"Yes, you do, actually. As a former cop I became pretty good at reading people," Alec said. "I can tell you're as straight arrow as they come." Then he added with a laugh, "Maybe the bar in Colorado is different from the bar in New York."

But before she could reply to that, he reached over and brushed her cheek. "I have to admit, I've never been attracted to a lawyer before. But then, I've never before been with such an attractive lawyer."

CHAPTER FIVE

ALEC CHECKED THE PASTA, then began tossing the salad. It had been some time since he'd cooked in a fully-stocked kitchen and it felt great. But at the same time he was starting to feel really uncomfortable with the game he was forced to play. He was damned sorry he'd agreed to do this job for Lou Sheridan. He'd rather concentrate on enjoying Zara's company and not think about the manuscript. Of course, if it hadn't been for the manuscript, he'd never have met her.

Though he was still somewhat in the dark about what was going on, his gut told him Zara was the accidental victim she claimed to be. The problem was, she wasn't eager to talk about the manuscript, and he knew he had to be careful about bringing it up. For the moment, though, he wanted to put all that out of his mind and focus just on her.

It was a nice evening and he had every reason to be in a great mood. He was in a good kitchen with quality ingredients, sipping a fine Bordeaux wine as he cooked. A full moon was rising over the mountain. Best of all, he was with a lovely, intriguing woman. Zara was unlike most of the women he'd known. For a guy who'd been cynical about romance, she was a refreshing change.

Glancing through the doorway, he saw she was still out on the veranda, gazing out at the sea. She'd been there for fifteen minutes. He could tell she'd been trying to figure him out as well and hadn't quite decided about him yet. Alec found himself wanting to please her—and not just to manipulate her.

Seeing that everything was in good shape, he took his wineglass and the bottle, and joined Zara on the veranda. Zara's back was to him and she hadn't heard him coming. He stopped to admire her. She was a tiny thing, but womanly and sensuous. She had fabulous legs. And he loved her hair. She'd put it up and she looked positively elegant, though the wisps of curls at her neck were more sexy than anything else.

Zara Hamilton had an innocence that appealed to him, yet she was intelligent and strong—a person couldn't go into law without having grit. But she wasn't hard. To the contrary, she had a softness, almost a gentleness that he found very, very appealing.

He again found himself wondering how much

he really cared about the ten grand. The money would come in handy, but at what cost? He certainly wasn't going to strong-arm her just to get the book for Lou. Maybe, since she'd gotten the damned thing by accident, she'd be willing to part with it just to get it off her hands. But how did he broach the subject when she hadn't said a word about it, as of yet?

He could simply ask her about it. But to do that he'd have to admit that he was working for the NYPD. She'd never trust him if he told her he'd been less than honest...and the fact was, he cared a hell of a lot more about what she thought of him than he did about doing the job.

He had hoped that she might be forthcoming when he'd told her about Benny Bandini. When she hadn't opened up, perhaps he should have come right out and said that Bandini was a soldier in the Pantano family. Zara couldn't have ignored that. But the opportunity had passed. All he could do now was wait and see how the evening turned out.

Just then, Zara looked back over her shoulder and, seeing him, turned around. "I had a feeling you were there, watching me," she said.

"I hope you don't read minds, too."

She smiled, her full mouth so alluring he couldn't help thinking what it would be like to kiss her. "Hardly a gentlemanly comment," she said.

"We were both admiring the view," he said. "It's just that my perspective was a little more enticing than yours."

"Oh?"

"It's not often the woman in the scene can rival the scenery itself, particularly in a place like this."

"That line sounds a little too practiced, Alec," she said. "Have you used it before?"

"I'm happy to say no, I haven't."

"Really?"

"There may have been times when I would have liked to," he said, "but failed for lack of sufficient inspiration."

She smiled. "I think you'd better quit while you're ahead."

He sauntered over to her and lifted the bottle of wine as if to ask if she wanted any. She smiled and nodded, and he proceeded to pour her a glass. "Dinner will be ready in a few minutes."

"I've been enjoying the aromas," she said.

"Wait until you've eaten, Zara. Cooking is tricky. The mastery is in the subtlety."

"Subtlety is good in a lot of things." She gave him a smile.

"I couldn't agree more."

They sipped their wine. He leaned against the railing and looked down into her eyes.

"You know, I've never been to Colorado," he said. "I've read a lot about Aspen, of course."

"It's sophisticated in its way, but with a small-town feel."

"How are the restaurants?"

"We have some great ones. Visitors come from all over the world and they want more than just steak and potatoes, which is a main staple in the West." She gave him an inquiring look. "Are you curious enough to come sample it?"

He gave her a broad grin. "You do read minds, Miss Hamilton."

"If you did make it to Aspen, I'd be happy to show you around town," she said, taking a hasty sip of wine.

Alec felt something pass between them, an awareness, a connection. He wanted to kiss her. Instead, he lightly touched her hair and said, "I think it's time to eat. Shall we go inside?"

"By all means. I'm famished."

He put his hand on her waist as they went through the door. He caught a whiff of her perfume and felt an ache in his heart. That was a definite warning signal. He was falling fast and better be careful. But then, he didn't want to be too careful.

Alec had resigned himself to a carefree bachelor life. Now suddenly, he found a woman he could care about—maybe too much for his peace of mind.

How could he have ever guessed he'd fall hard and fast for a woman lawyer from Colorado? There was also the little problem of the Mafia being after her. But he could deal with that, if she could. Fate, he decided, had a perverse sense of humor.

ZARA COULDN'T RECALL a candlelight dinner that she'd enjoyed more. It was romantic, but it was also very relaxed. Alec felt like a friend she'd known forever, though they hadn't yet known each other a full day. And the food! For the fifth or sixth time she told him how much she enjoyed the seafood pasta, what a great cook he was.

"You really should open a restaurant," she told him. "If the dishes you served were only half as good as this, it'd be a great success."

"You're very kind."

"I'm serious."

"I have to admit the bug has been biting me again of late," he said. "I'm not sure the Caribbean is the place for the sort of thing I want to do."

"Have you considered returning to New York?" she asked.

"Not really. The restaurant business is big in New York and if you put together the right combination of cuisine and ambiance, you can do well. But it would be going back and I want to look ahead. I've got a pioneer spirit in me. I thrive on challenge and adventure." He fingered the stem of his wineglass, staring at it wistfully.

Zara watched him with fascination. She wanted to say, "Have you considered Colorado?" but knew that would be forward. Besides, the relevant tomorrows were the next five or six days.

"Believe it or not, the idea of Colorado has been going through my mind since you talked about the Aspen restaurants earlier. It would be an interesting change of scene," he said.

Zara blushed. Once again this evening, she felt as if he'd been reading her mind.

"Quite a jump from this to the Rocky Mountains," she said.

"Well, the Rockies have a lot of appeal. I didn't mention it earlier, but I'm a skier," Alec said. "The grandparents of my best friend in high school had a place in Vermont. We'd go every winter—as much for the girls as the snow. But we got to be pretty good...."

"At what?" Zara quipped.

"At both," Alec replied, smiling.

"I believe it," Zara said, unable to resist smiling back.

He reached across the table and put his hand on hers. "I've been on my best behavior. Give me credit for that. And let me tell you, it hasn't been easy."

He toyed with her fingers. Chills ran up her spine and she had trouble looking into his eyes. "Why hasn't it been easy?"

"Because I find you extremely attractive."

"Even though I'm a lawyer?"

"Yes. Even though you're a lawyer."

There was desire in his eyes. For the first time she was a little bit afraid. This had gone awfully quickly and it could go quicker still if she indicated she was willing.

He continued toying with her hand and she trembled, hoping he hadn't noticed.

"Do you believe in parapsychology, astrology and all that stuff?" she asked.

"You mean fortune-telling?"

"Yes."

"I believe in extrasensory perception," he said. "I think we have powers beyond what we're aware of. I also think there's a lot of hokum out there." He drew his fingers lightly up the inside of her forearm. "How about you?"

She tried to ignore his touch, but couldn't. Alec seemed to arouse her so easily. It was amazing. "I guess I'm rather skeptical," she said.

"You know, there's a restaurant in Chinatown in New York that's sort of...I don't know what...developed a cult following, you might say. People claim the fortunes in the cookies really come true," he said.

Zara's eyes rounded as she listened, wondering if he could be talking about Madame Wu's place.

"The last time I was in town I went there with my cousin," he continued. "She insisted that I had to find out what my future would be."

Zara was almost afraid to ask. "Did you?"

He shrugged. "Let's see, it was something like, 'You will find true happiness in a faraway place.' I told my cousin if it meant anything, it was that I'd better get back to the Caribbean and not waste my time in New York," he said, chuckling.

"Have you found happiness here, Alec?"

He gave her a penetrating gaze. "Well, I haven't been unhappy."

"That's not quite the same thing, is it?"

He caressed her fingers, looking at them as though they were some rare and treasured object.

"Frankly, I haven't given Madame Wu and her fortunes a lot of thought."

"Oh," Zara said, "so you did go to Destiny House!"

"You know it?" he said, startled.

"I went with some friends two nights ago."

"How about that? Small world."

"Yes, I guess it is."

"So, what was your fortune?" he asked.

She colored. "I don't believe in that stuff."

"Well, tell me anyway," he insisted.

"It was dumb."

"What?"

"'Never judge a book by its cover.'"

She noticed something strange in his eyes. It was just a flicker, and it passed quickly, but it made her wonder.

"Doesn't sound awfully exciting," he said casually. "What do you figure it means?"

"I'm sure I don't know."

"How about that beach bums may have hearts of gold?" he said with a wink.

"Or maybe wolves sometimes parade in gentleman's clothing," she offered.

Alec drank the last of his wine. "Which brings me to my next suggestion," he said. "How about a walk on the beach?"

"Where did that come from?" she said.

"Come on," he said, rising from the table, "too much thinking is dangerous."

"For whom?" she quipped, getting to her feet.

He stepped over, took her hands and drew her to him. "For all concerned," he murmured. Then he lightly kissed her.

Zara had been wanting him to kiss her for hours, though a part of her had been afraid—probably the same part of her that had been wary of this trip. But now that she was in his arms, she felt her tension fade and she melted into his embrace. Alec's kiss deepened and she realized the heavy pounding of her heart was no accident.

After the kiss ended, she pressed her face into his chest, savoring his masculine scent. And as Alec toyed with a loose tendril of her hair, Zara decided that Madame Wu might have hit a bull's-eye, after all.

CHAPTER SIX

THEY STOOD IN THE SAND, staring at the moonlight reflecting off the water. Alec squeezed her fingers, as if signaling that his thoughts were running parallel to hers. Zara had let this move along faster and further than she had with any other man. Was that a good sign, or a bad one? There was no doubt what Arianna would think. Her twin had once called her a prude because she'd said she never even liked kissing a guy unless she really cared for him. Not that her sister was fast, but Ari wasn't afraid of experimenting. Zara wasn't like that. Until now, that is, when she began to feel that maybe Arianna had the right idea, after all.

Alec gestured toward the water. "Pretty, isn't it?"

"Just lovely."

"Ever had a moonlight swim in the sea?"

"I've skied by moonlight," she said.

"There's nothing as sensuous as your skin being caressed by the warm water."

"You make me wish I'd brought my suit," she murmured.

"You don't need a suit. In fact, it's much better without one. That way you can really feel the water."

"If you're suggesting we go skinny-dipping, Alec, you're talking to the wrong twin. Arianna might do something like that, but not me."

He gave her a funny look. "How did your sister get into the conversation?"

"I don't know. I guess I was thinking about her. But you might as well know I'm the shy one in the family."

"You don't strike me as being shy," he said.

"Well, let me put it this way. I don't think I know you well enough for a moonlight swim."

"Then I guess we'll have to wait until you do know me well enough," he said, putting his arm around her shoulders. "And if you'd rather not ever, that's fine."

They continued walking. Zara liked it that Alec had been so understanding—in spite of her defensiveness. That wasn't like her. Maybe she was afraid. A romantic adventure with a stranger was tantalizing, but she was all too aware that there could be a downside.

When they got to the end of the beach they looked out at the water again. Alec talked for a while about his boat and the romance of the sea, but she hardly heard a single word he was saying. She was imagining what it would be like to swim naked with him. Of course, it wasn't something she'd normally do. But sometimes a person had to travel to get away from themselves. Could that have been the meaning of her fortune?

"I'm boring you," Alec said, interrupting himself.

"No, not at all."

"Sometimes I talk too much," he said.

"If I wasn't listening closely, it was because I was thinking of you."

"Oh?" he said, raising his eyebrows, waiting for her to explain.

Zara had a sudden crisis of confidence and wondered if she should have kept her thoughts to herself. "I was just imagining what it would be like to go swimming with you, now in the moonlight, and everything...." she said, feeling her face heat up.

"When the time is right, we will," he replied, caressing her cheek. "But you know what? I should be getting you home."

"You're probably right, but it was a wonderful evening," she said, looking up into his eyes.

Reaching up, she pulled his face down and

kissed him. Alec responded by kissing her back. It was a deeper, more passionate kiss than before.

"So, you're the shy one in the family," he whispered into her ear as he held her against him.

"I guess there are sides to me I didn't even know," she replied.

"I like and respect the woman I picked up at the airport," he said, kissing her on the end of the nose. "So I am going to take you back now."

He took her hand and they started back to the house. Zara wasn't sure what to think. Part of her wanted to kick him in the shins for not carrying her off and making love with her, but the other part of her wanted to embrace him and thank him for being so good, so understanding.

Soon they came to the bluff where the house sat. Hand in hand, they climbed the narrow path that led up to the terrace.

Zara was the first to reach the door. When she looked inside, she gasped. Dishes had been shoved to the side, many were on the floor. In the middle of the bare spot was her small evening bag, turned upside down, the contents spread all over. She rushed in, Alec right behind her.

She checked her wallet. Her money and the passport were still there.

"Anything missing?" Alec asked.

Zara poked through her things. "No. What could have happened?"

"This isn't an ordinary burglary," he said. "Whoever was here was sending you a message."

"Yeah," she said, grimly. "And I know exactly what that message is."

AS SHE HELPED Alec clean the mess, Zara realized that her evening had gone from a delight to a disaster. She didn't want to make too much of it, but she was really frightened.

Alec may have been more concerned than he was letting on. He made a few lighthearted jokes, but there were hints of seriousness between the smiles. Once the place was back in order, he went around the house, locking windows and doors.

"I probably should have done this before we went for our walk," he said. "I'm really sorry, Zara."

"Hey, it's not your fault. Mr. Bandini is after me, not you."

He gave her a faint smile, but the remark didn't seem to make him feel any better. He moved toward her, though, taking her by the shoulders.

"I don't know what your sister is mixed up

in," he said, "but it's certainly complicating your life unnecessarily."

"The irony is, I don't even have it."

"Have what?"

She sighed. "I was hoping the issue was moot, but apparently I have to let Mr. Bandini know I don't have the damned manuscript anymore."

"You don't?" he said. "I mean, you don't have what manuscript?"

She told him about the mix-up at the airport in New York and how some Mafia-type had mistaken her for her sister, and how she'd been followed to the Caribbean.

"But he gave you the manuscript, right?" Alec said. "Are you saying you didn't bring it with you?"

"No, I brought it, all right, but I gave it to Mark to take back to Arianna."

"They're harassing you, but for nothing," he said in an ironic tone she didn't quite understand.

"How do I let them know that I'm just an innocent bystander?"

"That's the problem," Alec said, rubbing his chin. "You can't."

"So, what *do* I do?"

"First, I take you home. I'm sorry. I haven't been much of a bodyguard. Clearly, we were followed here, and I didn't realize it."

"I'm glad I came, though. We had a nice dinner. And a lovely walk on the beach."

Alec tweaked her nose. "Yeah, but you'll be better company if I keep you in one piece. Come on, let's get back to your hotel."

They left the house then. She felt a little creepy as they drove in the darkness through the dense vegetation to get to the road. On the way back to the Maison des Caraïbes, she appreciated his efforts to lighten her mood by telling her stories about the crazy antics of a group of tourists from the Midwest who had chartered his boat, but she couldn't shake her feelings of uneasiness.

When they reached the hotel, Alec pulled into the circular drive and parked. Zara glanced over at him and instantly he understood her dread.

"Why don't I walk you to your room?" he said.

She was glad for the offer and didn't even attempt to decline. "Thanks."

As they made their way through the grounds in the bright moonlight, Zara took his arm. When they got to the entrance of her bungalow, she handed him the key. He opened the door, and stepped inside, turning on the light. Then he froze. She looked past him and saw that the room had been ransacked. "Oh, my God."

"Looks like they've decided to leave no stones

unturned," he muttered. "And so much for hotel security."

Her eyes filled as she glanced around the room, but it was as much out of anger and frustration as fear. "Damn!" she said. "Alec, what am I going to do?"

"Well, you aren't staying here," he said. "You're coming with me to my boat."

There was a certainty in his voice, the most determination she'd heard from him yet. And a resolve. Under any other circumstances she would have protested. Instead, she turned and hugged him, taking comfort in his embrace.

"Gather up your things," he said, going to the phone. "I'll notify the desk. And you might want to change into something more comfortable."

Zara felt relieved, so relieved that the implications hardly mattered. If Alec Perrin represented a danger to her, it was a danger she was willing to accept.

THEY DROVE TO THE Cul-de-Sac du Marin, where Alec's boat was moored. He explained that he ferried himself to and from the shore in a rubber Zodiac which he left at the home of Philippe Deveureux, the friend who owned the taxi. That way his Zodiac was secure whenever he was ashore. At Philippe's house Alec briefly talked to his friend before returning for Zara and her suitcases.

Following a path in the moonlight, they arrived at the tiny dock where the Zodiac was tied up. "I asked Philippe to keep an eye out for anyone suspicious," he explained. "That's one nice thing about a boat—it's like being in a castle, surrounded by a moat."

"A platoon of marines would be nice, too," she said.

"I'll keep you safe from the bad guys," he said, helping her into the Zodiac. "I promise."

Zara liked hearing that, but there was a question he hadn't addressed—would she be safe from him? But once they were alone, the mood would undoubtedly change. Who could say what the fates had in mind for them then?

There was barely a ripple on the placid waters of the cove as they puttered along. With the bright moon overhead, Zara could almost see the greens on shore and the blues of the water.

When they reached Alec's boat, he helped her up the ladder and onto the deck, then lifted up her suitcase. Zara glanced at the dark shore, at least a quarter of a mile away. As Alec joined her on deck, she nervously took his hands.

"Thank you for being my friend," she said.

He kissed her on the forehead. "Never has being a friend to someone been so tough,'' he said. "Come on, I'll show you to your stateroom."

Alec took her bags and led her down the dark companionway, holding her hand. The first thing he did was light a lantern. The guest cabin, which he took her to directly, was small but cozy. His cabin—the crew quarters as he called them—was aft. The air was close and he opened the two port holes, giving her a bit of cross ventilation.

"This is awfully nice," she said, "but I want it understood I'm paying for this."

"No, you aren't."

"Yes, I am."

"I won't accept a dime."

"Well, I won't stay unless you agree to let me pay."

He put his hands on his hips, looking especially sexy in the flickering light of the lantern. "Are you prepared to swim ashore?"

"If necessary."

Alec did not look upset, though he did appear a bit frustrated. She wasn't sure, though, if it had anything to do with her paying or not paying. His body language told her what he really wanted to do was kiss her.

"We'll discuss this in the morning," he said. "It's late and I'm sure you're tired. I'll let you get to bed."

Before turning to go, he reached out and touched her cheek. "You've had a rough day, but for me it's been a memorable one. I'm going to remember our walk on the beach for a long, long time."

Zara nodded. "Me, too."

"I guess it's pretty obvious how attracted to you I am."

"I'm attracted to you, too," she said.

"That's going to make staying on good behavior difficult," he said softly. "I hope you realize that."

"It's going to be difficult for me, too."

"I wish you wouldn't say that, because I'm trying very hard to be a gentleman."

She took a deep breath before plunging ahead. "What if I told you that isn't what I want?"

He swallowed hard, looking into her eyes. "What do you want, Zara?"

She gazed at him for a long time, then decided to be honest. "I think I'd like that swim you talked about earlier."

"It is a beautiful evening," he said. "And the water's warm."

"I know."

Alec went to the closet and took out a couple of terry robes. He handed one to her. "Do you want to undress here or up on deck?"

"Here," she said.

He left the cabin. Zara hugged the robe to her breast. She couldn't believe it! She, Zara Hamilton, was having a romantic adventure! She'd never dared to think in those terms before, but then she'd never been with Alec before. He made everything seem natural and right. Even the forbidden.

When she arrived on deck a few minutes later, she found Alec's clothing in a pile. Looking out over the moonlit waters of the cove, she saw him twenty or thirty yards from the boat.

"The water couldn't be more perfect," he called to her.

Zara knew if she hesitated she'd never do it, so she untied her robe, let it slide onto the deck, then dove into the water. She took several strokes before coming to the surface. It was heavenly—warm, sensuous. Absolutely perfect.

Alec hadn't moved. Nor had he said anything. Using the breaststroke, she swam toward him, stopping a few feet away. She treaded water.

"You're right," she said, "it *is* nice."

"I don't know why I'm surprised at your pluck," he said.

"Pluck? Audacity is more like it."

"The many sides of Zara."

She inched toward him, her pulse racing at the

knowledge that they were both naked. Alec clearly wanted to touch her and the simple truth was she wanted to touch him.

He offered his hand and she took it. No longer having to strain to stay afloat, she was able to relax. She felt weightless, his hand her only connection with the solid world.

Alec continued to support her, but made no attempt to draw her to him. His gaze seemed intense. Looking into his hooded eyes made her heart trip. His grip was firm, but still not demanding.

"What are you thinking?" she asked.

"That I'd like to take you into my arms."

"I thought so."

"What are *you* thinking?" he asked.

"How much I like this."

Alec pulled her a bit closer so that their faces were only a couple of feet apart. Zara touched his face affectionately, then spun suddenly and swam away, laughing. The feeling of the water on her bare skin was exhilarating. This was turning out to be the most sensuous experience of her life.

After a while she stopped and looked back. Alec hadn't moved.

"What would you do if I swam back to the boat now?" she asked.

"Follow you," he replied with a laugh.

She swam back to the boat and climbed up the ladder hanging over the gunwale. She was glad for the faintness of the light, but didn't feel at ease until she had put on the robe.

He starting swimming back to the boat with long powerful strokes. When he got to the ladder, she turned the other way, facing the shore and the scattered lights on the darkened land.

Behind her she heard Alec stepping onto the deck. She heard him put on the robe, then move behind her, resting his hands on her shoulders. Lowering his head, he kissed her neck and she closed her eyes, letting her head fall back as she reveled in the feel of his lips on her flesh.

Alec continued kissing her, pressing his lips to the shell of her ear and caressing her with his warm breath. When the tip of his tongue grazed her ear, she moaned softly. Turning into his embrace, she kissed him deeply, giving herself up to her desires.

After a moment Alec lifted her into his arms effortlessly and carried her down the companionway to her cabin. He put her on the bed and stood over her, the shadows from the lamplight playing on his face. Then, reaching down, he loosened the tie of her robe and pushed back the flaps so that he could see her.

"You're beautiful," he said, his voice husky with emotion.

His eyes were glistening and hers were, too. Zara knew this would not end until they'd made love.

When he began to remove his robe, she took in his lean, deeply tanned frame. His chest was covered with a dense mat of hair and she eyed it as he lowered himself beside her, his eyes moving back and forth between her face and breasts. Her heart tripped wildly as his skin brushed up against hers.

He kissed her, turning her nipples hard as stone. Even before he began kissing her breasts, and feathering his hands up and down her hips and thighs she was liquid and ready, craving him.

He entered her gently, but she tensed anyway. Then she began to relax and their bodies undulated. Her excitement rose rapidly and within a few short minutes she was on the verge of climax. The pleasure, her need, were overwhelming. She'd never wanted a man this badly, and experienced such a need to be possessed.

Her orgasm came moments after his. They lay together afterward, his heart thudding against her breast, their breathing ragged. But she felt so complete, so whole, so fulfilled.

"Oh, Alec," she whispered, feeling totally drained.

"You're wonderful," he murmured against her neck. Then he pulled his face back so he could see her. He pushed a strand of moist hair back off her forehead. "I want you to know that this wasn't why I brought you here," he said.

"And it wasn't why I came," she replied.

"Why did you come?"

She caressed his rough cheek. "I wanted to be with you," she said softly.

"Nothing you could say would make me happier," he said, kissing the tip of her nose.

She continued to stroke his face. "Do you realize we haven't even known each other one day?"

"A day, a week, a month. It doesn't matter, Zara. This is very special."

"Vacation romances are supposed to be."

"I don't regard this as a vacation romance."

"Alec," she said, pressing her finger to his lips, "I don't even want to think where I am or how we met. I just want to enjoy being with you right now."

She then closed her eyes, luxuriating in his nearness as she slowly drifted into sleep.

CHAPTER SEVEN

"SHE GAVE IT TO WHO?" Lou barked into the phone receiver.

"To some guy named Mark. Her sister's former fiancé. He was waiting for her at the hotel when we arrived," Alec explained.

Lou Sheridan sputtered on the other end of the line. "That's a bunch of garbage, Perrin. Either you're trying to snow me or she snowed you. First you tell me she's an identical twin, now you're saying she's already unloaded the manuscript."

"It's the truth and if you don't like it, tough. Our deal was I'd either get you the manuscript or find out what happened to it. I held up my end of the bargain. Case closed. So long, Lou."

Alec hung up the phone, feeling strangely content. After paying the clerk for the call, he left the post office, stepping out into the early morning sun. Taking a deep breath of the wonderful fragrant air, he headed back up the street to where he'd left the taxi. He found Emile sitting on the fender.

"Bonjour, my friend," he said to the gendarme. "Beautiful morning, isn't it?"

"Alec," Emile said, "if I didn't know better, I'd say you're in love."

"My god! I had no idea it shows," Alec said with a grin.

Emile laughed. "Well, I have good news."

"What's that?"

"Early this morning we arrested the gangster, Bandini. He was trying to charter a private plane to take him off the island. He is now in jail."

"Ah, that *is* good news."

"So, Mademoiselle Hamilton's problems are over."

Alec considered that, frowning. "But that's not good news for me, Emile."

"No?"

"I would like an excuse to protect Miss Hamilton from Bandini for a few more days."

"Truly? Are you serious about the woman?"

"I'm serious about wanting to get to know her better. Ms. Hamilton and I need to get away for a while, Emile. And when we get back, then we'll discover the good news."

"Which is why you have all the supplies in the taxi," the policeman said, tossing his head.

"You're an excellent detective, Emile."

"And you, Alec, are a rogue," Emile said.

"Yes, my friend, but a rogue with a good heart and good intentions!"

WHEN ZARA AWOKE, it was morning. She was lying naked on the bed and she was alone. Alec was gone.

She dug an oversize T-shirt out of her suitcase and went into the main salon, but there was no sign of him there either. Calling out, and getting no response, she looked in the aft cabin, but it, too, was empty. Deciding he must be above, she went up the steps to the deck.

Squinting in the bright light of the midmorning sun, she looked around, but there was no sign of Alec. The Zodiac was gone. He must have gone ashore.

Taking advantage of the solitude, she decided to go for a swim. Removing her shirt, she dove in the crystalline water. It was heavenly. To the north she could see a jagged mountain with emerald green slopes. The rich foliage surrounding the cove created a feeling of seclusion, though she was able to make out a few rooftops in the distance.

After a refreshing swim, she climbed back aboard, scampering below deck. To her delight, there was water in the tiny shower. She got in, rinsed off, washed her hair, and wrapped a towel around her. When she'd finished, Alec had returned. He was in a T-shirt, shorts and Top-Siders.

"Ah," he said, taking her in his arms, "what a delightful sight."

He kissed her lightly on the lips.

"Where were you?" she asked. "When I woke up you were gone."

"I went ashore for supplies. I thought you might want breakfast."

Only then did Zara realize she was hungry. "Actually, I'm famished."

"Breakfast it'll be. But I've got a proposal for you," he said. "What would you think of a short voyage to Saint Lucia? It's the next island down the chain to the south. It's British."

"Why do you want to go there?" she asked.

"I thought it would be good to get away from Martinique for a while. You'll be able to relax. And I'll have you all to myself."

Zara fiddled with the neckline of his shirt as he drew her close. "What'll it cost me?"

"Just four or five more days like last night."

"That's taking advantage of me, you know."

Alec kissed her softly on the lips. "Yes. But I have no scruples."

"Finally, I'm seeing the real Alec Perrin," she teased.

He grinned. "What do you think I am? A gigolo?"

"You didn't get to be the lover you are by accident."

"Tell me, then," he said, stroking her cheek with the back of his fingers, "would you care to continue your education before or after breakfast?"

"If I were a lady, I'd at least wait until after breakfast...maybe even after lunch," she added with a laugh. "But I guess there's no point in pretending."

"God, do I love a reasonable woman," he said, pulling the towel from her and taking her naked body into his arms.

ZARA LAY ON THE DECK, staring up at the cloudless blue sky. After five days of snorkeling, swimming, eating Alec's scrumptious cooking and making love, there was no question about it, she'd found paradise. The past few days had been the most carefree, romantic, sensual, blissful interlude of her entire life.

Alec, she could tell, was happy, too. Half an hour earlier, after her swim in the cove, he'd lathered her with sun lotion and told her to relax because he was going into town to get some provisions for their last meal in Saint Lucia. They were anchored in the bay, two hundred yards from shore, the rooftops of the nearest houses visible in the trees. Tomorrow they would set sail for Martinique and then she would board a flight for New York.

They hadn't talked a lot about what would happen after he put her on her plane at Le Lamentin airport, but he'd made it clear he didn't want their relationship to end. He'd said he wanted to visit her in Aspen, and she'd said she'd like that very much. She'd talked about returning to Martinique, and he'd said he'd like that, too.

That morning she'd awakened feeling sad. It would be their last full day together. She'd noticed Alec seemed kind of blue, as well. Could this be more than a vacation romance? Madame Wu's fortune had been silent about the long-term future.

"Finding romance in an exotic place does not necessarily mean it's just a fling," Alec had said when she'd told him about the second fortune. "Don't forget, I got a fortune at Destiny House, too. I'm supposed to find true happiness in a faraway place, and I'd say I have."

They'd joked about it, but neither had forced a serious conversation. Despite her strong feelings for Alec, Zara still wasn't sure what lay in store for the both of them. Alec had uttered words of love, but she'd sensed a certain reserve, as if an untold truth were nagging at him. Either that, or her own insecurities were showing. The proof would be in what he said when the time for their farewell arrived. She'd take her cue from him.

As she lay in her bikini, drying off in the sun, Zara heard the faint putter of an outboard engine. It seemed early for Alec to be returning, but in the Caribbean, time had a way of drifting by quickly. She was glad he was back, though. For all her doubts she'd come to love him. Very much.

The Zodiac was getting closer. Zara decided to feign sleep. When she'd sunned herself the day before and drifted off to sleep while Alec was swimming, he'd come back and awakened her with a kiss, then they'd made love. Maybe he'd do the same again.

In a few minutes the Zodiac was alongside. Zara heard him coming up the ladder. She did her best to relax so he'd believe she was sleeping. She heard him on the deck. Then, oddly, she heard him clear his throat.

"Excuse me, Miss Hamilton..."

It was a strange voice. Her eyes popped open

and she saw a beefy guy in his early fifties. Shrieking, she jumped to her feet, snatching up the towel and wrapping it around her.

"Forgive the intrusion. My name is Lou Sheridan. I'm with the New York Police Department." He took a small leather case from his pocket and showed her a badge.

Zara was stunned. She searched the man's face, trying to understand. "What are you doing here?"

"I've been looking for you in Martinique the past four days before I learned you'd come to Saint Lucia. I was in Castries last night, and the local police were good enough to make some calls around the island. Is Alec on board?" he asked.

"No, he went ashore for provisions."

Sheridan, who was perspiring heavily, scratched his thinning dark blond hair. "It's just as well. You're really the one I want to talk to."

"Me? What about?" Zara tucked the towel between her breasts, regarding him warily.

"I'll be direct," Sheridan said. "We've had a gentleman by the name of Sal Corsi under surveillance for weeks. Corsi had access to some very sensitive, fully documented information concerning two prominent organized crime families."

"I think I know what you're talking about."

"I'm sure you do. We learned that Corsi passed a manuscript on to you at JFK a week ago. We'd be very interested to know what happened to it."

"I received the manuscript, yes. Unwillingly, I might add, because the man mistook me for my twin who's an editor at a New York publishing house. My intention was to give the manuscript to my sister."

"Then you aren't Arianna Hamilton?"

"No, she's my sister."

"But you're traveling under her passport, are you not?"

Zara explained how that had come about.

Sheridan scratched his head. "We contacted Miss Hamilton's office—Arianna Hamilton's office—and they assured us she was in the Caribbean on vacation."

"Arianna was happy to have me switch places so she could get away from it all. But I'll be glad to show you my Colorado driver's license if you don't believe me."

"If you don't mind."

Zara went below to get her wallet. While she was in her cabin, she slipped on a cover-up and returned to the deck where she found Lou Sheridan mopping his brow. She showed him her identification.

"I'll be. What about the manuscript? Where is it?"

Zara told him about Mark's visit to the hotel.

"Son of a gun," he said, shaking his head, "So Perrin was telling the whole truth."

She felt her stomach drop. "What are you talking about?"

"Oh, so Alec never told you, huh?" Sheridan hesitated for a minute. Then he plunged ahead. "I guess you would have found out sooner or later. I hired Alec to get the manuscript from you. Cost me a couple of grand and he didn't even produce it."

"Wait a minute," she said, incredulous. "You're saying Alec was paid to get the manuscript. That my meeting him wasn't accidental?"

"No, ma'am. Though, if it's any consolation, Alec must have a high regard for you because he seems to have continued with the charade after the show was over."

Zara turned bright red. "The rat," she muttered through clenched teeth. The more she thought about it, the angrier she got.

"Miss Hamilton," Sheridan said, "I'll have to apologize. I had no idea it was a sensitive issue."

"No need to apologize," she said, looking

past him toward shore. "You've actually done me a favor. For the first time I see the real Alec Perrin, and he's not the man I thought he was." Unable to control her anger, she turned and began pacing. "It was the other fortune!" she said out loud. "Never judge a book by its cover. That was what Madame Wu was really trying to tell me!"

"Ma'am?"

"Oh, nothing."

"I've obviously upset you," Sheridan said. "If there's anything I can do…"

"Are you going back to New York?"

"Yes. As soon as I can get back to Martinique."

"I'd like to bum a ride from you," she said. "In exchange, I'll answer your questions, though I warn you, I know virtually nothing."

"For starters, I'd like to learn as much as I can about this fellow you gave the manuscript to."

"When we get to New York, I'll put you in touch with him. Would that help?"

"That would be a great help."

Zara cast an angry glare toward the shore. "Give me five minutes to pack, Mr. Sheridan."

ZARA WASN'T ON DECK when Alec got back. Could she have gone swimming? he wondered.

A wave of panic went through him as it occurred to him she might have gotten into trouble in the water. He looked in all directions, but saw nothing. Maybe she was asleep below. Fighting back his fear, he rushed to her cabin. The bed had been stripped, the closet was empty and her suitcase gone. Then he noticed a note on the bed. Snatching it up, he read—

Dear Alec,

All good things must come to an end, but not always in the way you expect. While you were gone, Lou Sheridan paid a visit. He was relieved to learn that your reports to him have all been accurate and that you weren't deceiving him. I must say, I didn't share his joy.

My only regret is not finding out how you were going to tell me. If I may leave you with a compliment, let me say that your skills as a lover are exceeded only by your skills as an actor. Thanks for the meals and good times. May all your pigeons be as easy to trap. Happy hunting, Alec.

Zara

Alec crumpled the note and dropped down on the bed, stunned. He felt as though he'd been kicked in the gut. "Damn!" he shouted. If Lou Sheridan had been there, he'd wring his neck. But then, he knew he had only himself to blame. All week he'd been wrestling with how to tell her. The problem was, he didn't want to ruin it when everything was going so smoothly. Now, in spite of his good intentions, that was exactly what had happened.

He checked his watch. Obviously she'd left with Sheridan. Well, he'd just have to follow her. Do whatever it took. Zara Hamilton was going to hear the truth, and she was going to hear how he really felt—whether she wanted to or not.

CHAPTER EIGHT

ZARA AWOKE the next morning in Arianna's bed. She was miserable. Her plane had arrived at JFK around midnight in a rainstorm. Her taxi into Manhattan had gotten into a minor fender bender. New York at night had seemed especially forbidding. And she hated, positively hated Alec Perrin.

She'd hardly slept, thinking about him. How could he have been so cruel, leading her on that way? Cynical. That's what he was. He'd even spoken of love. What a fool she'd been to believe him!

To top everything off, she'd found out that their romantic voyage to Saint Lucia hadn't even been necessary. Benny Bandini had been arrested before they'd left Martinique!

Just thinking about it, she began to cry again. That was the worst part—she was letting Alec Perrin get to her. Reason told her that the most she could have expected was a vacation romance. So why then did it matter that it had ended with a rude awakening? Even if he'd played it straight with her, goodbye would still have been good-bye. She would have been right where she was now, alone in her sister's apartment, preparing to return to Aspen. The only difference was she wouldn't have been disillusioned. Was it that big a deal? Did it matter that it had ended with a rude awakening?

Well, yes it did. And the only reason she could think of besides her wounded pride was the fact that she'd been harboring hope that their relationship wouldn't have ended at the airport—that somehow, some way, they'd have gotten together again. Boy, had she ever been naive!

Getting out of bed, Zara went into the kitchen and put the kettle on. Arianna didn't even own a coffeepot. Living the fast life of a New Yorker, all she had time for was instant coffee. She pictured her sister in Aspen, sitting in her house with all that open sky, all that silence, and all that time on her hands. Poor Arianna was probably going stir-crazy, chomping at the bit to get back to the Big Apple.

Waiting for the water to boil, Zara noticed the pile of mail on the counter that the super had brought up during their absence. The letter on top caught her eye. It was in her sister's handwriting and it was addressed to her. She tore open the envelope and read the brief note.

Zara

God, that manuscript looks like *dynamite* all right! Maybe this will be the project that makes my career! Hope you weren't too inconvenienced having to deal with it, but appreciate you getting it to me. This thing is so big, I've decided to drop out of sight for a while to study it before I talk to my boss. Mark insisted it couldn't be in either Aspen or New York, and that I can't tell anyone. Beyond that, the less said, the better. I'll be in touch.

Ari

P.S. Your friend, Lina Prescott, called, desperate to talk to you. I gave her your hotel number in Martinique, but she said you'd gone.

Zara read over the note again, laughing at the line about not being too inconvenienced. If she only knew! The rest of it—the breezy ambiguity, the off-to-slay-the-dragon tone—was vintage Arianna. The cryptic reference to Mark was also typical. But at least it sounded as though Mark had used what leverage he had with her. Maybe their little chat in Martinique had helped. Of course, if Ari went underground for a while to work on the book, she wouldn't get the full story until Christmas.

The postscript gave her pause. Why would Lina want desperately to talk to her? Could something have gone wrong with her pregnancy? She decided to give her a call and put her mind at ease, just in case it was truly important.

The kettle was beginning to boil so she went over to put some coffee crystals in a mug. She checked the clock. It was still early in Aspen, but Lina often went down to her shop before eight to do paperwork. Zara decided to have her coffee first, then give her a call.

As she sat at Arianna's little kitchen table, looking out at the drizzle, she couldn't help but think of the sunny Caribbean and those idyllic days she'd spent with Alec Perrin. And they *had* seemed idyllic—at least until she found out what the man was really like! But why was she so bitter? Arianna would have laughed it off. Why couldn't she?

When she'd finished her coffee, Zara went to the phone in Arianna's small living room. She'd put her troubles behind her by focusing on other people's problems. That was one of the benefits of law—when you were busy fighting other people's battles, you tended to forget your own.

She dialed Lina's number. Her friend answered

on the second ring. "Hi, Lina, it's Zara," she said. "I understand you've been trying to reach me."

"Oh, thank goodness you called," Lina said. "I've been pacing for a week. I'm just sick."

"Is it the baby? You did get pregnant, didn't you?"

"Yes, but now I'm not so sure it was a good idea."

"Lina, what's wrong?"

There was a sob on the other end of the line. Finally she spoke. "I had a call from the clinic. A nurse. She warned me in confidence that the embryo the doctor planted in me was stolen."

"Stolen? What do you mean?"

"Used without the mother's permission."

"Oh, my God..."

"Just answer one question. Can they take my baby away from me?"

Zara thought for a moment. The last thing Lina needed to hear was a dissertation on fraud or breach of contract or lack of good faith. "Lina, that baby is in your womb, and not a thing is going to happen to it. I need to know more to give you an informed opinion, but for now I want you to take it easy. The cavalry is on the way."

Lina's response was half laugh, half cry. "I wasn't sure if I should call the doctor first, or wait for you to get back. I finally decided to wait."

"You did the right thing. I'll be there tomorrow. You and your baby are the very first things I'll take care of."

"Oh, good," Lina said with a sigh.

"In the meantime, just relax. Okay?"

"I'll try."

"I'll call you tomorrow, as soon as I get home."

"Thanks, Zara. I feel a lot better."

Zara hung up. Welcome back to the real world, she told herself. But she had to admit it made her feel somewhat better to get back in the saddle again. That way she'd be productive—at least during the day. Only the nights would be a problem. But if images of swimming with Alec in the warm Caribbean Sea came to mind, she'd simply have to force herself to think of something else.

Returning to the kitchen, she made herself another cup of coffee and sipped it as she watched the rain. Tears welled in her eyes. It was a lot easier to tell her clients that things would be all right than it was to tell herself that.

There was a knock at the door then. Reminding herself she was in New York, she went to the door and, getting up on her toes, peeked through the peephole. It was a man, but she couldn't see his face.

"Who is it?" she said.

There was no answer.

"Hello? Who's there?"

"Zara, it's me, Alec."

Her heart began to pound like crazy. She looked down at herself. She was in the T-shirt she slept in. Her hair was a mess. Her eyes were puffy. Not to mention the fact that Alec Perrin was the last person on earth she wanted to see.

"I'm afraid I'm not dressed," she said through the door. "I can't talk to you."

"Zara, please open the door. I really have to speak with you. I don't care what you look like."

"Well, *I* care how I look!" She realized that wasn't quite right. "I mean, it doesn't matter because I'm not opening the door."

"Zara, if necessary I'll break the damned door down. Open it. Five minutes and I'll leave, if that's what you want."

"Leave now."

"Please. Just five minutes."

She opened the door, giving him a stern glare. "I look like hell, which is fine," she said, "because you deserve it."

"You look fabulous to me," he said contritely. "Like an angel."

"Please. I've heard enough of your sweet talk already, Perrin. Spare me." She went over and dropped onto the sofa, crossing her legs as Alec closed the door. She checked her watch. "You have four minutes and thirty seconds left."

His browny-blond hair was mussed and it looked as if he hadn't shaved in a couple of days. In fact, he appeared just as he had the morning they'd met. Then she'd found it alluring. Now half of her was ready to scratch his eyes out.

"I came right from the boat," he explained. "First flight I could get on. There's only one possible reason I came here, Zara," he said. "Because I love you. I can't stand the thought of you never hearing me say that."

"Alec, please don't insult my intelligence."

"I have absolutely nothing to gain by coming here."

"So, what are you trying to say?"

"That I didn't tell you about Lou hiring me, or that Bandini was arrested, because I didn't want you to leave me before we had a chance to get to know each other."

"Liars generally don't want people to know them for what they are."

"How was I supposed to know I was going to fall in love?" he lamented. "Once I had, it was too late because I already had the job. And I didn't do a thing to harm you. Just the opposite. When I realized you were in danger, my mission was to protect you."

"Alec, did it ever occur to you the truth might work?"

"Yes."

"Then why didn't you tell me the truth?"

"Because I didn't realize it until I found your note. But I intended to tell you everything. Our last night over dinner. I was going to look you in the eyes and let it all come out."

"Easy for you to say now."

He dropped to his knees. "Forgive me. Don't you see, I was blinded by love. A day late is better than never. It's the only mistake I've ever made. Honest. Up till now I've been perfect. And I'll be perfect again, if you'll help me."

She couldn't help herself. She began laughing. "You can't imagine how ridiculous you look," she told him.

"Just say you believe me, you forgive me, and that you'll have lunch with me. You don't even have to say you like me."

He seemed so sincere. But he'd sounded sincere in Martinique, too. "You really expect to come waltzing in here, apologize, and think I can forget what you did?"

"Not forget," he said. "Forgive."

"You're asking an awful lot, Alec. And I still don't believe you."

"What will it take to convince you?"

"That's the problem. I can say I forgive you, and maybe out of simple human decency, I can. But that doesn't change my feelings. I could never trust you, Alec, so there's no point in discussing it further."

"All I'm asking for is a chance."

"A chance to do what? Pull the wool over my eyes again?"

"My intentions were good, Zara, and I didn't betray you."

"No, you took advantage of me."

"If I'm guilty of anything it's being weak, and of being so much in love with you that I feared spoiling things between us, and losing you."

She looked into his eyes and felt herself wavering. "Alec, I wish you wouldn't do this. It's an insult to us both."

"Have lunch with me. That's all I ask."

"I thought five minutes were all you were asking for," she said, checking her watch. "Your time's about up, by the way."

"Lunch," he said.

Zara shook her head. Then she sighed. "You know what hurt the most? I felt like a fool."

"Now you don't have to because I can be the fool," he said.

"And you expect me to go to lunch with you?"

"Trust me. It'll be the experience of your life."

"You're cooking?"

"No, even better."

"Better?"

"Trust me."

ZARA COULDN'T BELIEVE IT when their taxi pulled up in front of Destiny House. Alec had showered and shaved and actually looked pretty good. In Aspen he'd have fit right in. The lunchtime crowd at Madame Wu's gave him a few stares, but that was it.

They'd talked enough that she no longer hated him. She had given him the forgiveness he'd wanted, which meant she was now in roughly the position she had expected to be in when they were to have said their goodbyes at the airport. The big difference, of course, was that she was still holding back some, if only to protect herself.

During lunch she talked about going back to Aspen and the workload waiting for her. Alec was listening, but she could tell his mind wasn't on her words. Neither of them ate much. When

Zara pushed back her plate, she said, "It was a good meal, but I don't know if it was the experience of a lifetime."

"It's not over with yet," he said, signaling for the check.

Madame Wu approached, a knowing smile on her face. "And now your fortune," she said, extending a tray with two cookies on it. "Good luck."

Zara stared at the cookies. "Which one shall I take?"

"Let's ask the expert," Alec said. "Madame Wu?"

"This one is for the lady," she said.

Zara picked up the one she'd pointed to. Alec took the other. Both Madame Wu and Alec were watching her. She had a funny feeling.

"What?" she said.

"Open your cookie," he replied.

She had an ominous feeling, amplified by the look of expectation on Alec's face. She broke the cookie in two and picked up the slip with the fortune that had dropped to the table. It read, "Ask him to go with you."

Her mouth dropped open. She gazed up at Madame Wu, who was grinning. Alec was busy getting the fortune out of his cookie. Zara snatched it from his fingers. His read, "Say yes, but warn her you may never leave."

Her eyes flooded with tears. Laughing, Madame Wu went off to tend to her other customers. Zara looked at Alec. He took her hands, kissing her fingers.

"I know we've got a lot of things to settle, Zara," he said. "And the Aspen restaurant market may not be my cup of tea. But if we get along as well in the Rocky Mountains as we did in the Caribbean, we just might have a future together, somehow, some way."

"You sound pretty sure of this," she said, feeling the last vestiges of her uncertainty crumbling.

"It's not just me, sweetheart," he murmured. "Madame Wu has never missed yet. I don't know about you, but I'd really hate to ruin her average. Let me go with you to Aspen."

Zara thought for a moment, looking into his eyes. Her heart filled with love for Alex. "Under two conditions. First, you have to promise you'll never lie again."

"I promise."

"And the second is, you'll do all the cooking."

He gave her a wily look. "So it *was* my truffle soup, after all!"

Smiling, she gave him a kiss.

Just then Madame Wu returned. She had her tray and there were several fortune cookies. "Miss Hamilton," she said, "I think maybe you want to take a cookie to your sister."

"Arianna would be thrilled, but I thought one of my last two fortunes belonged to her. Does this mean they were both mine?"

"Maybe so. Did two things happen to you...two different things?"

Zara nodded.

Madame Wu looked pleased. "Take this one for your sister," she said, pointing.

Zara took it from the tray, wrapped it in a napkin and put it in her purse.

"Wait a minute," Zara said. "Could I have another for my friend Lina?"

"If you want," Madame Wu replied.

Madame Wu stared at the remaining cookies on the tray. "That one for your friend," she said.

Zara took it. She wrapped it in a paper napkin, took a pen out and marked the napkin so she'd know this cookie was for Lina, and put it in her purse.

"Any more?" Madame Wu said.

"No, if you do as well for Arianna and Lina as you did for me, the world will be a very happy place," she said, glancing at Alec.

He squeezed her hand and gave her a kiss.

"Life is very unpredictable," Madame Wu said, giving her a mysterious smile. "For your sister and your friend, only time will tell."

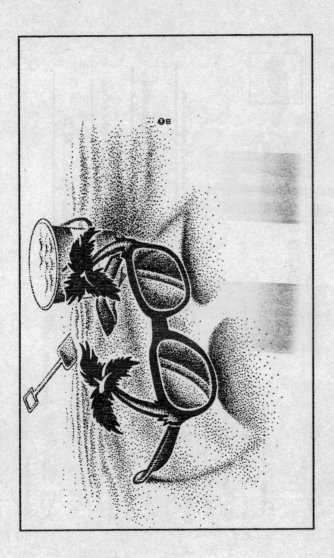

POSTCARD

Dear Arianna,

You were right about all of it —
the book, the gangster and
Martinique. It was the
adventure of a lifetime. But you
didn't know about the sexy ex-
New York cop who came to my
rescue. Ah, romance! The next
wedding night be mine!

Love,
Jana

P.S. Did I tell you how cute
Alec was?

_____ Arianna Hamilton

xxxxxxxxxxxxxxxxxx

xxxxxxxxxxxxxxxxxx

New York, N.Y.

THE DREAM DOC

M.J. Rodgers

Dear Reader,

There are two reasons I like going to Chinese restaurants. One is the superb green tea. And two is the traditional fortune cookie that arrives at the end of the meal.

I don't know anyone who can resist breaking open that cookie to get at the message inside. My dinner companions at these restaurants over the years have been lawyers, doctors, engineers, artists, business managers, secretaries, homemakers, plumbers, accountants—people from all walks of life, rooted in logic and reason, full of both formal and practical wisdom.

And yet, like myself, each and every one of these people eagerly reaches for and reads that long, skinny slip of paper they pull out of their fortune cookie.

What are we looking for? Surely we don't believe those fortunes could come true? Or do we? Could it be we yearn to find a touch of magic in this often too-practical world?

Laura Lacen is about to discover the magic that accompanies her mysterious fortune as she meets "The Dream Doc." I hope you will enjoy her story and the full-length sequel to it, a December Harlequin Intrigue novel called *The Dream Wedding*.

And I also hope that all your fortune cookies are filled with the magic of your fondest dreams.

CHAPTER ONE

"WHY DO YOU really want to work at the Institute of Dreams, Ms. Lacen?"

Laura Lacen uncrossed her legs, trying to relieve the cramp in her left calf. The heel of her shoe snagged her panty hose. She leaned down to give the cramping muscle a sturdy rub. A jagged fingernail ripped her other stocking.

"Ms. Lacen, I asked you a question," Dr. Quinn said, his deep baritone rolling over her like thunder.

Laura straightened in her chair. This interview was beginning to rank right up there with last month's drilling at the dentist.

"Perhaps you didn't hear me when I told you the first time, Dr. Quinn," she said with her sweetest tone and smile.

She knew perfectly well he had. It irritated her that he was making her repeat this lie. And, Laura always looked and sounded her sweetest when she was irritated.

"The research experience at the Institute of

Dreams will help me to home in on my course of study when I do my graduate work," she continued.

"So you didn't enroll in graduate school this fall because of indecision?"

Why did every question out of his mouth sound like an accusation?

"No, Dr. Quinn. My aunt's death caused me to miss this year's admissions deadline. I've been accepted in next year's class."

Dr. Nathaniel Quinn continued to focus his intense, penetrating stare on Laura. She was becoming more certain by the second that he was deliberately trying to make her nervous.

He didn't have to try so hard.

The second she'd walked into the Las Vegas hotel suite for the interview, everything about this man had put her on edge.

Her uncle had told her Nathaniel Quinn was nicknamed "the dream doc" at the Institute of Dreams. What her uncle had failed to mention was that Quinn also looked like a dream.

Deep tan lines intensified the bold forehead, cheekbones and chin of his blatantly handsome face. The sun-bleached ends of his wavy brown hair curled over his collar. His massive shoulder muscles bunched tightly beneath his sorrel cotton shirt, radiating enough kinetic energy to cause the hair on Laura's arms to stand on end.

But it was his restless brown eyes—sprinkled with gold dust and swimming in suspicion—that sent a warning chill though her chest.

Laura had opened refrigerator doors and felt more warmth.

She'd given Dr. Quinn no reason to distrust her. So why did he?

"Ms. Lacen, the Institute is not a temporary testing ground for wanna-be researchers unsure of their graduate course studies. We need people who know what they want and are ready to commit."

"I must not have made myself clear," Laura said. "I *want* to give the research assistant's job a try. I'm willing to *commit* to the year specified in your ad."

"A year? My work could take a decade to complete."

"If you're looking for a permanent employee, why did your ad specify you wanted someone for only a year?"

"I want someone who is flexible, Ms. Lacen."

No, what you want is someone else, Laura thought.

She leaned back in her chair and crossed her arms. She was certain her interviewer-cum-inquisitor was just going through the motions. She wasn't getting the job.

In truth, she was relieved. She hadn't wanted to be his assistant in the first place.

Still, whatever prejudice made Nathaniel Quinn decide against her, at least he should have been more subtle about it. Laura had had her fill of arrogant males dismissing her professional goals as though they didn't matter. More than her fill.

There was no way that she'd make it easy for Quinn to reject her application. Matter of fact, she was just stubborn enough to make it as hard as hell.

"I meet every qualification listed in the ad for this position," Laura said.

"Do you even know what we do at the Institute?" he asked.

"I think you know that would be impossible since you make everyone you employ take a secrecy pledge."

Dr. Quinn lurched forward so fast in his chair that he made Laura jump. The force of his deep baritone vibrated every vertebra up her spine.

"Did your uncle tell you about our secrecy pledge?"

"Is that why you're upset? Because Everett got me this interview?"

"I am not upset," Nathaniel Quinn said as his mountainous shoulders assaulted the back of his chair. Considering the force of the blow, Laura was surprised the chair survived.

"I just don't approve of nepotism, Ms. Lacen."

"What nepotism? Granted, my uncle has control over some of the purse strings for the Institute. But he has no authority to make judgments on the people you hire to do its research."

"Are you going to deny that he delays distribution of your aunt's money to those who don't see things his way?"

No, Laura knew her uncle too well to deny it. Still, she had no intention of admitting Everett's failings to this suspicious man seated before her, who obviously had plenty of failings of his own. She firmly believed in family loyalty. It was what had gotten her in this mess in the first place.

"Dr. Quinn, let's leave my uncle out of this, please? Besides he wasn't the one who told me about your secrecy pledge."

"Then who did?"

"Your personnel officer mentioned it just before setting up this interview in a hotel suite ninety miles away from the Institute. You have to admit the wall of concealment surrounding whatever you do out there is high."

"Ms. Lacen, you openly admit to being ignorant of our research. Yet, you say you want to take part in it. I find your attitude illogical."

"How you study dreams may be a mystery, but the fact that you study dreams is common knowledge. It's not illogical for me to be interested in dream interpretation."

"Isn't it?"

Laura's annoyance once again intensified the syrupy pleasant tone of her voice. "My undergraduate degree is in psychology, remember?"

"The job opening is in my department. I'm a research biologist, not a psychologist. My focus is *quite* different."

Laura uncrossed her arms and leaned forward. "I'd be interested to learn how a biologist studies the dreaming mind. Do you approach it from a biochemical standpoint?"

"I am not here to discuss my work. Your application for the research assistant position is the topic."

Laura leaned back in her chair and crossed her arms again. "Excuse me for presuming to ask questions about the job for which I'm applying. I have no idea what came over me."

Laura watched as his lips thinned to the width of paper sheets. She was delighted to see her dart had hit its target. She fully intended to send a few more its way.

"Perhaps you wouldn't mind telling me what is so problematic with your position that it's remained vacant for the last six months?" she said.

The gold dust in Nathaniel Quinn's eyes suddenly seemed to shift and reshape into solid golden bullets, aimed at her as though ready to fire. A warning shot up Laura's spine.

He positively roared his words at her. "How do you know how long the position has been open?"

Laura nervously uncrossed her arms. "The personnel officer at the Institute must have told me."

He loomed over the table toward her. "Personnel would not inform an applicant of that."

Damn, this guy was intimidating. Why did he get so upset every time she mentioned the little she knew about the job?

Laura reminded herself that the worst Dr. Quinn could do was deny her this position. Since he had already decided to do just that, she had nothing to fear. Right?

She sat up, making her spine ramrod straight. She met his angry eyes with a pair of her own.

"My uncle must have mentioned how long the position's been open. I see nothing wrong with his having done so. Now you tell me what's wrong with the job.''

He stared at her for a long uncomfortable moment before answering. ''Nothing's wrong with the job. Good research assistants are damn hard to find. The young men consider partying in their off hours more important than staying awake on the job. The young women leave to get married or start looking at me like I'm husband material.''

''Being a good-looking doctor must be such a heavy burden to carry,'' Laura said, her sarcasm barely veiled by the softness of her voice.

She leisurely leaned back in her chair. ''Perhaps your problem has been in employing those dewy-eyed youngsters who still lack good judgment when it comes to men?''

Laura watched his eyes flash at her. A delicious tingle dived down her spine. Another dart had hit home.

''The fact that you're twenty-seven, instead of the typical twenty-two, is not necessarily a factor in your favor, Ms. Lacen. Why did you delay going to college for five years?''

Even if this was an appropriate question for a prospective employer to be asking a prospective employee, Laura resented it.

"I was developing that good judgment about men," she said, with a defiant lift of her chin.

If Quinn asked her to explain that last comment, Laura was prepared to make him sorry. Very sorry.

"You're hardly suited for this job," he said.

Laura fumed as she faced the unfairness of his words.

"What do you find wanting in my qualifications? I was graduated at the top of my class. My last two undergraduate years I was an assistant to Dr. Dale Finholm, at the University of California in Berkeley. He's one of the acknowledged giants of psychological research. His evaluations of my work are glowing."

"A little too glowing."

"I beg your pardon?"

"Dr. Finholm did not require you to work graveyard shifts."

"I prefer night work."

"Nor did he insist you travel to a remote desert institute. Why aren't you assisting him during this next year?"

Because I was stupid enough to let my uncle talk me into seeing you today, Dr. Devoid of all Civility.

"Dr. Finholm didn't ask me to come back,"

Laura said aloud. At least, technically, that was true.

"He told me he wants you back."

Laura blinked in surprise. "You discussed me with him?"

"That's rather obvious, isn't it? Now, for the last time, Ms. Lacen. Why do you *really* want to work at the Institute?"

Laura knew Nathaniel Quinn had done his homework on her. The only way she'd get out of this one was to spin another lie.

Damn. She hated lying. Even if it was for a good cause. Maybe she could get away with an embellishment of the truth?

She let out an awkward half breath, half sigh that she didn't have to feign.

"Another research assistant has signed on with Dr. Finholm this year. He's the reason that I have decided not to return."

"What bothers you about this other research assistant?"

"He has a strong romantic interest in me and does not take rejection well. He's been acting quite…crazy. The situation has grown most trying."

Yes, it had, but nothing she couldn't handle. Rob was twenty and just suffering from an older-woman fixation.

Laura watched the gold dust in Quinn's eyes settle into a new and expected emotion. "Those situations can be...awkward."

It was the nicest thing he'd said to her since the interview began. Still, she sensed the only reason he believed her was because this was a problem he faced—and more than once, she'd wager.

Yes, this dream doc's devastating good looks probably plucked the eager heartstrings of any and all impressionable females under the age of fifty. No, better make that ninety.

Fortunately, Laura was no longer the impressionable type.

"What opinion do you hold about the dreaming process?" Dr. Quinn asked.

Wait a minute. Could it be he was actually asking her a question that related to the job opening?

"I don't have an opinion," she said, shocked into telling the absolute truth. "My classes and research with Dr. Finholm involved behavior analysis, not dream interpretation. I haven't given dreams much thought."

"And yet you're suddenly interested in devoting the next year to assisting me in their study?" he accused more than asked, his distrust etched into his every syllable.

I'd rather run barefoot through a dozen angry scorpions, Dr. Total Lack of Warmth and Charm.

"I'm prepared to keep an open mind," Laura said aloud. "After all, that's what being a scientist is all about. Hire me and you'll find I can be a fast learner and a solid contributor."

She followed up her politically correct words with an equally politically correct smile. Let him find fault with that.

"This interview is over," Quinn said abruptly, nothing appropriate about his tone nor politically correct about his expression.

Laura lost her smile. She rose to her feet and slung her bag over her shoulder. She swept toward the door in as quick a stride as her damn high heels would allow.

Why had she bothered to wear them and her best business suit to this pointless interview on what promised to be a scorcher of a day? She could have shown up in her much more comfortable running shoes, shorts and T-shirt for all it mattered.

"Just a moment, Ms. Lacen."

She had reached the door when Nathaniel Quinn's deep baritone blasted out its demand. And there was no mistaking his tone. It was a demand.

She was tempted to ignore it, and just storm out, slamming the door behind her.

It was what her uncle would have done. Indeed, she had seen Everett Thaw do a lot of door slamming in his time. But, in the end, it was her Aunt Molly's words that she heeded.

Don't let anyone make you into something less than you are.

Laura had already done that often enough to know Aunt Molly was right. A person had to be true to herself. Otherwise, she lost her true self and became nothing but a reflection of others. Laura had no intention of becoming Nathaniel Quinn's reflection. This man's rude manner was his problem—not hers.

Laura turned to face him, her smile polite, her tone reasonable.

"Is there something else?"

He said nothing for a long moment, just stared at her.

As their gazes locked this time, a new emotion was apparent in his eyes. It spawned an odd rush of sensation inside Laura. For a very long moment, she couldn't quite catch her breath—or bring herself to break contact with those arresting eyes.

"You'll be told my decision," he said finally,

looking back at her application sitting on the table before him.

Laura already knew Nathaniel Quinn's decision. These last window-dressing words didn't fool her.

She pivoted sharply, snatched open the door and marched out, closing it behind her with a nice comforting snap. Not exactly a bang, but it helped to punctuate her current pique while still maintaining her sense of personal dignity.

MICHAEL SANDS STEPPED out of the second bedroom of the hotel suite where he had been eavesdropping on Nate's interview.

"You heard it all?" Nate asked.

"Yes," Michael said. He slipped into the chair Laura had occupied only a moment before. "You were a bit hard on her."

"Hard on her?" Nate repeated, surprised at Michael's assessment. "I think I was remarkably polite considering the fact that she sat in that chair, looked me straight in the eye and then lied her head off."

Michael steepled his fingers beneath his chin, his expression thoughtful.

"Actually, I was rather impressed at how well she refused to be intimidated by your battering tone. She has guts."

"What she has is gall," Nate corrected. "Interviewing her was a waste of time. I don't know how you talked me into it."

"She's well qualified."

"Come on, Michael. We both know Everett is behind her application. He's obviously trying to get her into our midst so she can report back to him something he can use against us."

"Yes," Michael agreed. "His attempted bribes to our regular employees have failed. Everett probably thinks getting his niece to fill our vacancy is the next logical step. Still, you have to admit that stuff about Dr. Finholm's other research assistant getting a little crazy over her did have the ring of truth."

Nate nodded in response to Michael's words. He had a vivid mental image of Laura's long, rich, mink-colored hair and wide indigo eyes— and that go-to-hell look she had flashed him every time her tone had become its sweetest.

She was the kind of woman who could make a man go crazy, all right. Throughout their interview, his impulse to laugh in the face of her audacity had warred with his impulse to grab her shoulders and shake the truth out of her.

And then there was that other, much more primal and disturbing impulse that swept through him every time her eyes had locked so boldly with his.

Nate got out of his chair and marched over to the window. He dug his hands into his pockets and stared out at the blinding desert morning sun.

"I can't imagine how Everett thought we'd fall for the ploy," he said. "Our hiring his niece would be like pulling the Trojan horse into our camp."

"Aren't you overlooking the opportunity she presents?"

Nate swung back to Michael. "Opportunity? What are you talking about?"

"Put your anger aside for a moment and look at this with that practical scientific researcher's mind of yours," Michael said. "If Everett Thaw fails to get his niece into our midst to act as his spy, he's only going to try something else. He might even offer our regular employees so much money that one will finally break down and become his pawn. At least if Laura Lacen comes to work for us, we'll know who the spy is."

"You're serious? You want me to hire her?"

"With a little charm you might even be able to bring her over to our side."

"Charming women is your department, Michael. If you want to defuse Everett's plan, why don't you hire her?"

"I don't have an opening. Besides, your wing is the safest place. One day you'll be publishing the results of your research in the journals that matter. There'll be nothing she can tell her uncle about your work or clients that could hurt us. What do you say, Nate?"

Nate wanted to help thwart Everett Thaw's petty little war against the Institute. He owed both Michael and the Institute that—and a lot more. Michael had been the only one to give Nate and his work a chance.

But when he imagined the lovely, lying Laura Lacen working closely by his side, he was seized with an overwhelming and unreasoning urge to run.

"You've been without an assistant for a long time, Nate. You've worn yourself out, trying to do everything. Taking into consideration our isolation and the conditions of secrecy we impose, I doubt you'll get a better qualified candidate."

"She's coming to spy, not work," Nate grumbled.

"Still, her outstanding academic record and Dr. Finholm's glowing reports tell us she's driven to do well. Once Laura Lacen is at the Institute, I believe her high work standards will kick in and she'll apply herself to the job."

Nate dug his hands deeper into his pockets. "I don't think I can work with her."

Michael got to his feet. "Why don't you hire her contingent on a two-week probation and find out?"

Leave it to Michael to come up with a perfectly logical answer to every one of his concerns. Damn him.

Nate exhaled in defeat. "All right. Two weeks."

Michael was smiling as he reached the door. "Buck up, Nate. At least she's a knockout. If she does nothing else, she's going to decorate your lab quite nicely for the next couple of weeks."

Thinking about Laura Lacen decorating his lab did nothing to assuage Nate's qualms. Quite the contrary.

"I CAN'T BELIEVE IT," Laura said as she hung up the phone.

"Who was it?" Everett Thaw asked.

Laura returned to her seat at the large dining room table, empty except for her and her uncle. It was on quiet evenings like this that she most missed her Aunt Molly and the noisy dinner guests she always gathered around her.

"Well?" her uncle asked impatiently as he meticulously cut up his baked chicken breast into pea-size pieces. Laura had watched this ritual often. For a portly man, Everett appeared to have a very small throat.

"That was the personnel office at the Institute of Dreams."

Everett squinted at his wristwatch. "Calling at eight o'clock in the evening? Isn't that just like those people. Incompetent, inconsiderate, insensi—"

"They hired me," Laura said.

Everett stopped his tirade. His head shot up. "What? Laura, this is wonderful! And you were so negative about how you had done in the interview. See, I told you they couldn't turn down talent like yours."

"I don't understand it," Laura said, still struggling with the shock. "Dr. Quinn was barely civil to me."

"That's just him. He's barely civil to me, too."

"No, there was more to it. He acted distrustful. Everett, are you sure you've never said anything to him or the others at the Institute about your suspicions concerning Aunt Molly?"

"And alert them? Of course not. These matters have to be handled subtly."

"Then why did Dr. Quinn treat my reasons for wanting the position with such skepticism?"

"No one trusts anyone at that place, Laura."

"Everett, I don't know about this. When it was all hypothetical, it sounded harmless enough. But now that I have the job, I'm having some major second thoughts about this spying stuff."

"Laura, you listen to me. Your aunt was duped by these people into leaving the bulk of her estate in trust to them. The lawyers tell me if I can prove the Institute of Dreams was guilty of undue influence, I can break the trust. Now that you'll be on the inside, you can get that proof!"

"I have only two weeks."

"Two weeks? What do you mean?"

"I'm on a two-week probation."

"Oh. Well, no matter. You can do it."

Easy for him to say. "You're asking a lot of me, Everett."

"Me? You think I'm asking this for myself? Laura, this is for your aunt—the kindest, gentlest person who ever lived."

Everett paused as a tear gathered at the corner of his eye. Laura knew her uncle had his faults. When he'd married her rich, widowed Aunt Molly twenty years before, everyone in the family said it was for Molly's money. It probably was.

But, Laura also knew that Everett loved Molly. When Molly took Laura in when she was ten,

Laura saw daily the love that flowed between her aunt and second husband. Everett made Molly very happy. Laura would always be grateful to him for that.

"Molly always talked about leaving her money to you and me," Everett continued. "Yet, a month after going to the Institute, they brainwashed her into turning her back on those promises."

"It's not like she disowned us," Laura said. "I have the special fund she left to help me through graduate school. I can make it on my own after that. And she did leave you this house and the grounds. With the salary you earn as administrator of her trust, you'll be comfortable for the rest of your life."

Everett Thaw put down his knife and fork. He looked at Laura with an exasperated expression on his puffy face. "This is not about me or you being financially comfortable. This is about those people at that place deliberately duping your aunt so they could take her money. Do you want to see them get away with it?"

"If they really did that to Molly—"

"If? Laura, do you believe Molly would make such momentous changes out of the blue a month before her death?"

Laura had to admit her uncle had a point. Aunt

Molly was known for taking forever to make up her mind, especially when the decision involved money. And she had never talked about the Institute of Dreams. There was something fishy about that sudden rewriting of her trust.

"No," Laura admitted.

"So, are you going to let them get away with it? They will, if we don't come up with some proof."

Laura sighed. "All right. I'll do what I can."

Everett beamed with delight. "I knew I could count on you."

He got up from the table and chugged his way into the study. He was back a moment later.

"This is only an artist's rendition," he said as he handed Laura an eight-by-ten-inch sketch. "They won't allow any photographs to be taken."

Laura studied the drawing of the four-wing building, sitting atop a high mesa. It looked like a giant white bird that had come to rest on the red rock. The muted colors of the gilded desert valley were lovely beneath a brilliant blue sky.

"That's the Institute of Dreams?" Laura asked, surprised at the beauty she found in the building's architecture and the rugged remoteness of its setting.

"They deliberately built it out in the middle of nowhere," her uncle said.

Laura set the drawing beside her plate. "You never told me why Aunt Molly went to the Institute, Everett."

Her uncle plopped down in his seat and let out a deep, sad breath. "It was a couple of months before her death. She'd heard the Institute helped people in her situation."

"Helped how?"

Everett shook his head angrily as he picked up his fork. "With some stupid mumbo jumbo dream stuff. I should have objected. Only, by that time there was nothing any *real* doctor could do for Molly. I thought if going to this place could give her any comfort..."

As Everett's sentence trailed off, Laura could see the new moisture collecting in his eyes.

"Did they bring her comfort?" Laura asked gently.

"She never told me a thing about what they were doing to her there," Everett said, anger creeping into his words. "I should have known they were taking over control of her mind. It wasn't like her to keep things from me."

"She never even told me she was ill," Laura said, not able to keep the disappointment out of her voice. "All of a sudden, she was just... gone."

"She didn't want to interrupt your studies and jeopardize your graduation, Laura. She knew how hard you were working to make up for lost time."

Yes, that sounded like Molly. Still, Laura wished she had known. She would have given anything to have been there for her aunt. Molly had always been there for her.

She owed her so much!

"Dr. Quinn's wing is here," Everett said, redirecting Laura's attention as he pointed at the artist's sketch with the prongs of his fork. "There are several other researchers at the Institute. But the two big wings are run by Nathaniel Quinn and the founder and director, Michael Sands."

"Did one of them see Molly?"

"I don't know. If there aren't central files, you'll have to check each wing. But be careful. They'll be watching you."

"Watching me?" Laura repeated, uneasily.

"Well, of course. These people don't trust anyone, remember. Make sure they are occupied elsewhere before you go searching. It wouldn't be good if you got caught."

Caught?

For no reason that made any sense, Laura got

a sudden mental flash of being caught in the strong arms of an angry and suspicious Dr. Nathaniel Quinn. Quivers of both fear and excitement shot through her.

She thought of that Chinese dinner she'd shared in New York the week before at Destiny House with Zara and Darcy. What had that silly fortune said that she'd ended up fishing out of her tea? Oh, yes. "Beware of..." it had begun, the rest blurred into blots of ink.

Maybe she shouldn't have laughed off that warning so easily. Just what did await her at the remote Institute of Dreams?

CHAPTER TWO

"LAURA LACEN?" A burly security guard with a big black handlebar mustache squinted at her.

"Personnel just sent me over," Laura said, smiling anxiously as she pointed to the new ID badge pinned to the lapel of her white lab coat.

The guard's eyes dipped to check his list. Laura drummed her fingers nervously on the counter of his station. She felt like a fraud. She was a fraud. She wasn't a grateful new employee ready to do her best for the Institute who'd hired her. Actually, she was a spy ready to find the evidence to bring it down.

She glanced around at the spacious rotunda in the center of the building. The floors and walls were gleaming white marble. Its glass-domed ceiling arched high up toward the heavens.

"Oh, yeah," the guard said, a distinctive nasal tone to his voice. "Here you are." His small gray eyes rose once again to her face. "So, Dr. Quinn has finally hired himself a new research assistant.

Welcome aboard, Ms. Lacen. You've passed the gauntlet.''

"Gauntlet?"

"Our Dr. Quinn is known to be mighty particular in his selection of research assistants.''

The hefty guard got to his feet. "I'm Bittle. No first name. No title. Just call me Bittle. Come on. I'll show you the way.''

Leading off from the rotunda were the four wings of the building. Each wing was demarcated by a phase of the moon which was inscribed above its white door.

Laura followed the guard's lead to the door marked with the half-moon. He leaned down to unlock it.

"When do I get a key?'' she asked.

"Only the doctors have keys. Don't worry. A guard is always on duty. And at night, it's mostly me. I'm sort of a fixture. Been here since the Institute opened.''

Bittle stepped aside for her to enter. Laura was taken aback by the sight of the long, empty hall stretching before her.

"Which one is—'' she began.

"Dr. Quinn's office is the last door on the left,'' Bittle answered, anticipating her question.

The idea of coming face-to-face with the suspicious gaze of Dr. Quinn once again was enough to glue Laura's feet to the floor.

"Now, don't you worry, Ms. Lacen. He hasn't murdered any of his assistants yet. Well, at least, I haven't found any of their bodies lying around. So, I guess they got out okay."

Laura's eyes darted to Bittle's face. His mustache twirled up at the edges. He was making a joke, thank heavens. She let out a little sigh of relief.

He patted her arm reassuringly.

"You just have first night jitters. You need anything, you pick up the nearest in-house phone and dial 0. It will ring me at the guard desk. Okay?"

"Thank you, Bittle."

"No problem." As Bittle shuffled his hefty bulk back to his station, Laura forced herself to face her misgivings.

Okay, so you're a spy. So what? If these people took advantage of Molly, they deserve to be spied on.

Laura squared her shoulders and set off down the long white wing. For Molly, she could do this. For Molly, she *would* do this.

NATE WAS JUST ending a telephone conversation when he heard the knock on his office door.

He called out for whoever it was to enter. He looked up to see Laura step inside.

"You're prompt at least," he said, checking his watch. It was precisely 9:00 p.m.

"At the very least," she said, dryly.

He knew his comment and tone had been querulous. He hadn't consciously meant them to be.

But, he'd been on edge all weekend thinking about her being here tonight. And, now that she was here, he couldn't ignore how her white lab coat set off the dark richness of her long hair. Or miss that sparkle of challenge in her deep indigo eyes. It wasn't only her spying that was going to be difficult to deal with the next couple of weeks.

Nate rose from his chair. "I'll show you the lab and acquaint you with your duties later. Something's come up that I have to attend to first."

Her eyes flitted to the computer terminal on his desk. "I'll wait for you here."

"No, you'll come with me," Nate corrected, lightly taking hold of her arm. He hadn't gone two steps when the warmth of her galloped through him like a cavalry charge. He released his hold in immediate retreat.

Touching her, even casually was *definitely* not a good idea.

As soon as they stepped into the hall, he closed

and locked the door to his office. He knew that she'd find nothing in his computer, even if she got inside. It was just the principle of the thing.

"Where are we going?" she asked, as she effortlessly kept up with his extralong stride down the hallway. She was wearing running shoes—the better to sneak around in, no doubt.

"To see a friend of mine," Nate answered. "Security put him in the guest waiting room at the front of the wing."

"I don't want to intrude on your private conversation," Laura said, too nicely.

I know what you want, Laura Lacen—a chance to go snooping.

"My friend just wants to tell me about a case he thought I'd find interesting," Nate said, aloud.

They quickly reached the end of the hall. Nate opened the door. He held it open and stepped aside, waiting for Laura to pass into the room before him.

As she did so, he got a whiff of her, clean, lemony scent. She smelled good. Way too good.

"Nate, it's great to see you," a hearty voice called out from inside the room.

Nate stepped forward, closed the door behind him and grasped the hand of the big man with the big voice. "Frank, it's been too long."

Senator Frank Mason had a mat of well-groomed auburn hair and an air of sincerity about his likable features. Nate knew both had helped Frank keep his political seat for two previous races.

"Kathy and I got tired of inviting you and Reba to dinner and getting turned down," he said. "We decided we were going to wait until you two had time for us. Isn't that right, honey?"

Kathy Mason stepped to her husband's side. She was tiny and blonde, dwarfed by her husband's bulk. It surprised Nate to find her here. He thought he would just be seeing Frank.

"How is Reba?" Kathy asked.

"Reba moved out eight months ago," Nate said.

"We have been out of touch," Frank said, giving Nate's arm a buddy nudge. "Sorry, old man."

"It was for the best," Nate said, feeling uncomfortable that Laura was hearing this. He turned to her. "This is Laura Lacen, my new assistant. Ms. Lacen, this is—"

"Senator and Kathy Mason," Laura interrupted, holding out her hand. "Senator, I'm a great admirer of your insistence on running a clean campaign."

She turned to Kathy. "And Mrs. Mason, your wooden figurines of our endangered desert wildlife are beautiful. I'm particularly impressed that you donate all your earnings from them to safeguard our natural resources. If you were running against your husband, I'd have a hard choice this November.''

While Frank and Kathy thanked Laura, Nate held back his surprise at the genuine warmth in her words. He didn't know she had it in her.

Nate gestured toward the sofa. Frank and Kathy obliged by taking a seat. "So, what's up?" Nate asked.

"That case I mentioned to you, Nate," Frank began, as uncharacteristic worry lines broke out on his brow. "It's our son, Cagan."

"He's paralyzed," Kathy said before her husband could go on.

Nate looked over at her. He could now see the signs of definite strain in her face that he had missed on their greeting.

"Paralyzed?" Nate repeated.

Frank took his wife's hand in his and held it firmly.

"It happened two weeks ago," Frank began. "Cagan's high school football coach is the real gung ho type. He's had the team on a high-protein diet and out practicing this summer so they'd be in top shape for the coming season. Cagan came home after practice one day and collapsed on the kitchen floor. Kathy and one of her colleagues at the environmental league found him. He couldn't move his legs. He still can't.''

"What has the doctor said?" Nate asked.

"Three doctors have done complete physical workups on him. No strained muscles. No torn ligaments. His nerves and reflexes are fine. The X rays show his spine and leg bones are perfect. None of the doctors can find anything physically wrong.''

"Is he in any pain?"

"No. He's in remarkably good spirits, too. The last doctor suggested we have him psychoanalyzed.''

"No!" Kathy protested, her voice high and tight. "It's not all in Cagan's head. His paralysis is not due to his inability to accept a traumatic event. We're not taking him to an analyst!''

Kathy's outburst surprised Nate. She was a woman who prided herself on keeping cool in every situation. He didn't think he'd ever heard her raise her voice before.

Frank wrapped his arm around his wife and pulled her to his side. "It's going to be okay, honey. Take it easy.''

Kathy nodded numbly as she leaned against her husband.

"I'd like you to look at Cagan," Frank said to Nate.

"The facilities here aren't equipped to run the kind of tests—"

"The conventional tests have already been done. I'll have the doctors send them over. Running more won't change the results. Nate, I was listening all those times you were talking about your work. I know if anyone can find out what's wrong with Cagan, it's you. Will you try?"

Nate knew Frank Mason was a proud man. Not once in the fifteen years they'd known each other had he ever asked Nate for a favor. Until now.

"Where is Cagan?" Nate asked.

"Waiting outside in the car."

"You were pretty sure of me."

"I was," said his friend. "I am."

"Give me a break, Nate. I can move this thing," Cagan Mason complained as Nate steered his wheelchair down the long corridor.

Laura noticed that Nate immediately released his hold on the back of the wheelchair.

"So, show me what you can do," Nate said.

As Laura looked on, the husky youngster propelled the wheelchair forward with ease. He turned his head of auburn hair and grinned back at them. He had the mark of his father's good looks on his face and the healthy glow of youth in his eyes.

Laura had never seen anyone who appeared like they needed a wheelchair less.

"I'll cancel the nurse," Nate said.

"Why? I'd love some cute little candy striper giving me a bath," Cagan said with a grin.

"Okay, but the last time I asked a Las Vegas hospital to lend us a nurse, they sent me a guy who was an ex-marine."

"Uh, on second thought, I think I'll pass."

"Wise choice. So what's with this paralysis thing?"

Cagan shrugged. "What the hell, Nate. I thought it'd be a good way to get the babes. The sympathy angle and all. Only when they drop by the house, Mom won't even let them in."

"So other than the fact that your mom is ruining your love life and you can't walk, everything else okay?"

"Yeah. Sure. I figure if I have to spend much more time in this chair, I'll just set my sights on the Special Olympics."

Laura admired Cagan's good spirits—and the way Nate didn't challenge his false bravado.

As Laura walked beside Nate, she thought about the warmth in his voice when he'd greeted Frank Mason. And the concern in his eyes when he saw Kathy's distress. When he teased Cagan like one man would another, he obviously did so to make the boy feel good about himself.

Nathaniel Quinn could be very kind. It made her all the more curious as to why he was so brusque with her. She stole a look at his profile. His eyes swung almost immediately to hers.

"How much farther is the lab?" she asked, quickly looking away. She had once again found it very unsettling to be staring directly into those restless brown eyes of his.

Nate moved in front of the wheelchair to push open a large swinging door at the end of the hallway. "We're here."

Laura's first impression of the lab was that its walls and floor were the same dazzling pristine white as the rest of the Institute.

As they walked through she noticed it was divided into cubicles that made up separate sleeping rooms. Each was equipped with a bed, dresser, nightstand and lamp.

"I'm putting you in this last cubicle, Cagan," Nate said, stopping in front of it. "It's number twelve—the best room in the house."

"Cool." Cagan wheeled himself inside to take a look.

"I've heard of sleep labs, but this is the first time I've seen one," Laura said to Nate as they stood just outside Cagan's cubicle. "How do you tell when someone's dreaming?"

"Come on. I'll show you." Laura followed Nate into a compact, glass-enclosed room at the back of the lab.

"This is the soundproof control room," Nate said, as he closed the door behind them. "The volunteers in each of the sleep cubicles wear a custom-made, lightweight mask. It contains electrodes that sense when their eyes begin the rapid eye movements during sleep, or what we call the REM state. This REM state is the one we find accompanies most dreams."

"Yes, I've heard of REM sleep. What happens when the electrodes in the mask sense a dreaming state?"

"A red light will flash here above the cubicle number," Nate said, pointing to a control panel that took up a sizable portion of the tabletop.

"When a volunteer's dream is over, you'll wake them and ask specific questions designed to help them recall the details of their dream."

"How do I wake them?"

"This control panel also works as the intercom to the sleeping quarters. When you want to speak to the volunteer in a particular cubicle, you flip the switch for that cubicle here and it activates a sensitive two-way microphone located in the nightstand next to the bed.''

Nate paused to point to the tape machines built into the control panel. ''Every conversation you have with the dreamer is recorded, so it's not necessary to take notes.''

Laura's eyes roamed over the control panel, impressed by both its sophistication and the simplicity of its operation.

''My role appears to be a rather routine one,'' she said. ''I'm surprised you set such stringent qualifications for your research assistant.''

''On the contrary, Ms. Lacen. The qualifications are not stringent enough.''

Laura's eyes raised to Nate's. ''Why do you say that?''

''There are between ten and twelve volunteers in here each night. Each experiences four to five dreams at ninety-minute intervals during a sleep cycle. On the average, they'll spend about two hours in dreams by morning. Every one of their dreams has to be timed. The dreamer must be questioned with sensitivity and care to facilitate their recall. There is no margin for error. Not a moment of dream material can be missed.''

''I suppose it could get to be quite a juggling act at that,'' she said looking back at the control panel. "Who has been doing all this lab work for the last six months?"

"I have."

"And before that?"

"Mostly me. As I explained in our interview, good research assistants are damn hard to find."

She caught the edge of his scowl. He obviously included present company in that assessment.

"Why did you hire me?" Laura asked. She figured she might as well get the air cleared on this now.

"I need help. You're the only marginally qualified candidate who applied."

"*Marginally* qualified? You really shouldn't turn my head with such charming compliments, Dr. Quinn."

"You want charm, go back to Dr. Finholm and that Rob guy who showered your desk with flowers and candy every morning."

Her eyes darted to his face. "How did you know about Rob and the flowers and candy?"

"I checked up on your story, of course."

Of course. She should have known he would. So, he didn't want her here any more than she wanted to be here. And he wasn't pretending otherwise. Well, fine. That just made doing what she had come to do that much easier.

"So, are you going to show me how to work this control panel now?"

"You'll learn as we do."

"*We* do?"

"It's not a one-person job. I'll be here with you."

Uh-oh. Laura hadn't counted on Nate being with her the whole time. She was going to have to find excuses to slip away.

Out of the corner of her eye she caught a glimpse of Cagan's wheelchair as he explored his room. She turned back to Nate.

"I don't understand what Senator Mason thinks you can do for his son," she said.

"He hopes I'll be able to diagnose the physical cause of his problem. Or rule out a physical cause."

"And how are you, a research biologist, supposed to do that when three medical doctors couldn't?"

"I won't be approaching the diagnosis in the same manner they did."

"You must be involved in something more than just recording your subjects' dreams. What is it?"

"You took physiology, right?"

"Got an A in it," Laura said.

"Then you're aware that nerves constantly

feed into the brain from every part of the body, relaying the status of the body's comfort and discomfort levels."

"Which is why we get the messages to eat or sleep when we're hungry or in need of rest," Laura said, nodding.

"And, yet, subtle physical cues that are constantly being transmitted go virtually unnoticed."

"Which subtle physical cues are you talking about?"

"We aren't conscious of the secretion of enzymes. Or the building of bone or blood cells. Or the thousands of other functions occurring inside us every second."

"It would be kind of hard to focus on the outside world if we were so tuned in to all those functions, wouldn't it?"

"Yes. Which is precisely why our conscious mind isn't. And, yet, the subconscious mind records every one. At night it takes the signals about the status of the body and weaves the important ones into dreams."

"Are you saying you believe people's dreams reflect their *physical* health?"

"I believe their dreams can, when a problem exists."

"That's what you're doing in this sleep lab?

Diagnosing the physical problems that show up in people's dreams?''

"You sound surprised. It's not a new idea."

"It is to me."

"And, yet, Aristotle wrote that a disease about to visit the body is more evident in the sleeping than in the waking state. Then there was Hippocrates, the father of Greek medicine, who believed that dreams had the potential to point to physical ailments. And Galen, a second-century Greek physician, wrote of the foretelling of impending illness by studying dreams."

"These were the same guys who thought the earth was flat, too, right?"

A reluctant smile caught the edges of Nate's lips. Laura was amazed at how good he looked when he smiled, even reluctantly.

"Geography wasn't their forte," Nate said. "Medicine was."

"Has anybody looked into this dream diagnosis of physical ailments lately? Like in the last few centuries or so?"

His smile actually dented his cheeks this time. He looked even more attractive. Laura was beginning to wish she hadn't noticed.

"The sheer volume of the evidence detailing how patients' very own dreams have predicted their subsequent illnesses is growing daily,'' Nate said.

Laura leaned forward, momentarily forgetting her exasperation with Nate as the scientific possibilities piqued her interest.

''Have there been any controlled studies?''

''That's precisely what I've been doing here at the Institute for the last three years.''

''And you've diagnosed physical problems by studying dreams?''

''Some of the results have been quite promising.''

Nate had chosen his words carefully—like a true scientist. But Laura heard the undertone of excitement in his voice. She had always found dedication and enthusiasm quite infectious. And, this dream diagnosis idea had a very intriguing sound to it.

These next couple of weeks might not be so bad after all.

''Do you really think you can help Cagan?''

''I wouldn't even be trying if he wasn't Frank's son. But, if I can approach it right...''

Laura was aware of a hard excitement building in him. She was becoming aware of other things, too: the rough-and-ready set of his jawline, the shine of his thick, dark hair, the contours of his shoulders bunching beneath his white lab jacket, and the subtle scent of his spicy aftershave.

Without warning, his gaze met hers. The golden liquid glow of his eyes poured through her like hot honey. Laura felt the warmth deep inside her bones.

"Nate?" Frank Mason called from the doorway.

"Come in," Nate said. He tore his eyes away from Laura and flashed his friend a tight smile. He was still reeling in response to the roller-coaster ride Laura had just taken him on.

Laura refused to be intimidated by the fact that he was her boss. She openly countered his every scientific premise with an amused skepticism that was keeping him firmly on the defensive.

And, then, she went in for the kill by passionately listening to him talk about the possibilities of his work. When he saw the pure feminine interest aimed at him in those mind-melting indigo eyes, he knew he had lost the will to fight.

"Nate, you okay?" Frank asked as he stepped to Nate's side next to the control panel.

Nate followed his friend's anxious gaze. Only then did he realize that he was gripping the sides of the tabletop so hard his knuckles were white. He released his hold.

"Yeah, fine," he lied, taking a very deep breath. "Just a little...preoccupied."

Frank studied Nate's face, then glanced over at Laura and smiled. "Can't say I blame you."

Nate knew Frank didn't mean his comment seriously. They had always kidded each other about women. Normally, Nate would have kidded back. But, at this moment, Nate didn't feel in much of a kidding mood.

"So, Cagan getting settled okay?" Nate asked, intent on changing the subject.

"The security guard is showing Kathy where to stow away his stuff," Frank said on a more serious note. "This is really tearing her up. She cries herself to sleep nearly every night."

"Cagan'll be okay, Frank," Nate said, briefly resting his hand on his friend's shoulder.

Frank sighed. "We'll be back in the morning to pick him up."

"I'll let security know to expect you. Best therapy for you both is to focus your energies on campaigning. Get Kathy out there with you and take her mind off this business."

"These days I seem to have lost the campaigning spirit. I'd rather be by her side to see Cagan through this thing. Uh, Nate, who are those people?"

Nate turned toward the front of the lab where

Frank was pointing. "Those are my study volunteers arriving for their nightly dream session," he said.

Frank looked at his watch. "I'd best collect Kathy and get out of here so you can get to work. Nate, thanks."

"Hold your thanks until I do something worthy of it."

Frank's eyes met Nate's. "You've given me hope. Believe me, that's worth a lot."

As soon as Frank left, Nate's thoughts raced right back to Laura.

He was convinced he could resist this attraction he had for her, if only he wasn't so certain that she was attracted to him. But, he was certain. He had felt it the instant their eyes had first met. And every second since.

He reminded himself she'd come to spy on him. He knew that if she could, she'd find something her uncle could use against the Institute. He was going to have to keep his crazy urges for her in check over the next fourteen nights.

Fourteen nights. Heaven help him. He had a sudden sinking feeling that this was going to be the longest two weeks of his life.

CHAPTER THREE

"I HATE TO disappoint you, Nate, but I'm one of those people who doesn't dream," Cagan said, resting his head on his pillow.

Laura watched Nate pick up a feather-thin black mask lying on the nightstand. He handed it to Cagan.

"Everyone dreams," Nate said. "Every night. You just haven't been remembering your dreams. Tonight, I'll wake you up after every one and make sure they become part of your conscious memory. They'll tell us what we need to know."

Laura listened to the confidence-inspiring conviction in Nate's tone as she stood watching from the doorway. She had been carefully keeping her distance ever since that look he'd given her in the control room earlier.

It hadn't been the look of a research scientist. It had been the look of a man. And it had made her feel very much like a woman.

She hadn't counted on this complication. Still, when it came to men, she considered herself a graduate of the school of hard knocks. And, as such, she knew better than to let a physical attraction override her good sense.

"You really think remembering my dreams is somehow going to cure me?" Cagan asked, turning the mask over in his hands.

"All your dreams have to tell me is why you can't walk," Nate said. "We'll work on the cure afterward."

"This all sounds pretty weird."

"Yeah, well computers sounded pretty weird to a lot of people twenty years ago, Cagan. Now those same people are using them to run everything from toasters to turbo jets."

"So, what do you want me to do?"

"Just relax and dream."

Cagan nodded as he fixed the mask over his eyes.

Laura returned with Nate to the control room. He hung his lab jacket on the coat tree near the door. She kept hers on. She had dressed lightly for the desert's warm night. The Institute's air-conditioning was too efficient for her comfort.

Laura took one of the two chairs in front of the control panel. She looked out at the sleep cubicles spread before her, thinking about Nate's words to Cagan.

"Were you deliberately trying to get Cagan to

believe in dream diagnosis back there?'' she asked.

''Believing you'll have a helpful dream predisposes anyone to having one,'' Nate said as he slipped into the chair beside her.

''So, you're counting on the power of suggestion. It sounds as though you believe the conscious mind controls what we dream.''

''Unless it's receptive, it can block a message getting through.''

''What do you mean?''

''The communication between conscious and subconscious is accomplished through an intricate dance. The dream is the music that brings them together.''

Laura thought over the dance image, visualizing the partners trying to match steps. ''So, the conscious mind has to learn to harmonize to a different mental beat—the dream beat.''

''That was well expressed,'' he said, a quiet sincerity in his tone.

Laura felt a deep swell of pleasure at his small compliment. It surprised her. She was normally not one to be swayed by praise. But, she had a strong feeling that Nate said only what he really believed to be true, which made his praise special.

Strange. She wasn't quite sure when it was she

had decided that about him. Or why she felt so sure that she was right.

"These files contain the background data of the volunteers here tonight," Nate said, passing her a thick folder. "Wake them gently or they'll lose the delicate fragments of their dreams. Calling them by their first name is also helpful. Work on trying to sound like a friend, not a scientist."

Laura leafed through the pages Nate handed to her. They contained several brief biological and biographical sketches.

"Will I be entering the details of their dreams into their computer file later?" she asked.

"No. I'll take care of entering the salient facts from the dream content off their tapes."

So, there *were* computer files on all the volunteers. That's all she wanted to verify.

"Have the volunteers here tonight had any dreams indicating physical illnesses?" she asked.

"Not this group. Two such dreams occurred in the first year, one in the second."

"What were the illnesses?"

"One was a silent heart attack that took place during the dream. It was later verified by the dreamer's doctor. The second was a dream that predicted a virus attacking the body. Twenty-four hours later, the dreamer came down with a very bad fourteen-day flu. Last year a volunteer dreamed he had a black lump on his lung. A subsequent X ray revealed a lung tumor.''

"And dreams told you about each of these physical problems. That's rather amazing,'' Laura said, meaning it.

"Still, three studies contain too few individuals to yield any statistically significant results. But, finding definitive dream imagery relating to real, previously undiagnosed physical problems in even three subjects is encouraging.''

"What happened to the dreamer with the heart attack and the one with a lung tumor?''

"Both are doing fine. Their dream imagery of illness helped them to seek an early diagnosis and treatment. They both have probably added many more years to their lives.''

And, Nate cared that they did. Laura heard it in his voice, saw it in the small lift of his lips. Nathaniel Quinn was using dreams as a diagnostic tool because he cared about saving lives.

Laura leaned back in her chair and looked at Nate with new eyes.

Had she been going about this the wrong way? Could she find out what she needed to know without all this unsavory spying stuff? It was worth a try.

"Nate, was my Aunt Molly one of your volunteers?''

His eyes swept over her and then quickly swept away. "I am not at liberty to discuss your aunt with you." The stiffness in his voice was unmistakable.

"Why not?" she asked, not able to hide her disappointment.

"Because everyone who comes here to the Institute receives a sworn statement that we will never divulge anything about them unless they give us permission to do so."

"Nate, she's dead. How could you hurt her by telling me?"

"Her death doesn't change the confidentiality of her records or the Institute's pledge to her."

"She was my aunt. I have a right to know what was done for her here."

"She told you whatever she wanted you to know."

"She didn't tell me anything. I was away at college."

"She could have called you. She obviously chose not to."

Laura fumed at the unfairness of his words. He was clearly implying Molly had no trust in her— only in the Institute. Laura knew that wasn't true.

"Look, Nate, I'm an employee here now. I'll be privy to a lot of private information about your volunteers. What's the big deal?"

"The big deal is the Institute's sworn word to your aunt. Your job requirements do not necessitate your being given any information about your aunt's case."

"Are you saying you didn't personally see her?"

"I'm saying it's none of your business."

Laura swallowed the angry phlegm that had collected in her throat and took a deep, steadying breath.

All right. She had tried to get the information in an aboveboard manner. Nate's refusal to speak left her no choice but to sneak around to get it. Her conscience could be clear.

She saw one of the volunteers head for the rest room. A plan moved forward in her mind.

"When does the show start?" she asked, deliberately wiping everything but polite inquiry from her tone.

"Our subjects take some time to fall asleep. None of them will be entering a REM state for at least ninety minutes. I suggest you use the intervening time to study their biographies."

"I'll answer nature's call first," Laura said as she stood.

"There's one right over there in the corner," Nate said absently, gesturing with a wave of his hand.

"One of the volunteers is using it," Laura said as she brushed by Nate's hanging lab coat on the way to the door. "I'll use the rest room in the hall outside the lab."

Before Nate could say another word, Laura was on her way. And hidden in her hand was the key to Nate's office that she had surreptitiously slipped out of the pocket of his lab jacket.

Now was her opportunity to get to those computer files.

From the way Nate had described his ongoing experiment, Laura couldn't see Molly fitting into it. Molly already knew she was ill and what was wrong with her.

Still, the computer terminal in Nate's office might be networked with all the Institute's files. And if it was, Molly's file and who she saw would be in there somewhere.

Laura kept a leisurely pace as she approached the front doors of the lab. As soon as she had let herself into the outside hall, however, she moved quickly. The first room on her right was Nate's office.

She fit the key into the lock and turned the knob. She stepped inside the dark room, flipped on the overhead light, then closed the door behind her.

The large beige metal desk in the center and

beige leather couch in the corner were strictly utilitarian. There was a four-drawer metal file cabinet in the corner. Nate's framed doctorate degree was the only decoration on the otherwise bare walls. It was not a showy office. It was an office where someone worked.

She opened the file cabinet in the corner. The first three drawers contained an assortment of office supplies—pens, paper, blank recording tapes. The final drawer had a pillow and light blanket stuck in it. Laura decided Nate must use that couch in the corner for more than just visitors.

She circled his desk and sat down in his large leather chair, feeling dwarfed by its bulk. She turned on the computer.

When the booting process was over, she was relieved to find herself looking at a menu and not a password request. She choose item five—Volunteers. When prompted for a name, Laura typed in: Molly Lacen Thaw.

The computer message read, "Name Not Recognized." Laura cursored down the options. She selected the only other heading that seemed to fit—Guests. Again the computer prompted for a name. Again, Laura typed in her aunt's. This time three items of information were returned.

The computer showed her aunt's first visit to the Institute had been a year before her death.

That was strange. Everett said Molly first came to the Institute two months before her death, not a year.

Laura also noted that the date of Molly's last visit was the day before her death. Under the final heading, Status of File, was entered, "Inactive." It was followed by a five-digit number.

Laura tore off an old calendar sheet from the desktop and jotted down the number. She went back to the main menu. She found no Inactive heading. She soon realized that the software had been designed to retrieve data only for someone who knew specifically what they were looking for and how to request it.

That wasn't her. She gave up, switched off the computer and stuck the piece of paper in her pocket. Now what?

Laura started when she heard the key in the lock. A second later, the door swung open. It simply happened too fast. There was no time to run. Or hide. He was looking right at her.

She was caught.

CHAPTER FOUR

"WELL, HELLO," the elegant stranger in the white lab coat said as he closed the door behind him. He had a distinctly deep and rhythmic cadence to his voice that Laura found almost hypnotic. "I didn't expect to find you here," he said.

Laura forced herself to stand and meet his advance.

"I'm Laura Lacen, Dr. Quinn's new assistant," she said in a voice that she hoped didn't sound as weak and wobbly as her knees felt.

"I'm Michael Sands." He leaned across Nate's desk and held out his hand, flashing her the kind of smile that could melt the nail polish off a woman's toes. "Welcome, Laura."

His handshake was warm and firm. Interest, not suspicion, showed on his face.

And what a face.

She wondered if it was part of the job requirements for every doctor at the Institute of Dreams to look like he had just walked out of one. First Nate, and now this tall, sandy-haired Adonis with the piano key smile dressed in an impeccable summer suit.

Laura was very relieved that Michael Sands did not seem to find it strange that she was alone in Nate's office. After her experience with Nate and her uncle's warning, she had been expecting suspicion from every doctor at the Institute.

"Have I interrupted you, Laura?" he asked pleasantly as he released her hand.

"No, I just came in to make a telephone call, Dr. Sands."

"Please, call me Michael. Shall I step outside and give you some privacy?"

"No, no. It's over. I mean I got a busy." Laura knew she sounded nervous. Hell, she was nervous. She'd never been good at lying. And, there was something about this Michael Sands that made her feel he could see right through her.

"Were you looking for Nate?" she asked, changing the subject.

A mischievous twinkle lit Michael's eyes as he leaned over the desk toward her and lowered his voice. "No, I'm here to steal."

Laura was certain she must have misunderstood. "Excuse me?"

Michael walked over to the metal file cabinet. He opened the second drawer and pulled out a blank recording tape.

"I just ran out," he said, holding up the tape. "And Nate's are the best ones around to filch. They're so sensitive you can hear the proverbial pin drop on them. You won't tell on me, will you, Laura?"

"Tell? Oh, you mean about taking the tape."

Michael's solemn nod was accompanied by an index finger pressed against his lips, clearly a signal for silence. But there was something about the accompanying sparkle in his eyes that made Laura suspect this charming man was putting her on.

He coaxed her out from behind the desk with a beckoning wave of his hand. He draped a companionable arm across her shoulders as he headed them both toward the door.

"Laura, I need you to help me with something."

"Me? What?"

"Nate's my friend as well as my colleague. He's been working way too hard for way too long. Now that you're here, I want you to use your influence to get him to relax."

"My influence?" Laura laughed. "Michael, I have no influence over Nate. He doesn't even like me. He growls at me most of the time."

Michael's blue eyes shone. "When it comes to

Nate, a growl is a definite—if reluctant—sign of affection.''

Michael's words caused an odd stir in the pit of Laura's stomach. She was still reeling from it as he led them into the hall, closing the door to Nate's office behind them.

"You really think Nate likes me?" Laura couldn't stop herself from asking.

Michael captured her hand and blew a kiss across her knuckles. "How could he resist liking you?" Then he straightened and treated her to another one of those devastating smiles. "See you around."

As Laura watched his long-legged, ground-eating stride down the hall, she wondered if Michael had seen Molly. She could imagine Molly being charmed by him. Hell, she could imagine the entire female population donning goofy smiles for the guy. He wasn't just good-looking. He made an effort to be charming.

Unlike another doctor at this Institute she could mention.

Laura turned around to head back to the lab and ran right into that other doctor. She jumped. "Nate! You startled me!"

He caught her arms within his two strong hands in an attempt to steady her. The branding strength of his touch and the look in his arresting eyes did anything but steady her. Her blood started to pump in a most alarming manner.

It was at that precise moment that Laura made a disturbing discovery. The growly Nathaniel Quinn could get beneath her skin in a way that the charming Michael Sands never could.

"I see you've met Michael," Nate said, releasing her as suddenly as he had held her.

"He's very...nice," she said, stepping back, still far too aware of the lingering warmth of Nate's hands.

"You sound surprised."

"I am. I expected him to be more like you."

Laura watched in amazement to see a small smile lifting the sides of Nate's mouth. "You really shouldn't turn my head with such charming compliments," he said, repeating her earlier words.

Oh, God, he looked wonderful in that smile. Her heart pole-vaulted to the other side of her rib cage in a jubilant arc.

Nate opened the swinging door to the lab and waited for her to precede him.

Laura could feel her nerves sparking as she stepped past. She walked quickly in front of him, eager to get to the control room and slip the key back in his white lab jacket pocket before he noticed it was missing. Her heart was beating way too fast.

She was going to have to find out where the inactive files were soon. Being around Nathaniel Quinn was getting more and more disturbing by the minute. And far too dangerously exciting.

"IN THE DREAM I swallowed a pit," Judy Holstern's taped voice said sleepily. "It was a hard pit. I could feel it embedding itself in my intestinal wall. It was making me sick."

"Sick in what way, Judy?" Nate's taped voice asked.

"Queasy. I told my husband about the pit. He refused to be sympathetic. He told me I was overreacting. I told him that peach pits had arsenic in them and maybe this was a peach pit. He laughed. I felt so sad I began to cry. That's when the dream ended and you woke me up to recall it."

Nate stopped the tape and took off the earphones. He was concerned about what Judy had related about her dream. Very concerned.

He felt Laura's eyes on him. "Who's still here?" he asked, trying not to look at her. It was bad enough that every nerve in his body seemed to have set a new magnetic heading in her direction.

"Cagan is getting dressed," Laura said. "Everyone else is gone except Judy in cubicle number nine. She's waiting for her husband to pick her up. It's her last dream that is bothering you, isn't it? That's why you keep playing that tape of it."

Nate nodded, stretching his arms above his head as he tried to coax the stiffness out of his shoulders.

His muscles always felt tense after nearly nine hours bent over the control room table lost in his subjects' dreams. Still, he had to admit the task had been a lot easier with Laura working beside him.

He was amazed at how quickly she'd memorized all the volunteers' names. He had assigned her the task of timing and recording most of the dreams. She hadn't missed a single one. But, what amazed him the most was the way she questioned the dreamers, her voice so soft and unintrusive that she seemed to barely rouse them awake. She'd been perfect, a natural.

"Are you going to tell me what is it about Judy's last dream that's bothering you?" Laura asked.

"The pain she talks about in her intestines," Nate replied. "It's not the first dream she's had about it. Last Wednesday, it was a caterpillar munching away at the lining. Once again, her husband was in the dream and she was telling him about it.''

''Where's that earlier recording? I'd like to hear it.''

Nate noted the genuine interest in her voice. ''It's filed away with the inactive tapes. It won't help to review it. I just told you its pertinent aspects.''

''A caterpillar and a pit are quite different images,'' Laura said after a moment. ''How do you decide what they mean?''

''I don't try. It's the repetition of a similar physical complaint in a dream state that interests me. The reported pain in her intestines is what's important.''

''Her husband didn't come across as very sympathetic in her dream tonight. I wonder if there's a problem with the marriage?''

''Attempting to figure out the emotional dramas in a volunteer's dream isn't our job, it's theirs.''

Laura cocked her head. ''They study their own dreams?''

''That's why they come here—because they're interested in understanding their dreams. Most of them keep dream journals.''

"But you never discuss their dreams with them."

"I do when a physical problem is revealed in them."

"So you'll discuss Judy's dreams with her?"

"Right about now," Nate said, getting up.

"I'd like to be there."

Nate nodded, pleased at her continuing interest. As they made their way to Judy Holstern's sleep cubicle, he remembered Michael's comment about Laura applying herself once she came to the Institute. It appeared Michael was right. But it was too bad that Michael had found her in Nate's office earlier.

She would have made an excellent assistant if she hadn't come here to spy. Maybe after stealing his key and searching his office, she'd be satisfied there wasn't anything to find and give it up.

Yeah, and maybe the moon would fall out of the sky tonight.

"I DO REMEMBER those two dreams about intestinal pain," Judy Holstern told Nate as he and Laura sat on the edge of the bed in her sleep cubicle. Judy was fortyish, chubby with short black hair, nimble eyes and a generous mouth.

"Did you record any other dreams like them in your home journals?" Nate asked.

"I think there might have been one this last weekend. I'll check when I get home today."

"Are you experiencing any physical pains?" Nate asked.

"Not...exactly."

"But there is something?"

"Well, it's really my husband, Paul," Judy said. "You have to understand, Dr. Quinn. Paul and I met in high school, married right after graduation twenty-five years ago. We're very close. We're all each other has. No kids, no other family, just us."

Nate wanted to hear about the intestinal pain, not about her married life. He remained politely attentive, however, hoping Judy would get to it soon.

"When I first signed up for your study, Paul was on the night shift at the furniture refinishing plant. It worked out fine. We were both gone at the same time. But, then the plant relocated out of the country. Paul was forced into an early retirement. Now, when I'm here, he's alone at night. He's really grumpy when he picks me up in the morning."

Judy paused. Nate waited.

"And when he's grumpy, your intestinal pain begins to bother you?" Laura asked.

Judy nodded so briskly Nate understood this

was the question she'd been expecting. "It's gotten so I just pretend to eat. The mornings I've taken more than a bite or two, I've actually had to excuse myself from the table and run to the rest room."

"This began when your husband lost his job?" Laura asked.

"Actually, the first month or so we just kind of enjoyed his not having to work. But, it's been three months now. He's been looking for another job, but there aren't any. He's getting grumpier and grumpier with every passing day."

"Mrs. Holstern, the physical pain you're dreaming about has me concerned," Nate said, gently refocusing the topic of conversation. "I want you to make an appointment with your family physician and have it checked out."

"Even our...lovemaking has suffered," Judy said, showing no sign she had heard Nate's warning. "This last month he's barely even touched me. I feel awkward telling you about these personal things, but—"

"As well you should!" a loud voice suddenly barked out from the doorway.

Nate swung around to see Paul Holstern glaring at them.

Holstern was a tall, wiry, rough-looking man with graying hair, graying jeans and a graying anguish tightening his features. He came forward with jerky steps.

"Why are you telling these strangers about our...such personal matters?" Paul demanded.

"It was part of my dreams," Judy said.

"You're dreaming about these private things and then discussing them? You said your dreams were silly, nonsensical things. I never would have let you come here if I had realized—"

"*Let* me come? You do not direct my life, Paul Holstern."

Paul's face flushed. "You have no right talking about what we do or don't do in the privacy of our home, Judy."

"And you have no right barging into a room where I'm having a private conversation with a scientist about an important experiment in which I'm involved!"

Paul Holstern glared at his wife. When she glared right back, he turned, stomped out of the sleep cubicle and slammed the door shut behind him.

Judy let out a strangled sound and fell across the bed.

Laura wrapped her arms around Judy and hugged her, saying nothing, letting her cry. After several moments when Judy's sobs began to subside, Laura released her firm grip and produced some fresh tissue from her lab coat pocket.

Judy took it and dabbed at her eyes. "I should have known Paul would get all huffy over this. But, it's so unlike *me* to fall apart this way. It seems like lately the least little thing makes me cry. I'm sorry. I..."

"You have nothing to be sorry for, Judy," Laura said firmly. "Men can be absolute imbeciles. It's either cry or hit them over the head. Too much good china gets ruined in the latter case."

Judy sighed. "It's his pride I've wounded now. He'll never understand my need to talk about these things."

"Come on," Laura said smiling. "Let's retire to the sanctity of the ladies' room where you can wash off that smeared mascara, and we can bash men to our hearts' content. Wait until I tell you about this unbelievable jackass I used to live with."

Laura winked at Nate over Judy's bent head. She led her out of the cubicle.

Nate found himself smiling. Laura had handled that well. It was clear what Judy had most needed at that moment was a sympathetic female ally.

"Nate. There you are."

Nate turned to see Frank standing just outside

the cubicle. "I've been looking all over for you," Frank said.

Nate stepped out of the cubicle and closed the door behind him. "Sorry. I was in conference with a volunteer."

They walked to Cagan's cubicle where Nate could see Kathy was waiting. He nodded as they approached her.

"I just talked to Cagan," Frank said. "He seemed quite surprised to realize how much he dreams. He also said he'd given you the okay to talk to us about one of his dreams."

"What was it about?" Kathy asked. "I was in the rest room when Frank and Cagan talked. I didn't get a chance to hear."

"Remember that red bike I got him for his tenth birthday?" Nate asked.

"The racer with all the fancy gears," Kathy said, nodding. "He loved that bike, Nate. Rode it into the ground."

"He was riding it again last night in his dream. He told me Denise, Frank's new media consultant, was mounted on the handlebars."

"Denise?" Frank said. "Oh ho. Cagan didn't mention that part to me."

Frank paused to smile at Kathy as he wrapped his arm around her shoulders. "Looks like our son is growing up, honey.'' Nate noticed Kathy's returning smile was less than enthusiastic.

"I take it this Denise is a looker?'' Nate asked.

"A very cute twenty-three-year-old,'' Kathy said. "Cagan's been rather taken with her. I'm not...comfortable with his attachment. So, what else was in this dream?''

"Cagan had entered a race. He struggled with the extra weight of Denise on the handlebars. Halfway through the race, his energy gave out and his legs went numb.''

"You mean he became paralyzed in this dream?'' Kathy asked.

"It's a very hopeful sign,'' Nate assured. "It tells me that Cagan's subconscious is well aware of his paralysis and is weaving it into his dream images.''

"So, what's the next step?'' Frank asked.

"To continue to pay attention to his dreams. This one implies that exertion preceded the paralysis, which fits in with the fact that he'd just come from football practice when it happened.''

Nate looked back at Kathy. He was alarmed to see she was clutching at her stomach. A big tear rolled down her cheek.

"Kathy, what is it?'' he asked.

She buried her face in a tissue. "I'm just... afraid for him.''

"Kathy, his dreams are going to tell us what we need to know to help him," Nate said, with as much reassurance as he could muster. He hoped to hell he was right.

"Dry your eyes, honey," Frank said. "If Cagan sees you crying, you know it'll upset him."

Kathy wiped her eyes and took a couple of deep breaths in an obvious attempt to compose herself.

"You must think I've become a big wimp," she said to Nate.

"Naw. Just a little wimp," Nate said, coaxing a smile out of Kathy.

Kathy turned into Cagan's cubicle. Frank didn't immediately follow her inside. He lowered his voice.

"Maybe it would be better if you didn't share the content of Cagan's dreams with Kathy any more, even when Cagan okays it."

"Why?" Nate asked.

"You heard how she overreacted about his dreaming of Denise. I don't want to upset her any more than she already is."

Before Nate could respond, Frank had slapped him on the shoulder and stepped inside his son's room.

It wasn't so much what Frank asked, as the

worried way he had asked it, that made Nate uncomfortable.

Before Nate had a chance to think much more about it, a movement caught his eye. He looked over to see Laura back in the control room. He made his way to join her.

"I thought you'd still be with Judy Holstern," he said, stepping inside the control room a moment later.

"Her husband came back for her," Laura said absently, her attention clearly elsewhere.

And that's when Nate realized that the control board was lifeless and dark. His eyes followed Laura's gaze to the floor.

The electrical wires that had fed into the control panel were wrapped around one of the legs of her chair. They had been ripped away from their connections.

CHAPTER FIVE

"SORRY TO DISAPPOINT YOU, but I was able to solder the electrical connections back into the control panel today," Nate said. "We're ready for tonight's session."

Laura bristled at the sarcasm shooting through Nate's every syllable as she stood next to him in the control room Tuesday night.

"Look, for the hundredth time. I did not rip out those wires. I found them lying on the floor when I returned to the control room after seeing Judy Holstern and her husband out to their car this morning."

"Yeah, right."

"Oh, for heaven's sake. Why would I rip out the wires to your precious control board?"

"You tell me."

Laura had no doubt that Nate had snared the wires on her chair leg. She distinctly remembered it was he who had pushed the chair beneath the table on their way out to talk to Judy.

Clearly he had no intention of admitting he'd been careless.

Laura sat down in her chair in front of the control panel.

"I suppose I might as well confess," she said in a deadly calm tone. "Some women leave a trail of broken hearts behind them. I leave a trail of ripped electrical wire. Normally, I enjoy wrapping it around the throat of some big, dim-witted male. But, alas, you weren't in the room at the appropriate moment this morning."

She looked up at him and deliberately smiled.

His sudden laughter burst forth like thunder through the small control room, racing her blood to a heady new beat. Damn, but he had a great, big, wonderfully hearty laugh!

When it was over he was actually smiling at her. Her heart pounded beneath that smile. Way too hard.

"Okay. I might have jumped to a wrong conclusion or two," he said, magnanimously. "I suppose the leg of your chair could have snagged the wires unintentionally. We'll put the incident behind us."

Laura shook her head in disbelief. First he treated her like some wire-ripping maniac. Then he had the nerve to smile at her like that while accusing her of trying to cover up a careless act for which *he* was responsible.

Who ever said that men had fragile egos? This guy's could take a direct hit from a sledgehammer and not show a dent.

"So, you going to tell me what happened with Mr. and Mrs. Holstern this morning?" he asked, just as though everything had been satisfactorily resolved.

Laura let out a deep sigh and reminded herself that she was here for Molly. For Molly's sake she would not murder Nathaniel Quinn. At least, not yet.

"Paul was still acting pretty tense and uptight when Judy got into their car this morning," Laura said. "He seemed much more relaxed when he walked her into the wing tonight. He's apparently forgiven her for talking about their sex life. And she's forgiven him for yelling at her. She kissed him goodbye."

"Maybe after hearing about your jackass, hers didn't seem so bad."

"I didn't get a chance to tell her about my jackass. Paul was waiting for us when we left the cubicle."

"So, what did your jackass do?"

Laura turned to Nate, surprised at his question. Did he really want to know? Or was this just his way of apologizing for his behavior over the wires? Probably, the latter. Still, if he could make an effort, she decided so could she.

"His name was Bill," Laura said. "He was twenty-three. Handsome, smart. Studying to be a tax attorney. I was a dewy-eyed nineteen. The plan was I'd drop out of college to work to support us so he'd get through school faster. After he completed undergraduate and graduate school, he'd support me through my degrees."

"But it didn't happen that way?"

"After he got his education, Bill changed his mind about putting me through school. He wanted me to marry him, have *his* kids and keep *his* house. His exact phraseology."

"I take it you didn't buy into Bill's Plan Number Two?"

"He considered me quite unreasonable about it, too. He kept telling me that the bottom line was I didn't need to waste all that time and *his* money on getting a college education since he was going to take care of me. He reminded me that there were thousands of women who'd jump at the chance to marry a good-looking, educated man who'd just landed a high-paying job."

"And what did you say to that?"

"I told him to go find one."

"Did he?"

"In record time. Six months later he married some dewy-eyed nineteen-year-old. Last year he left her and their two kids for a lady lawyer who specializes in divorces. He brags she'll make sure he doesn't pay a dime in alimony."

"The jackass label seems a bit tame for Bill," Nate said. "Several other more colorful nouns spring to my mind."

Laura smiled at Nate's response.

"So what happened with you and Reba?" she asked.

It was like the lights had been suddenly switched off in his eyes. They stared out at nothing, dark, unmoving, lifeless.

"I don't have room for a woman in my life," Nate said after a long silence. It wasn't so much the words as the total lack of emotion in them that gave Laura pause. For no reason that made any sense at all, she suddenly felt sad.

Nate shuffled some papers on his desk. "I want you to handle the dream recording on all the subjects tonight except Cagan and Judy. I'll be here to assist you with the others if it becomes necessary, but I want to concentrate on them."

Laura could see that their frank exchange was over. She was more disappointed than she knew she should be. She'd felt good telling him about

Bill. She'd felt even better at his understanding response.

It made her want to know more about him. She told herself it was the budding psychologist in her—not the woman—who was curious. But neither that budding psychologist nor the woman was buying the explanation.

"So, HOW IS IT GOING, Ms. Lacen?" Bittle asked as he opened the door to Nate's wing on her fourth night at the Institute.

"I've missed you the last two nights," Laura said.

"I've pulled weekend duty so I had to take a few extra nights off during the week."

"You have to work the weekend? That must be rough."

"Naw. I volunteer. I got no other place to go since I lost the missus a couple of years ago."

"Bittle, I'm so sorry."

"Yeah, she took off with the electrician who was doing some repairs in Dr. Quinn's wing."

"Oh," Laura said, surprised and relieved to learn his wife wasn't dead. Bittle didn't look all that relieved, however.

"Yeah, she was one of Dr. Quinn's volunteers. Only, pretty soon she and this alligator-boot-wearing electrician were sneaking off to the archives to fool around.''

"The archives?"

"It's where the inactive files are sent.''

Archives? Inactive files? Bingo. "Where are the archives?" Laura asked in her most nonchalant tone.

"They're in the basement, right beneath our feet. Here I was right above them and they were down there—"

"How would I get to them?''

"Why would you want to? Nothing but old tapes, the fuse boxes and a cold concrete floor. Not that *that* stopped them.''

Clearly, his wife's infidelity was not an issue Bittle had come to terms with yet.

"I have some research to do for Dr. Quinn,'' Laura said, pleased with her improvisation. "I need to refer to some of the old tapes. Is there an elevator?''

Bittle gestured with his thumb. "Just stairs. You go right past that column over there. Door's just on the other side.''

"Is it locked?''

"Dr. Quinn will have to give you his key. None of us guards are allowed to let anyone down there but the doctors.''

"I see. I don't have time to do my research

during the week. Dr. Quinn keeps me too busy.
I'll be back this weekend. You'll be working the
night shift on Saturday?''

''Same hours as during the week.''

''See you then, Bittle,'' Laura said, walking
into Nate's wing.

Somehow, she'd get that key. Somehow, she'd
find Aunt Molly's records. Somehow, she'd
sneak them out of the Institute.

Somehow, she'd bring an end to this unsavory
spying business. She had to.

Working closely beside Nate each night was
wreaking havoc with her emotions. If it had just
been a physical attraction, she knew she would
be handling it a lot better.

But it wasn't just a physical attraction. She
liked him. A lot. What's more, she respected
what he was trying to do.

She was quickly getting in over her head. It
was time to get out. Before she was swept along
by Nate's dedication to his work. Or drowned by
the warmth in his remarkable eyes.

''I WAS IN THIS really cool red Firebird with the
side flames and all,'' Cagan said. ''I was flying
along, doing at least ninety. Denise sat right next
to me. She was wearing this really short black
leather skirt. I went to shift. I grabbed her

knee by mistake. We laughed. She looked me up and down. I sucked in my gut real hard. Tried to be cool. My gut started to hurt I'd been sucking it in so long.

"Then I heard these bangs. *Pop. Pop.* I knew a tire had blown. The car went from ninety to like nothing in no time. We stopped, dead. I got out and looked at the rear end. The tires were flat. Both of them. Denise started to walk away. I wanted to follow her, but my legs were flat like the tires. My dad drove by in his car. He was going to pick Denise up until I waved and yelled. When he saw my flat tires, he stopped and picked me up instead."

"Anything else, Cagan?" Nate asked after a moment.

"I...uh...nothing. The dream just sort of stopped there. I woke up and it was morning and you were asking me questions."

"Thanks, Cagan." Nate switched off the microphone.

It was Cagan's only dream since Monday night that dealt with his problem. Nate was particularly interested in the stomach pain Cagan had described preceding his paralysis.

It rang a bell, albeit a faint one. Where had he heard about that combination of stomach pain and paralysis before? He was going to have to hit the medical journals today.

Nate checked his watch. It was almost seven on Saturday morning. He heard Laura's low-pitched laughter skipping through the control room, like silk sheets slipping off a warm bed. She was getting dream material from a volunteer.

The warmth in her voice when she probed for dream elements worked like a lubricant, aiding the volunteers to recall their dreams. The recorded dream material had increased by a third this last week under her soft guiding voice and encouragement.

And it all came so naturally to her—the warmth, the gentleness, the understanding. Nate now realized she was a natural at this job because she was just being herself.

Nate looked at her. He'd been looking at her far too much for his sanity this last week. But, it was irresistible.

Her rich mink hair curved across her cheekbones, like a fragrant, silken hood. He wanted to touch it, to see if it could possibly feel as thick and rich and soft as it looked. Being so near to her like this, night after night, seeing firsthand the genuine sweetness inside her—it was driving him wild.

Laura finished with the dreamer and switched

off the two-way mike. By the time she turned to him, Nate was carefully studying the control panel.

"Any physical symptoms?" he asked.

"None. But, I've been meaning to talk to you about Cagan. Have you noticed that he seems to be holding back on sharing all his dream material?"

"It's hard for a young man to bare all. Makes him feel too vulnerable. As long as he gives me the parts that deal with physical ailments, I don't care if he censors his emotions."

"Nate, I never realized how emotionally revealing dreams could be. This week has really opened my eyes. You're gathering a lot of potentially useful dream data in this study."

"That part doesn't concern me."

"I think it should. What Judy Holstern told us about her changing relationship with her husband supports an emotionally based problem. Plus, every subsequent dream she's had this week seems to deal with it in some way."

"Emotional confrontations with her husband that leave her feeling queasy in her waking life do not explain her physical intestinal discomfort while she's dreaming."

"But, Nate, what if Judy's physical pain in her dreams is psychosomatic because of the emotional pain she feels in her relationship with her husband?''

"Physical pains in a dream are not psychosomatic. They can be taken literally, unlike the emotional drama surrounding them.''

"If you're so certain that emotional messages in dreams *can't* be relied on, why are you so sure that physical ones *can?*''

"Before I began my current research, I interviewed more than a hundred people who had dreamed of physical problems. In every case, their dream images were traced to a real physical problem.''

"*Every* case?''

"Every case. What's more, I have never come across a case of physical pain being present in a dream and not resulting in a waking ailment.''

Laura scooted her chair a little closer. "Couldn't that also be true of emotional pain as well? I've been reading a lot of psychological journals this last week about dream images and what they represent. What if Cagan's last doctor is right and his inability to walk is emotional?''

"Then those of you in the psychoanalytic camp will have plenty of time to convince him he's all screwed up.''

Laura looked up at Nate in some surprise as

he rose to his feet. The heavy irritation that rode his tone was unmistakable.

"Ouch," she said. "Where did that come from?"

"Experience." The word buzzed the air like an angry bee.

Laura rose. "You've been psychoanalyzed. And you didn't like what the analyst told you."

She saw the accuracy of her guess registering in the sudden tightening of his jaw and golden flash of his eyes.

"Anyone who says that just because you dream about snow it means you're emotionally cold is projecting, not diagnosing."

"Is that what that psychoanalyst said to you when you mentioned you had dreamed about snow?"

Nate had to give it to Laura. She was smart and quick.

"Reba was that psychoanalyst, wasn't she?"

Too uncomfortably smart and quick. "Did Michael tell you?"

"No, your face did," Laura said. "You get that exact same look in your eyes whenever I mention Reba or psychoanalysis. So, Reba was a psychologist. And you let her psychoanalyze you."

"*Let* her, nothing. From the first, I couldn't

say or do anything around her that didn't end up getting psychoanalyzed.''

"You realize, of course, that psychologists aren't supposed to act that way. I'm also surprised she overlooked the fact that since you were brought up on the East Coast and now lived in the Southwest desert, you were probably dreaming about snow simply because you missed it."

"How do you know where I was brought up?" Nate asked.

"An educated guess. The medical degree on your office wall is from the college of medicine at Penn State. Did Reba consider your geographical background before making her diagnosis?"

Nate exhaled heavily. "No. Reba only considered the fact that I decided not to continue our relationship."

"Sounds to me like she was trying to use the tools of her profession to punish you for that."

"You're not bad for someone with psychological training," Nate said, smiling. He knew he was feeling too pleased that Laura was taking his side in the matter. Entirely too pleased.

"Actually, I have to chalk this one up to experience. Bill lobbed a lot of negative barbs at me on his way out, too."

Nate lost his smile. "Like what?"

Laura leaned her hip against the tabletop and stared out into the sleep lab. Her arms and back were suddenly as rigid as posts.

"Like how anyone who got freaked out by a little smoke didn't have the guts to make it through college on her own."

"What did he mean by that crack?"

Nate watched as memories clouded Laura's eyes like faded pictures in an old locket.

"I was ten when our house caught on fire," she said. My parents died. A fireman got me out in time. I can never forget that night. Waking up to the searing pain of the smoke in my eyes, my throat, my lungs. Being trapped inside a room full of smoke. Once, when I was baking some chicken for Bill and me, I left the kitchen for a moment. When I returned, the room was full of smoke. I screamed and ran out of the apartment."

She paused to sigh. "It was only some grease that had caught on fire. Bill put it out, aired the room, laughed at my neurotic overreaction."

"And used the incident to try to weaken your confidence when it suited him," Nate said, ire infusing his tone.

She flashed him a quick grin. "You're pretty good for someone without psychological training."

He smiled at the way she had used his own words on him.

"Bill's manipulation might have worked if it hadn't been for my Aunt Molly," Laura said. "She took me in after my parents died. She taught me to value and be true to myself. Remembering that lesson helped me to break away from Bill. Molly's gift was the greatest one I ever received. I loved her so. And then one day she was just...gone. I never even got to say goodbye."

Laura's voice fluttered on those last words. Nate watched as her eyes filled with soft, shimmering tears. He covered her hand with his.

Her eyes slowly rose to his. The warm invitation in them suddenly fused every nerve cell in his body into one bold, electrified pulse.

Before he could consider what he was doing, he had slid an arm around her shoulders, the other around her waist and pulled her to him. He pressed his mouth against hers in a soft, gliding motion, tasting its smooth surface as his lips quested and questioned.

She was an explosion of fire and honey on his tongue, too incendiary to control. A tardy alarm sounded somewhere inside his brain.

He might have heeded it, pulled away, if her lips hadn't opened to his, if her body hadn't softened against his, if her arms hadn't circled his waist.

The next instant he was lost to all but the feel of the warmth of her response, to the knowledge that she was welcoming him.

His arms wrapped tightly, possessively around her. She gave a sigh of pure pleasure that sizzled in his ears.

The heat of her breasts and belly rubbing up against him robbed him of all sanity. His fingers pressed against her back and through her hair as his mouth increased its friction against hers with ever-growing greed. And still he could not seem to bring her close enough, kiss her deeply enough.

The loud voice unexpectedly intruding into the control room struck Nate's ears like a blow.

He released Laura instantly and jumped back, his head twisting around to locate the intruder. His breath was ragged. His heart was racing.

"Mom, what's wrong?" Cagan's raised voice asked. "What are you doing here so early?"

"I need to say something to you privately, before your father gets here," Kathy's voice answered.

Nate's eyes darted to the control panel. He realized then that he must have inadvertently flipped on the mike to the number twelve sleep cubicle when he leaned over to kiss Laura. He was just about to turn it off when Kathy's next words stopped him.

"No matter what you have seen, Cagan, your father and I will always be together. Please believe that. Please."

"It's okay, Mom," Cagan said, sounding anything but okay. And no wonder. Kathy was sobbing loudly.

Nate switched off the mike, perplexed by what he had just heard, but still too preoccupied with his overwhelming reactions to Laura to give it much attention.

But when he turned back to Laura, she was no longer there.

He just caught the flash of her white lab coat out of the corner of his eye as she swept out of the control room.

LAURA HIT THE BUZZER as she stood outside the locked doors to the Institute Saturday night.

"Please state your name," a voice said through the intercom.

She recognized the nasal tone immediately.

"It's Laura Lacen, Bittle."

The door opened. Bittle's familiar black, bushy mustache preceded his chubby face by at least an inch.

He smiled as he stepped back for her to pass. "Archives?"

"Yes. Got to get that research done for Dr. Quinn before Monday," Laura lied.

"You sign in over here, Ms. Lacen," Bittle said pointing at a tablet on the guard's desk in the Institute's central rotunda.

Laura stepped up to the desk and noted that the four people who had signed the weekend log-in sheet earlier in the day had already signed out. Outside of Bittle, she was the only one in the building. She scribbled her name on the fifth line and entered the time of 9:05 p.m. Then she pretended to search her pockets.

"Oh, no," she said, making her voice sound as plaintive as possible. "I forgot Dr. Quinn's key to the archives! I live an hour and a half away! What am I going to do?"

Her soulful sounds and expression had the desired effect on Bittle. He got out his keys. "All right, I'll let you in. But don't you go telling anyone. It could cost me my job."

"You are a knight in security guard uniform, Bittle."

"You mean I'm a sucker in a security guard uniform," Bittle grumbled, but he was smiling when he opened the door for her.

Laura quickly slipped inside the archives,

flipped on the light switch and then closed the door.

The fluorescents in the ceiling hummed reluctantly to life. She found herself at the top of a long wooden staircase, leading down into a deep cavern of a room.

There were no windows. Nearly every inch of the concrete floor was lined with storage cabinets. Outside, the warm September night had been pleasant. In contrast, these archives were as cold as a cave. Laura shivered as she descended the steps in her shorts and tank top.

She was tired and dispirited. She'd given up even trying to fight the feelings that had robbed her of sleep all day.

Even now—many hours later—just thinking about that kiss and mind-melting embrace she'd shared with Nate made her body hum for more.

She knew there would have been a lot more if Cagan and Kathy's voices hadn't erupted into the control room. She couldn't deny her feelings for Nate any longer.

She was halfway in love with him. And that other half was just a step away. It was a step she knew she mustn't take.

Not that she believed Nate had any part in coercing Molly into leaving her fortune to the Institute. He wasn't that kind of man. She couldn't feel this way about him if he were.

Still, she knew if someone at the Institute had duped her aunt, her uncle would bring down everyone working there.

And Nate would discover that she had only come there to spy on him. And he would hate her.

The thought sent another chill through Laura. It was time to get Molly's records. It was time to find out if she really had been coerced. Laura prayed with all her heart that she hadn't, that there was another explanation for her odd behavior.

And if she had? Well, then let Everett take whatever legal action was necessary. Laura wanted no part of it. Indeed, she was sorely sorry she had gotten involved in the first place.

The last wooden step creaked as Laura descended to the concrete floor of the archives.

Manila envelopes stuck up in the metal storage units lined up like soldiers. There were hundreds of them. Laura snatched the scrap of paper out of her pocket and read off the number that she had gotten off the computer—the one that had been assigned to her aunt's inactive file.

Her eyes traveled up and down the outside of the storage units. It took quite a while before she found a block with the right bank of numbers. She shuffled through the envelopes until she located her aunt's numbered file. She pulled the envelope out. She looked inside to see two cassette tapes.

Laura had planned to take whatever she found directly to her uncle. But, now that she held the tapes, the urge to discover what was on them was suddenly very strong.

If she heard something incriminating on them, she could warn Nate. Maybe he could disassociate himself from the Institute in time to save his work and reputation. It was worth a try.

Nate's lab would be empty. It wouldn't take long to play the tapes. She quickly climbed the stairs and opened the door leading into the rotunda.

"Finished already?" Bittle asked from the guard desk.

"As soon as I review these," she said, holding up the envelope. "I'll need to get into Dr. Quinn's wing now."

Bittle obliged by unlocking the door.

"If I'm on a coffee break when you leave, just sign out at the desk," Bittle said.

"Yes, I will. Thank you."

Laura hurried down the dark hall. She entered the lab and made her way to the control room at the back. She sat down and slipped the first tape into the built-in recorder. She took in a deep breath then hit the Play button.

A monotone voice—clearly computer generated—stated a date that was more than a year and a half before.

The sound of her aunt's voice suddenly filling the room made Laura sit straight up in her chair. So, the computer record was not in error. Molly had come to the Institute a year before her death. This was very strange. Why hadn't Molly told Everett?

"I saw Michael at an environmental benefit the other day," Aunt Molly's taped voice said. "I mentioned this strange dream I had the night before. Michael told me I must talk to you about it. He was most insistent I see you right away."

"Tell me about this dream," the deep baritone voice said.

Laura punched the Stop button on the cassette recorder, her fingers suddenly shaking, her heart sinking inside her chest.

It was Nate's voice on the tape! It was Nate who saw her aunt!

Laura did not want to hear the rest of the tape. And yet she knew she must. She had to know what role Nate had played. She pressed the Play button again. Molly's voice once again filled the room.

"In the dream I was swimming underwater through a silent, red sea. There were glowing, translucent white fish floating alongside me. It was very pleasant. Then the feeling of the dream changed. The white fish became agitated. They began to all rush in one direction. I was swept along in their mad dash. I feared what had caused them to become agitated. I didn't want to be swept along with them, but I couldn't seem to help it.

"Then I saw a big black octopus clinging to a piece of chalky-looking rock. The white fish attacked the octopus. The octopus didn't even flinch. It sunk its teeth into a chunk of the chalky rock. Pain shot up my back. I woke up."

"Did you still feel the pain in your back when you woke?" Nate's taped voice asked.

"Just a twinge," Molly answered.

"Michael tells me you've had a complete physical recently?"

"Couple of months ago. Everything checked out fine."

"Did you mention the pain in your back to your doctor?"

"I didn't notice it until the dream this last week."

"I want to send you to a radiologist friend of mine for a couple of special tests that wouldn't have been included in a regular physical. They're noninvasive and pain free. I'll call him now and get you scheduled for them later today."

"Today? Do you really think there is such an urgency?"

"I'm uncomfortable with that pain in your dream."

"But it was only a twinge when I awoke, Nate."

"Still, I'd rather error on the side of caution. Okay?"

"Okay, Nate."

The monotone computer voice came on again identifying a time and date. Laura recognized it as two days after the previous recording.

"The results are positive for invasive bone cancer," Nate's voice said. "The physical dream images were so clear I'm surprised Molly didn't realize. The rushing red sea was obviously her bloodstream. The glowing white fish were her white blood cells. They became agitated because they sensed the invading cancer. Only, by the time they got to it, it was too powerful for them to kill. It had already eaten into her spine."

As Laura listened to Nate's diagnosis, invisible icy fingers clutched at her heart. She had expected such news, since she knew Molly had died of bone cancer. Still, it was hard to hear.

"What's the prognosis?" another man's voice asked. Laura recognized the voice immediately as Michael Sands's.

"Not good," Nate said. "The oncologist identifies it as a fast-growing variety."

"Terminal?" Michael's voice asked.

"The oncologist says if we hadn't found it now, she would have been dead in six months," Nate answered. "As it is, even with aggressive treatment, he figures all he can do is buy her an extra six months at the most."

"This is going to be rough on Molly. On us, too. She's been our staunch supporter from the beginning."

"There has to be something we can do," Nate said.

"There is. Turn off the tape and I'll tell you about it."

Laura let the rest of the tape run out. The silence following Michael's last words was total and downright chilling.

Michael claimed Molly had been a staunch supporter of the Institute. Did Michael and Nate discuss a plan to convince a dying Molly to make the Institute the beneficiary of her trust?

Laura couldn't bring herself to believe Nate

would be part of such a plan. Still, she reached for the second tape, knowing she had to play it.

But, before she could put it into the recorder she stiffened, her senses suddenly alerted. Something was wrong. There was a smell of smoke in the air!

Laura swung around. A large, gray cloud was forming just outside the control room door. She dropped the tape, jumped to her feet and rushed to the door. She grabbed the handle and pulled it open. Billows of smoke rushed in at her.

Laura slammed the door shut, choking on the smoke, panic rising inside her. She ran to the house phone on the wall and punched in O, trying to reach Bittle. She punched it again and again. There was no answer. He must be on a coffee break!

An icy sweat broke out on her skin. She whirled around the room, desperately looking for another way out, already knowing there wasn't one.

She was trapped.

CHAPTER SIX

NATE STARED bleary-eyed at the clock on the corner of his desk in his office. It was nearly ten. He was sprawled out on the couch. The medical journal he'd been reading hours ago still lay across his chest.

He was weary, beyond exhausted. Memories of holding Laura in his arms, kissing her, feeling her response, had tormented him all day, robbing him of sleep.

The way she'd run out that morning, he knew she was not coming back. He reminded himself that she had only come to spy on him. He told himself it was better this way.

He might have convinced himself of that a week ago when all he knew of her was her physical beauty and strength of spirit. But in the past week he'd also come to know the quickness of her mind and the gentleness of her heart.

Nate closed the medical journal and let it drop to the floor. He switched off the lamp next to the couch, lay back on the pillow and shut his eyes, once again trying to blot out the memory of her beckoning blue eyes and silken laughter.

At first Nate thought the insistent buzzing sound to be nothing more than the woolly fog of fatigue in his brain. When he realized that it was the distant warning of one of the lab's smoke detectors, alarm flooded through him. He swung his legs off his office couch and charged out into the hall.

He grabbed the fire extinguisher off the wall as he raced for the lab. He pushed through the swinging doors, headfirst.

The smoke was a billowing plume in the back. He could see the blackened smoke curl out of the seams of the metal cabinet right outside the control room door.

The cabinet was not combustible material. Still, he knew that unless he stopped the smoke, the automatic sprinkler system would soon be activated, flooding the lab.

He rushed forward, halting a couple of feet from the cabinet. He raised the nozzle of the extinguisher, ready to give it a blast as soon as he opened the doors.

That was when he saw Laura.

She stood frozen in the glass control room on the other side of the billowing smoke, her eyes filmed with fear, her face the same white marble color as the walls.

A cold stone dropped into Nate's stomach as her words came back to him. *I can never forget that night. Waking up to the searing pain of the smoke in my eyes, my throat, my lungs. Being trapped inside the smoke-filled room.*

He knew she was seeing it again, living it again.

He sprung into action, kicking open the metal cabinet doors, smothering the burning blankets and pillows inside with bursts of carbon dioxide foam. He pulled out each piece of smoldering cloth and sprayed it thoroughly. He pointed the nozzle at the inside of the cabinet and emptied the rest of the contents of the fire extinguisher into it.

When he was absolutely certain the fire was thoroughly out, he dropped the extinguisher and snatched open the door to the control room.

He rushed to Laura and gathered her to him, holding her close.

"Laura?" He knew his voice was hoarse, a mere croak, but not because of the smoke he'd inhaled.

He felt a quiver snake through her. Her voice was tiny, barely a breath. "I couldn't get past the smoke."

Nate moved his arm to her waist. He led them quickly out of the smoky lab. He took her to his office, closed the door behind them, set her on the couch.

"I'm sorry, Nate. I'm...sorry."

He knelt before her and took her hands firmly into his. "Stop saying you're sorry, Laura. I'm not that jackass Bill."

She let out a long, slow sigh that shivered through her. "I'm so happy you're not him, Nate."

She withdrew her right hand from its imprisonment beneath his. She reached out to touch his brow, his cheek, to trace the outline of his lips. The gentleness of her touch sent a shaft of desire through him.

Nate closed his eyes tightly as he tried to quell the surge of his emotions. He captured her hand, kissed it. He told himself that she didn't know what she was doing to him, that she had been frightened, that it was a friend she needed now. But, when he opened his eyes again, her cheeks were flushed and the emotion darkening her indigo eyes was a lot more than friendly.

He leaned forward to brush his lips against hers, gently, searchingly. When she eagerly melded her mouth to his with a soft cry, exultation rose in his chest.

His hands dived beneath the edges of her tank top. When he found only her beneath, it nearly undid him. He pulled the top over her head and threw it aside.

He rained kisses down her warm, bare throat as he laid her across the couch. Her hungry little murmurs made his pulses leap. Her breasts filled his eager hands as she arched her back. He filled his mouth with the pinkness of her nipples.

All day long he had imagined making love to her like this, having her respond like this. And, now, it was happening. Every muscle and bone and blood cell in his body was beating with the incredible reality of it. With the incredible reality of her.

Laura locked her fingers in Nate's thick hair, pressing him closer, the intensity of her own desire a shock to her senses. His mouth and hands were firm, sure, eager as they caressed her skin. His eyes were alight with a golden heat that melted her insides.

He pulled down her shorts and panties in one swift move. His strong, powerful hands moved up her thighs, flooding her body with heat. There was such care and skill and sensitivity in his every touch.

It struck her then that Nate was making love to her in the same manner he did everything in his life: with bold confidence and a reverent, focused attention to every detail.

She wouldn't have wanted it any other way.

He separated her legs and caressed her intimately. She cried out at the sweet, sharp sensations rocking through her. His lips covered hers in kisses as his fingers opened her with flaming strokes.

"Nate." His name escaped from her lips with a moan. It was a deep cry, spawned from a ravenous need that was rapidly spiraling beyond her control.

He tore off his clothes and laid his full, hungry length on top of her, ready to respond to that need. She registered and reveled in every ounce of the solid, hot weight of him, the musky male scent rising like steam off his skin.

She wrapped her legs around him and took him inside her.

The smooth, steel heat of him was heaven. A rumble of raw need broke from his throat. She pushed against him, sending him deeper until he filled her completely. Their fingers intertwined. Their mouths sealed together, letting no breath escape as they breathed into each other.

Laura never knew anything could be so wildly erotic. To feel him surging so sleek and wet and full inside her, his huge hands clasping hers tightly with each thrust. To hear his strong heart pounding so hard it threatened to break through her rib cage and join with hers. To have her every breath drawn deep into him and his into her.

It was a full naked intimacy. Torrid. Lustful. Sizzling.

Laura shuddered at the intensity of the blinding release that spun through her beating core at the same time Nate's rich roar rumbled through her throat.

When Nate finally released her mouth, he was breathing hard and looking at her with such awe that she laughed with a breathless delight. That he could make her feel this incredible was amazing enough. But to know that she could make him feel this incredible, too… Ah, that was the stuff of dreams.

"I DON'T KNOW what's happened to me," Laura said with a heartfelt sigh. "I can barely lift an eyelash."

Nate chuckled as he combed his fingers through the thick, luscious richness of her hair. "I thought you said you got an A in physiology?"

"That was from studying the textbook. Until tonight, I never knew how great the application could be."

He kissed her forehead, inordinately pleased to hear it. Making love to her had been an impossible wish—and then in one dazzling, shimmering second it had happened. If it had been anything less than magic for her, it would have spoiled the magic for him.

She made a soft, settling sound as she nestled her head beneath his chin.

He wrapped his arms about her and drew her closer. Damn, this felt so right. So impossibly right.

"Nate, why haven't you asked me what I was doing in the lab tonight?"

He planted a soft kiss on the top of her hair.

"I don't have to ask, Laura. I know you were snooping around, looking for something you could give your uncle to use against the Institute. It's why you came to work here."

She turned in his arms to face him. She looked tousled and perturbed and incredibly lovely. "You knew?"

"Of course. Michael and I figured that it was better to keep an eye on you than worry about who next on the Institute's staff your uncle would try to bribe."

"Bribe? What are you talking about?"

"You didn't know your uncle has tried to bribe everyone from the janitor to the Institute's volunteers to dig up some dirt that he could use against us?''

Laura sighed as she rested back against Nate's shoulder. ''Everett never said a word about having tried to bribe anyone! Wait until I get my hands on him.''

''Why did you agree to spy for him, Laura?''

''I didn't agree to spy for Everett. I did it for Molly. I couldn't stand the idea that the Institute might have used undue influence on her in order to get her money.''

''So that's what all those questions concerning her treatment were about. What did you think we were doing, brainwashing her?''

Laura propped herself on an elbow and looked at him. ''You should know, Nate. I got her tapes out of the archives.''

''How did you know they were there? How did you get in?''

''I turned out to be a good spy. Please, don't make me apologize for it. What I'm trying to tell you is I listened to the first tape tonight. I know you persuaded Molly to see a specialist and added many months to her life. But, I don't know what else you and Michael did because I was panicked by the smoke before I could listen to the second tape.''

Nate's hands circled her shoulders. ''Laura,

are you telling me you need to listen to that second tape to be convinced that I didn't conspire to take advantage of your aunt?''

''No, Nate. I know you wouldn't do something like that.''

The smile that lit his eyes made her tingle with happiness. The tenderness of his quick kiss sent a tremble through her. She knew he affected her this way because she was in love with him. But, she also knew the fact that he had made love to her wasn't a declaration of his love.

She reminded herself that he had walked away from Reba. He might do the same with her. The thought made her heart sink. She forced herself to lean away from the wonderful drawing warmth of his body. She sat up, trying to regain some protective physical as well as emotional distance.

''It's getting late. I really should go.'' She reached resolutely for her clothes.

He captured her hands in his. ''Stay with me.''

His head lowered to her neck as he gently nibbled on her collarbone. Her muscles quivered as delicious little ripples of delight ran through her.

''This is a pretty small couch for two people to be sleeping on,'' she protested, her breath catching as his fingers feathered over her breasts.

''What makes you think we'll be *sleeping* on it?''

Laura's smile met Nate's as his mouth shifted over hers. Her resolve, her worries—everything melted away when he touched her like this. Everything but the splendid feel of him.

"SMELL THIS, LAURA," Nate said as he held up a burned piece of cloth Sunday afternoon. She moved to where he stood next to what was left of the blanket cabinet outside the control room.

"It smells oily, like wood varnish," Laura said.

"I've found bits of rags soaked in this stuff between the burned blankets and pillows."

"Nate, you're saying this fire was deliberately set? But, that's not possible. I would have noticed if someone had come in."

"Whoever set this fire didn't have to be here Saturday night. Rags soaked in this kind of oil produce tremendous heat. It takes hours, sometimes days, but eventually they spontaneously combust."

"My God," Laura said. "That means that anyone who was in the lab in the last couple of days could have stuffed the soaked rags in the cabinet with the pillows and blankets."

"That about says it all."

"But, why would someone want to burn down your lab?"

"This fire wouldn't have burned the lab. The sprinklers would have drowned the lab in a couple of feet of water as soon as a second smoke detector had been activated. Fortunately, I extinguished the fire before that happened. A flooding would have closed down the lab."

"Maybe that's what someone wanted. To close down your lab?"

"If so, it puts an entirely different perspective on that wire-ripping episode at the control panel, doesn't it?"

"I forgot about that," Laura said. "I guess we were so ready to blame each other for being careless, we never considered it might be someone else's deliberate doing. But the only people who were in the lab at the time the wires were ripped out of the control panel were the volunteers and their families who had come to pick them up."

"Which narrows down the suspects."

"This is crazy, Nate. Why would any of them want to close you down?"

"All I know is that whoever planted those rags soaked in oil knew they were going to cause a fire sooner or later. My guess is the person placed them in the cabinet sometime Friday night or Saturday morning, assuming that the fire would occur over the weekend. Now, the hard part is figuring out who."

"Maybe not so hard," Laura said.

"You have an idea?"

"I was just thinking that if I were the one who planted those oil-soaked rags, I'd be expecting to hear about a fire in the lab causing it to be closed down, right?"

Nate nodded. "Right."

"And, if I found out it hadn't happened, I'd think twice about coming back to the lab. That fire could start any moment."

"So you figure our saboteur will be the one who doesn't show up Monday night. That's not bad for someone who's studied psychology."

"There you go trying to turn my head with those charming compliments again."

Nate laughed before planting a quick kiss at the side of her smiling lips. "Come, Ms. Freud. We have a saboteur to catch."

LAURA AND NATE conferred in whispers as they stood just outside the control room door, counting noses. One by one the cubicles filled as the volunteers came in for the Monday night dream session.

"I don't understand it, Nate," Laura said, frustration riding her tone. "Everyone is here."

"It appears as though our saboteur has fooled us," Nate said. "Or is trying to."

Laura watched Paul kiss Judy Holstern on the cheek. He didn't look at all nervous about leaving his wife in the lab for her night's dream session.

Just before Paul headed out the door, Laura watched him turn and send a scowl in their direction. Or was it only a trick of the light?

"Nate," Frank Mason called as he and Kathy strolled up. "I got your message that you wanted a word. What's up?"

"I believe I know what's caused Cagan's paralysis," Nate said. "Can you and Kathy give me about an hour's time tomorrow morning?"

"You can't just tell me now?" Frank asked.

"There's something I have to check out first before I'll be sure. Besides, the dream sessions are about to begin. When we sit down together to discuss it, I don't want to be interrupted."

"All right," Frank said, sounding a bit peeved at being put off.

"Are you okay, Mrs. Mason?" Laura asked. Kathy was clutching her stomach. Her face had turned positively ashen.

"I must have eaten something that didn't agree with me," she said.

"Is that what it is, Kathy?" Nate asked, studying her face intently.

"Of course. Let's go, Frank," she said, clearly eager to be on her way.

"What was that all about?" Laura asked after the Masons had left the lab.

Nate shook his head. "A case of self-denial I would say. Come on. We have a big night ahead of us."

"I WAS WALKING in this swamp," Cagan said. "The air was really thick. I wanted to get out. I knew Mom and Dad were up ahead somewhere in the thick fog. I saw Dad going off to the right. He was with Denise. I yelled at him to stay with Mom so they'd find the way out together. He didn't hear me. I started to run after them. I got a stitch in my side. It was really hard to breathe. I fell into some quicksand. My legs wouldn't move. I was stuck. I…"

"Is that all you remember?" Nate asked, when Cagan didn't complete his sentence.

"Yeah. That's all."

"Okay, Cagan. Now go back to sleep."

"I heard most of that," Laura said after Nate turned off the mike. "Do you know how easily those images can be interpreted to describe Cagan's current emotional conflicts?"

"No, I don't. And, I don't want to know."

"You're a stubborn, hardheaded man, Nathaniel Quinn."

"There you go again trying to turn my head with charming compliments."

Laura chuckled. "That's Judy's light that just went off. Let me listen in. None of the others will be dreaming for a while."

"Okay," Nate said with an exaggerated sigh of feigned defeat. "But, don't expect to be spoiled like this all the time."

Laura's laughter danced in his ears.

"It was an awful dream, Dr. Quinn," Judy's agitated voice said. "Simply awful."

"Tell me about it, Judy."

"Paul was hiding from me. I kept searching through the house for him. But the house seemed to have so many more rooms than it did before. I was lost. I kept calling out to him, pleading for him to show himself. But he continued to hide from me. Oh, Dr. Quinn, I was so frightened I'd never find him!"

"It's all right, Judy. Go back to sleep."

When Nate flipped off the microphone, Laura was shaking her head. "I wish I knew what that meant. Does she believe her husband is emotionally hiding from her?"

"Laura, we are not here to—"

"—diagnose emotional dream images," she

finished. "But I can see now there are so many mysteries inside them to be solved! I now know what I'm going to be doing in graduate school."

It was twenty minutes later when Laura saw the shadow out of the corner of her eye. It gave her a start. She rested her hand on Nate's arm.

"To my left," she said. "Lying on the floor."

"Yes, I see," Nate said. "On a direct course to the blanket cabinet. Remember, Laura, that even though the control room is soundproof and in darkness like the lab, the light from the control panel illuminates our faces."

It wasn't easy for Laura to act natural and keep herself from staring at the shadow. Now that she knew the moment had come, her pulse was jumping and her hands had begun to perspire.

The shadow was cautious. It stayed anchored to the floor for several long minutes. Laura questioned another dreamer, then flipped off the mike.

And, every second her skin crawled with the knowledge that those eyes were watching her out there in the darkness. The seconds dragged by, weighed down by her enforced inaction.

When Nate's warning call finally came, Laura jumped clean out of her chair.

"Now!" he yelled.

Laura grabbed the flashlight and spun around.

Nate had already flung open the door of the control room and charged out into the sleeping area.

Laura raced after him. She reached the door just in time to see Nate tackle the fleeing figure to the floor. She ran over, flashlight at the ready.

But when she shone it on their saboteur's face, she could barely believe her eyes.

"Cagan!"

CHAPTER SEVEN

"AS YOU NO DOUBT realize, Cagan's phony paralysis and subsequent sabotage of the lab have raised some serious issues that need to be resolved," Nate said as he and Laura faced the three members of the Mason family early Tuesday morning.

"Serious issues indeed," Frank said, a scowl on his brow as he looked at his son. "Faking paralysis! Sabotaging Nate's control panel! Trying to set fire to his lab! I don't even know who you are anymore, Cagan."

"I didn't fake the paralysis, Dad," Cagan said, his voice a study in anguish as his hands grasped the arms of the side chair in Nate's office. He dropped his head. "At least not at first."

"You expect me to believe you?"

"Cagan is telling the truth, Frank," Nate said. "I've found out what caused his paralysis. He's suffering from an inborn error of metabolism. I had a test run on him this morning that confirmed it."

"Nate, what are you talking about?"

"Prophyria ALA-D is an inherited enzymatic defect. Cagan has it. I suspect Kathy has it, too. I couldn't help but notice that she's been suffering from abdominal pain and generalized muscle weakness. Those are other symptoms of the disease."

Kathy leaned forward, surprise clear on her face. "My doctor said it was just stress."

"Stress brings on the symptoms of the enzyme deficiency, Kathy. We'll give you the same blood test I ran on Cagan this morning. I believe it will confirm you have it, too."

"Why didn't Kathy or Cagan's other doctors pick up this enzyme deficiency?" Frank Mason asked.

"It's very rare, Frank. Most doctors don't even think to test for it. And Cagan didn't exhibit the severe abdominal pain and breathing difficulties that are common symptoms of an acute attack— except in his dreams. His dream content was what supplied me with the missing pieces."

"How could this lack of an enzyme suddenly make his legs paralyzed?" Kathy asked. "I've never had that."

"The metabolism problem manifests itself in different ways with different people," Nate said.

"But Cagan has been healthy all his life," Frank protested.

"Remember, Cagan had just returned from a strenuous workout. His coach had put him on a high-protein diet. Both physical stress and a reduced carbohydrate intake are known to be precipitating factors. Rest and the resumption of a normal diet is all he needed to bring him around. Cagan tells me that the paralysis of his legs left him the afternoon after the attack."

"Too bad he didn't bother to tell his parents," Frank said. His tone was little more than a snarl.

"Dad, I was afraid to. I thought you'd go away again."

"What are you talking about? I haven't gone anywhere."

"Ever since you hired Denise, you've been so caught up in media blitzes and campaigning that you stopped showing up at my practices. You even stopped coming home for dinner."

"What do you expect? I'm running for reelection."

"You've run before without running away from us. You haven't been there for me or Mom in months. That's why she let that guy from the environmental league kiss her that day I came home from practice."

"What?" Frank said, turning toward his wife.

"Is this true, Kathy? You let some guy kiss you?"

"Yes, Frank," Kathy said, tears forming in her eyes. "He kissed me. One silly, stupid kiss. The first kiss *anyone* had given me in months. Oh, Cagan, I've been so afraid this was all my fault! I thought you saw us kissing and it gave you such trauma that you became paralyzed."

"Aw, get real, Mom. You could have run that kiss on the Disney channel. I knew you were just feeling down because Dad was gone all the time. And when he did show up, all he talked about was what a great job Denise was doing."

"So, what you did is my fault now?" Frank said.

Despite the pique in his words, Laura could detect a look of guilt in Frank Mason's eyes.

"Dad, as long as I was in that wheelchair, you were home and you seemed to care about us," Cagan said. "I knew as soon as you realized the paralysis was gone, you'd be out the door again."

Cagan turned to Nate. "I thought you'd learn I could walk again by analyzing my dreams. I got scared."

"So, you pulled the wires from the control panel," Nate said.

"Yeah. And, I put the oil-soaked rags from

Mom's woodworking in the cabinet. I thought if a fire started, the lab would be shut down, and I'd be safe."

"What about last night, Cagan?" Nate asked.

"I knew I'd gone too far. I planned to get the rags back and put them in water so they wouldn't catch fire. That's what I was doing when you tackled me. I was going to sneak them out under my wheelchair like I sneaked them in. Honest, Nate."

"I believe you," Nate said. He turned to his friend. "The Institute won't be taking any action against Cagan, Frank. He's going to need to be followed up medically. But, as far as the rest is concerned, we'll forget it ever happened."

"I won't be forgetting it," Frank said as he got to his feet. He turned to his son. "Stand up, Cagan."

Kathy quickly rose and grabbed her husband's arm. "Frank, please."

"It's okay, Mom," Cagan said, standing and facing his father. "I deserve to be punished. What I did was wrong."

"You're damn right it was wrong," his father said. "You're grounded, Cagan. You go to school, you play ball, you come home, that's all. And just to make sure, your mother and I are going to be at every ball game and at home with you every night. Every single, blessed night.''

Frank smiled and opened his arms. Cagan came into them and hugged his dad. Frank circled his arm around Kathy's shoulder and kissed her cheek. She rested her head against his.

''I knew you'd come through for me, Nate,'' Frank said. ''I wish I could repay you for what you've done for me today.''

Nate smiled. ''Seeing Cagan walking and you guys together like this is the most satisfying fee I ever got, Frank.''

His friend nodded in understanding as he headed his family out the door. When the Masons had left, Nate was astonished to find Laura throwing her arms around his neck and giving him a warm kiss.

''Not that I'm complaining, but what was that for?'' he asked.

''For being you.''

Nate wrapped his arm around her waist and sat her on his lap. ''I plan to be me again. How about another kiss?''

Laura laughed. Before she could oblige, however, the phone rang. She picked it up. ''The incredible Dr. Quinn's office.''

Nate laughed. He nibbled on her earlobe as he listened in to Laura's side of the conversation.

"Oh, hi, Judy. It's Laura. What? You're kidding. That's terrific! I'll tell Dr. Quinn. Yes. Thanks for calling."

"And what was that all about?" Nate asked after Laura hung up the phone.

"You'll never guess. Judy Holstern's doctor just called with the news. She's pregnant! After twenty-five years of marriage, Judy and Paul are finally going to have a baby! She says Paul's grinning so hard he can't stop."

"So that's why she was experiencing physical discomfort in her dream state," Nate said. "Her body was sensing the growing fetus's demand for nourishment. That's amazing. I wonder if anyone is studying pregnant women's dreams?"

Laura laughed. "And, that, ladies and gentlemen, is the cool, dispassionate reaction of a man of science."

Nate's easy laugh turned into a smile.

"Laura, I talked with Michael this morning. We both believe that Molly would have wanted you to listen to her second tape."

Nate pulled the already loaded tape recorder out of the drawer of his desk. "Would you like to be alone?"

"No, Nate," Laura said quickly. "I want you here."

Nate nodded and pushed the Play button.

Laura recognized that same monotone computer voice recording the date and time. When she realized it was the day before Molly's death, a chill ran up her spine.

"The pain medication is no longer effective, Michael," her aunt's voice said. "If it weren't for the numbing dreams you've given me, these last few months would not have been endurable."

Laura stopped the tape as sorrow filled her heart. "I never knew Molly was in pain! Oh, why didn't she tell me?"

Nate held her for a moment before starting the tape again. "She'll tell you now, Laura. Listen."

"I'm glad the pain is under control, Molly," Michael's voice said. "Something else has brought you to see me today?"

"Yes. Everett knows about the seriousness of my illness. He's preparing himself. But, I've never even told my dear Laura I'm ill. She's working so hard to do well in college. I pick up the phone a dozen times a day to call her. Only to hang up."

"You're afraid to talk to her, Molly? I don't believe it. You're one of the strongest women I know."

"Thank you, Michael. But in this I am a coward. You see, Laura has lost her parents, been betrayed by the man she loved. I can't bear to tell her she's losing me, too. Do you understand?''

''I understand you don't want to cause her pain, Molly. But, do you understand that not being able to say goodbye to Laura is causing you great pain?''

''Yes,'' Molly sighed. ''Can you help me with this pain as you have with the other, Michael?''

''Yes, Molly. I will help you to say goodbye,'' Michael's liquid, languid voice promised. ''Come. Lie back. Relax. Feel your muscles go soft, limp. Close your eyes.''

Laura could feel the hypnotic quality of Michael's voice closing her own eyes and relaxing her own muscles.

''You are drifting weightless, floating, light as air. You rise gently upward toward a bright, beautiful warmth. It surrounds you, caresses your body, melts away all the pain as its full, healing light passes through you. Can you see the light and feel the warmth, Molly?''

''Oh, yes, Michael! It's wonderful.''

''Let it take you, Molly. Give yourself to it. Let yourself embrace the warmth as the light flows through you.''

Laura tried to remain merely a listener. But, the images evoked by Michael's words and the incredible soothing quality of his voice were sweeping her up into the bright, beautiful warmth. She could feel it caressing her body until she, too, was lighter than air.

"Laura is there with you, Molly. Right beside you in the warmth and the light. Can you see her?"

"Oh, yes, Michael. She must know why we're here. Her eyes are glistening with tears."

Laura could actually feel those tears on her lashes. And, suddenly, inexplicably, she could see Molly's face just as clearly as she could hear her taped voice.

"Laura, you have brought me such happiness," Molly said. "When you came to live with me, you filled an empty part of my heart to overflowing. I couldn't love you any more than if you were my own daughter."

Molly's gentle fingers touched the tears escaping onto Laura's cheeks. "Dear, don't be sad. I'm never going to leave you. Not really. All you have to do is think of me and I will be there—alive in your memories of love."

A wonderful look of peace descended on Molly's face as she said those words. The ache that had lived so long in Laura's heart eased and gently drifted away.

It took several seconds for Laura to realize that

Michael's voice had stopped and the tape was at an end. She opened her eyes feeling dazed. Nate was holding her close in his strong arms, the gold dust alight in his warm russet eyes.

"Nate, I know that was Michael's tape with Molly. And, yet, suddenly I was there with Molly and she was saying goodbye to me. I don't understand. How can that have happened?"

"We call Michael The Sandman around here, Laura, because of his ability to bring his clients very special daydreams. I suspect it was your love for Molly and your need to say goodbye that swept you into this last dream he brought to her."

Laura sighed deeply, her heart completely, amazingly accepting what her logic could not.

"I understand now why Molly left her money to the Institute. She wanted you and Michael to do for others what you had been able to do for her. After I read Everett the riot act for his reprehensible behavior, I'll make sure he accepts Molly's wishes. I promise you he won't be sending in any more spies."

Nate cupped her chin and kissed her softly. The gentleness of his touch made her heart swell with longing.

"So, are you going to take me off my probationary status this Friday?'' she asked, trying her best to keep her voice light.

His tone and manner grew very somber. ''That all depends.''

Laura looked away, almost too afraid to ask. ''On what?''

Nate's finger fit into the hollow of her cheek as he gently brought her eyes back to his. ''The department head of the graduate psychology program at the University of Las Vegas is a friend of mine. He also happens to be a staunch advocate of the emotional diagnosis of dreams. He wants to meet with you tomorrow at ten to outline your study plan.''

''Study plan? For graduate work?''

''I've told him you have access to all the data I've collected over the last three years. I could hear him salivate over the phone.''

Laura was so touched she found it hard to speak. ''Oh, Nate, you did that for me?''

''No, for me. Classes start in less than two weeks. I don't want you going away a year from now to attend graduate school in some other state. I want you right here from now on—with me.''

Laura caught her breath at the golden glow that had settled in his russet eyes. She wanted to believe what she saw there. With all her heart.

"Nate, when you told me you didn't have time for a woman in your life, were you just repeating another one of Reba's barbs?"

He grinned. "Damn, you're good for someone with psychological training."

Laura's laugh filled her throat with happiness as she wrapped her arms around his neck. "I love you, you know."

No, he hadn't known. Not for certain. She saw that in the big, beautiful relieved smile that drew back his lips and wrapped itself right around her heart.

"I love you, Laura," he said, his deep voice not quite steady as he held her tightly. "Stay with me. Work with me. Marry me."

"Nate, you mean it?"

"Of course, I mean it. I have no intention of ever letting you go. Good research assistants are damn hard to find."

Laura laughed as she melted into his kiss, joy singing through her soul. She thought of that fateful fortune cookie, certain now she knew what its washed away message had said.

Beware of the Dream Doc. For he will capture your heart completely and whisk you away forever to a world full of dreams.

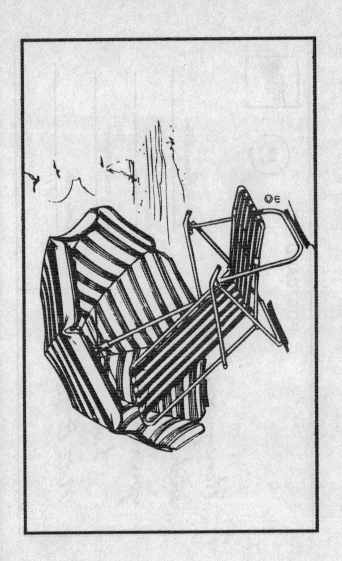

POSTCARD

Honeymoons are
such fun! So glad
you're not here!

Love,
Nate & Laura

Tara Hamilton

xxxxxxxxxxxx

xxxxxxxxxxxx

Colorado

DEAR DARCY <g>

Margaret St. George

Dear Reader,

The advent of the computer age has changed so many things, even romance. If you don't yet know someone who met Mr. Right on-line, chances are you will in the future. Two years ago a friend of mine fell in love with a man on-line, met him in person and married him. Their story is the inspiration for Darcy and Bruce's romance.

Writing Darcy and Bruce's story was a treat for me because I liked the characters so much, and because this is my first novella. And *Joe's Girl,* my January 1998 American Romance title, continues the fun! I hope you enjoy them!

Maggie

CHAPTER ONE

"ANNE, YOU'VE GOT to help me, I'm desperate." Darcy Connors cupped her hands around her coffee mug and sent a pleading look across the restaurant table.

Anne Clancy made a face. "I don't understand this. You're a bright woman. How do you get yourself in such messes?"

"Just lucky, I guess," Darcy answered with a weak smile. Raising a hand, she signaled the waiter for more coffee. "Do you want dessert?"

"Maybe. Are you having something?"

"Are you kidding? Do these thighs need cheesecake?" Darcy rolled her eyes. "If you're going to order dessert, do me a favor and order the chocolate cake. I'm the one woman in America who doesn't like chocolate."

"Your favor is granted," Anne announced, smiling after she ordered the cake.

"I hope that's the start of a trend." Darcy sighed and tried to look pitiful. "Seriously, Anne. I don't know what to do."

"For starters, you could tell him the truth. If

you'd done that in the first place, you wouldn't be in this mess now."

"Easy for you to say."

If Darcy had been blessed with Anne's classic beauty, she doubted she would have been tempted to, well, exaggerate a bit. Okay, a lot. All right, she had out-and-out lied.

But she didn't have masses of shining red hair; her hair was a shade usually described as mouse brown. And she didn't have Anne's vivid green eyes; Darcy's eyes were sort of a cross between gray and blue. And she wasn't a beauty. At best, she was mildly pretty. Mildly pretty was light-years ahead of cute, but not in the same universe as beautiful. Anne was beautiful, confident, and her life was glamorous and exciting.

Frowning, Darcy watched the waiter place Anne's chocolate cake on the table. "I thought models didn't eat stuff like cake," she said glumly.

"This will cost me an extra hour on the NordicTrack," Anne said, lifting her fork. "But it's worth it."

Darcy owned a NordicTrack, too. She considered it a vicious machine that hated her. The instant she relaxed her vigilance, it flicked her off onto the floor. Her theory about exercise was to start slow then taper off.

"Well?" she asked, watching Anne eat the cake. "Are you going to help me or not?"

"What you're asking is crazy. You know that, don't you?" Anne said, glaring at Darcy. "Give me one good reason why I should do this."

"Because we've been friends since the seventh grade. Because your mother likes me. Because I covered for you whenever you were late getting back to the dorm. Because I canceled a trip to Europe to be your maid of honor."

"Putting you in a wedding is a jinx. My marriage ended in divorce, and didn't you tell me that your friend Arianna's wedding didn't even take place?"

"That wasn't my fault," Darcy said quickly. "She broke off with her fiancé Mark Lindsay, *before* I even got a chance to march up the aisle as a bridesmaid in the wedding rehearsal. So there! Now back to the subject. You want reasons, I'll give you reasons. Because I've never asked you to do anything big for me before. Because—"

Anne held up a hand. "All right. Damn it, Darcy, I hate this." She pushed her empty plate away and sighed. "Start at the beginning and tell me the whole thing again."

"It started last year when I signed on to America Online. I posted back and forth on a bulletin board for chess enthusiasts. This guy was on the board—his name was Tom Arden. Then, I started posting on a board about mystery novels, and there he was again. He also showed up on a board discussing gambling.''

"I've never understood how you can be interested in gambling."

"What can I say? I love Atlantic City. Anyway, we kept popping up in the same interest groups, so we started posting each other privately.'' Gazing down at the napkin in her lap, she started pulling off little pieces, rolling the bits into tiny paper balls. "Well, eventually, we asked each other for a physical description.''

"And you described me!" Accusation gleamed in Anne's green eyes.

"It seemed harmless at the time. After all, Tom lived in Denver and I live in Manhattan.'' She shrugged. "Face it. I'm not exactly a beauty queen.''

"You could be, you just don't work at it.''

"I sort of borrowed you to make myself more interesting.''

"Oh, geez. What else did you tell this guy?"

Darcy drew a breath and emptied a handful of paper balls into the ashtray. "Computer programming is the dullest job on the planet. I didn't want him to think I'm some kind of computer nerd.''

"You're not a nerd, you're smart. Most of the time, that is. In every area but your personal life. So?''

"So, I told him I was a model. Every now and then I'd throw in something you'd told me. Like I had to go to Paris for a shoot. Or I had to sign off now because I had an early morning session."

"Damn it, Darcy."

"Well, how could I guess that Tom would move to New Jersey? I honestly thought we'd never meet. I really believed this would be one of those long-distance bulletin board romances that went nowhere." She shrugged again, pulled a big hunk off her napkin and rolled it into a ball in her palm. "You know the rest."

"He arrives next week, and since the two of you are finally in the same area he wants to meet in person, get married and live happily ever after."

Darcy felt a little sick inside. "Not exactly, but I think he'd like to explore that possibility. I mean, we've shared a lot of confidences and it's developed into a special relationship, but we haven't talked about love or the future or anything like that. Well, a few hints, but..." She raised her head. "Anne, he's wonderful. If it's possible to fall in love with someone you've never met, well..." She pushed a hand through the tumble of brown curls springing around her face. "I could just cry. I finally meet someone who seems to be everything I've ever wanted in a man, and look what happens. I've made it impossible for us."

They sat in silence, watching snowflakes drift past the restaurant window. Something about the moment reminded Darcy of the day she'd had dinner with her best friends from high school, Zara and Laura. They'd gone to Destiny House and it had been fun—just like old times—that was until the fortune cookies were served. Darcy's fortune had read: "Deception brings heartache."

No kidding. In Darcy's case, what had begun as an innocent deception with Tom was going to lose her the one man who had attracted her in years. You bet her heart ached.

Anne broke the silence. "Do I understand this right? You're asking me to pretend to be you, and break it off with Tom?"

Darcy nodded. She tried to swallow the lump in her throat. "I know it's a dumb plan. I know I should just tell him that I lied. But...I really care about him, Anne. And I'm ashamed of myself. I just...I don't want him to know that I deceived him. He thinks I'm the most honest person he's met. It's important to me that he never knows that I fudged the truth." A crooked smile twisted her lips. "Deceitful right to the bitter end."

Anne studied Darcy's face then reached to

squeeze her hand. "I'm sorry, sweetie," she said gently. "Are you sure there isn't some way to work this out?"

"I'm sure. I've thought about nothing else since Tom posted that he was moving to the New York area. But there's no good way to say 'I lied about how I look, I lied about what I do for a living, and I even lied about loving Mexican food. Isn't that amusing? Ha ha ha.'" She closed her eyes above a grimace. "Can't be done, my friend. I'm caught. Trapped. My E-mail romance is over. Finis."

"Who suggested that the two of you get together in person?"

"I think it was Tom."

Had he suggested a meeting? Or had she, in a forgetful moment? Darcy couldn't recall how the suggestion to meet had come about. But it was inevitable. Once Tom accepted the promotion to New Jersey, it would have been strange if they hadn't agreed to meet in person.

She placed her elbow on the table and propped her chin in her palm, staring out at the falling snow.

Anne sighed heavily. "I hate this. I can't believe I'm going along with this nutty plan. But, okay. I'll do it."

"Oh, God." Darcy released a long-held breath. "Thank you."

"But you owe me, Darcy Connors. For the rest of your miserable life. Got that? When my boring cousin comes to town and needs a date, you're it. When I need someone to water my plants while I'm out of town, that's you."

"It's me, anyway. Listen, if you do this for me, I'll bear all your children so you can keep modeling. If you get sick, I'll say, 'Here, take one of my kidneys. I'll be your slave for life.'"

Anne laughed. "Damned right you will be."

They grinned at each other. "Well, we might as well order more coffee, and you can tell me how this deal is supposed to work. And I'll need to know what you talked about in all those E-mail postings." Anne leaned back and shook her head. "I can't believe I'm going to do this."

"Me, either. But I'm glad and grateful that you are."

Was that really how she felt? No, Darcy didn't want Anne to meet Tom. She wanted to meet Tom herself. She wanted to know if he was as wonderful in person as he was in his E-mail postings. Was he as bright and funny and thoughtful and insightful? Was he the perfect man for her that she thought he was?

When she left the restaurant, she thanked heaven for the snow. Maybe no one would notice the moisture in her eyes.

From: Tom Arden
To: Darcy Connors
Subject: Arrival

My dearest Darcy, it was wonderful to set up my computer and find mail from you. I appreciate the nice welcome to the East, but you didn't have to order all this snow on my account.

No, I haven't found an apartment yet. I'm staying at my brother's place for a while. Thought I'd learn a little about the area before I commit to an apartment. How did the fashion shoot go? It seems strange E-mailing you when you're only a few miles away. I've thought about meeting you so many times. Now that it's finally possible, I'm feeling a little shy. The same for you?

> With affection,
> Tom

Darcy read the note again. It was shorter than their usual posts, and it sounded a little rushed and hesitant. Her eyes fastened on the final lines, and she chewed her lip in thought.

Was he subtly suggesting that they not meet? For an instance, hope flared in her chest. But she decided she was mistaken, merely indulging in wishful thinking. How many posts had they sent mentioning their desire to meet in person? They had talked about it countless times. Still, it might not be a bad idea to test the water. Maybe she could wiggle out of this and keep their relationship alive for a while longer.

She placed her fingertips on the computer keyboard, thought for a minute, then typed a reply.

From: Darcy Connors
To: Tom Arden
Subject: Glad you're here
My dear Tom, I'm happy that you're getting settled. If I remember correctly, the brother in New Jersey is Bruce, right? I remember the funny story you told about his brief marriage to the Las Vegas showgirl. Have you been to your new office? Are you happy about the move and your new promotion? Maybe you'll be the next Wall Street whiz kid. The fashion shoot went smoothly, thanks for asking. I know what you mean about suddenly feeling shy about meeting. Silly, isn't it? But I've heard of people being very compatible on-line, then they discover they just don't click in person. I think we'd be wise to at least consider that possibility.

Warmest regards,
Darcy

The next morning, before she left for work, before she brushed her teeth or got dressed,

Darcy rushed into the living room and checked her E-mail.

From: Tom Arden
To: Darcy Connors
Subject: Meeting in person
Dearest Darcy, I agree that we have to consider the possibility that we might not be compatible in person. As sad as that would be, I know these things can happen. It probably happens that way more often than not, in fact. I don't want you to think I'm suggesting we don't meet. We've talked about meeting so often, and it would be hard to justify not meeting when we're this close. It's a risk I guess we have to take. I want to say this. Your daily postings have become very important to me. If it turns out that we're not compatible, I imagine we won't continue to post each other, in which case I'll miss you very much. You're a special person, Darcy. You've made the past year interesting and exciting. What's your schedule for next week? Would dinner on Saturday work for you?

Affectionately,
Tom

Darcy stared at her computer screen. The plan she and Anne had concocted was going to be successful. Anne would gently say, "I'm sorry, Tom. I wish we were as good together in person as we are on-line, but...we knew this might happen."

Tom would be disappointed, but not surprised. He was aware their cyberspace relationship might not survive reality. In fact, his post had a whiff of goodbye in it.

Her shoulders slumped and she pressed her fingertips to her forehead. Losing him was going to open a hole in her life. She hadn't realized how eagerly she'd awaited his posts until she had to accept they would soon cease.

Tilting her head back, Darcy gazed at the ceiling of her apartment. She was twenty-eight years old and had never been married. Despite the efforts of matchmaking friends, she hadn't met a man in years who interested her. In fact, she was slowly developing a theory that the men in New York City were either married, gay, seriously crazy, or possessed of a personality about as exciting as a mushroom.

Was it any wonder that she had turned to her computer in the search for male companionship? Talk about safe sex. It didn't get any safer than a computer screen. But you couldn't cuddle in bed with a computer. A computer couldn't hold you when you came home from work feeling beat up by the world.

Still, she had found Tom on the computer. And Tom was the best thing that had happened to her in years. Which said everything there was to say about her recent social life.

And she was about to throw him away.

"You idiot," she whispered, blinking hard. "How could you do this to yourself?" But she knew how it had happened. Self-confidence had never been her strong point.

She reached for the telephone and called Anne.

"Did I wake you?"

"No," Anne said, yawning in Darcy's ear. "I'm reading the newspaper, having breakfast."

"Black coffee and a grapefruit, right?"

"Right. Have you done your workout yet?"

Darcy swung around in her chair to glare at the NordicTrack. She cursed the day she had brought the damned thing home. Now she felt guilty if she didn't use it.

"I hate to sweat," she said. Then added hastily, "But I'm going to do it. I'm up to five minutes a session."

Anne snorted. 'Five minutes. That isn't a workout. It isn't even a decent warm-up."

"The reason I'm calling…are you free for dinner Saturday night?" She sighed and her voice sank. "Tom wants to meet on Saturday."

"Swell. I can hardly wait." Anne's sigh was deeper than Darcy's had been. "Actually, I have a date Saturday night."

"How about lunch? Lunch might be better anyway. Throw down a salad, dump him, you're out of there in an hour."

"Listen, I've been thinking about something...."

Panic tightened Darcy's chest. "You aren't changing your mind about this, are you?"

"Nooo. But it occurs to me that I don't know this guy from Adam. I'm a little uncomfortable about meeting a stranger for dinner or lunch or whatever. You have to come with us. That way you can kick me under the table or something if I start to mess up. You know, if I say something wrong."

Darcy considered the suggestion. Of course she wanted to be there. She wanted to meet Tom, hear his voice, gaze into his eyes. If she didn't meet him, she would wonder about him the rest of her life.

"He's going to think that's strange," she said slowly. "Bringing a friend to the first meeting. The last meeting," she corrected. "But, of course, he doesn't know that yet. Let me think a minute."

"There's nothing to think about," Anne said firmly. "I've made up my mind. If you don't come along, I'm not going. The guy could be a serial killer or something."

"He is not!" Darcy said, shocked. "Besides, how are you going to dump him with me sitting there? I'm crazy about Tom. I don't want you to give him the heave-ho in front of me and embarrass him!"

"Look, I've dumped a hundred guys. We'll have lunch. We'll talk about his move and his promotion. Then, as we're leaving the restaurant, I'll take him aside and say adios, partner. It's no problem."

"I can't tell you how much I hate this." Darcy groaned and covered her eyes.

"Me, too. You should have thought about this before."

"All right, I'll see if I can work this out for lunch. You and Tom and me. God. I'll call you back with the details as soon as I know them."

She hung up, stripped off her bathrobe, and did an endless five minutes on the hated Nordic-Track, thinking it might loosen her up. During the eternity that she was walking and pulling, she stared at the computer screen, thinking about Tom.

He hadn't said that he was a hunk, but she'd picked up that impression. He'd mentioned dark hair, dark eyes. She knew he worked out regularly; he teased her about her love-hate—mostly hate—relationship with the NordicTrack. He'd been the one who talked her into buying the awful thing.

And Tom had been the one who introduced her to Tony Hillerman's novels. The person who made long-distance chess exciting. Tom was the only man with whom she could be silly or serious, philosophical or bitchy. She hadn't even told Anne, whom she'd known longer than she'd known Arianna, Zara and Laura, how painful high school had been for her. But she'd told Tom.

After her workout, she returned to her computer.

From: Darcy Connors
To: Tom Arden
Subject: Lunch instead?
My dear Tom, I'm free Saturday, but let's have lunch instead of dinner, okay? Dinner seems a bit formal for our first meeting. And if things don't go the way we'd like…well, it just seems that lunch might be a better choice. And would you mind terribly if I brought along my friend Anne? I may be from Denver originally, but I'm a New York girl now, and we New York girls have it drilled in our brains that it's not a good idea to meet a stranger alone. You're not a

stranger, of course. But there might be some awkward moments, and I think having a third person present would make it a little easier for us. If this plan works for you, we could meet at The Mealy Mouth at, say, twelve-thirty? BTW, I'm up to six minutes on the NordicTrack.

Looking forward to meeting you,
Darcy

The first thing she did when she returned from work was dash to her computer. She didn't even take off her coat or kick out of her heels.

From: Tom Arden
To: Darcy Connors
Subject: Good idea!
Hi Darcy, lunch works for me. And bring your friend along. If it's all right with you, I'll bring my brother Bruce, and we'll make it a foursome. He wants to meet you. No matter how this works out, I want you to know that you're terrific. I've enjoyed our chess games, the book discussions, the arguments about holding a face card with a pair or discarding it. (Always discard!)
 Looking forward to meeting you, too.

Tom

Darcy blinked at the tears welling in her eyes. "Dearest Darcy" had become "Hi Darcy." Apparently, she'd set the stage well. There wasn't much intimacy in their recent postings. And he seemed prepared to make a brief appearance then exit gracefully if it worked out that way. Which it would.

Blindly, she reached for the telephone and dialed Anne.

"We're all set," she whispered. "Lunch at The Mealy Mouth on Saturday at twelve-thirty. I'm going, and he's bringing his brother Bruce."

"Oh, great. Two serial killers. What shall I wear?"

"Something ugly. So he won't feel bad when you dump him."

Anne laughed. "Listen, help me out here. Did you say he was a stockbroker or an insurance broker?"

"Oh, God. He's a stockbroker. Anne, if you—"

"Don't have a heart attack, I was just teasing. Have a glass of wine and calm down. An hour and we're out of there, remember? It's going to work out the way you want it to."

The way she wanted it to. Sure. Driving a stake through her heart was exactly what she wanted.

A glass of wine didn't help. She was going to

be a nervous wreck until the lunch was behind her, and she was going to hurt like hell when it was over.

Not that it mattered, but it occurred to her that she only had two days to figure out what *she* was going to wear. It broke her heart to realize that Tom wasn't going to notice her. Even if Anne wore a grocery sack, Anne was going to be the only one Tom saw.

He would be sitting next to the person who knew he'd broken his arm in his senior year of high school and missed his last season of baseball, who knew that he regretted not having been able to say goodbye to his father before his father died. Darcy knew Tom had a secret ambition to write a novel some day, knew he dreamed of vacationing in the Greek Islands. She knew he had an onyx chess set, knew he was a whiz at video poker.

She would sit across from him at lunch, knowing so much about him, loving him, but he would never see her.

The realization was dismal enough to make a person want to eat a whole cherry cheesecake.

CHAPTER TWO

"HOW DO I LOOK?" Darcy asked anxiously. She and Anne had taken seats at the bar facing the restaurant door, and whenever the door opened, Darcy inspected the new arrivals with a mixture of dread and anticipation.

"You look wonderful. Did you color your hair?"

Darcy nodded. "The box said warm brown with red highlights. I dyed three towels, part of the kitchen counter, my blouse and some of my hair. I'm so nervous. Are they late?"

"Relax. We're early."

"Oh, sure. Relax. Easy for you to say."

Swiveling on the stool, Darcy studied Anne in the mirror behind the bar. Even though they had decided that Anne would ugly up to soften her rejection of Tom, she still looked gorgeous. Masses of red hair were piled on top of her head. The loose black dress she was wearing floated over her elegant curves. Her legs looked a mile long.

Darcy sighed. "Why couldn't I have an ugly

best friend? Then I'd look great by comparison.''
She tore her cocktail napkin into pieces, rolled
the pieces in balls, and arranged the little balls in
a circle around her drink. "But, no. You and
Molly Stevens are models. Why was I so dumb
as to pick models for best friends? I don't have
a single ugly friend. It's so depressing.''

Anne laughed. "You always sell yourself
short. I'd love to have your voluptuous figure.
And you have beautiful eyes, and lashes to die
for.''

When the door opened again, Darcy looked up,
then smothered a gasp. She gripped Anne's wrist.
"That has to be him! And he looks exactly like
I imagined he would! Oh Lord, he's sexy as
hell.''

Tom—that had to be Tom—stopped inside the
restaurant door, scanning faces with a searching
expression, his hands in the pockets of a dark
topcoat. Thick brown hair waved across his forehead, the color a shade lighter than his eyes and
eyebrows. His mouth was precisely as Darcy had
fantasized it would be, full and wide, a mouth
made for laughing and kissing and whispering
words of love.

A hot tingle raced through her body as she
stared at him. He was taller than she had expected, but every bit as great looking. This was

one fabulous man, everything she had hoped he would be.

"Wow," Anne breathed. "Who's the guy standing behind him? Is that Tom's brother? He's gorgeous!"

Darcy dragged her eyes away from Tom long enough to notice the man leaning to speak in his ear. Ninety women out of a hundred would probably have said that Tom's brother was the better looking of the two. But to Darcy's taste, Bruce was too pretty, too blandly perfect. Tom, on the other hand, had the type of craggy good looks that was unleashing an earthquake in her stomach.

Tom spotted them then, and he and his brother walked directly into the bar, halting in front of Anne and Darcy.

But Darcy had guessed wrong.

The pretty boy brother shocked her by smiling broadly at Anne and extending his hand. "Hi. I'm Tom Arden and you have to be Darcy Connors." Smoothly, he converted a handshake into a kiss, bringing Anne's fingers to his lips. "You're more beautiful than I imagined."

Anne stared and a light blush tinted her cheeks. "I'd like you to meet my friend, Darcy." She caught herself and dazzled Tom with a smile. "Sorry, I'm Darcy. This is my friend, Anne. I guess I'm more nervous about finally meeting you than I realized."

Darcy resisted an urge to roll her eyes. Staring at him, she extended her hand. Tom didn't kiss *her* fingertips. He gave her hand a perfunctory shake and immediately turned back to Anne.

"This is my brother, Bruce."

Bruce shook Darcy's hand firmly and smiled into her eyes. "I'm pleased to meet you." His hand was large and warm. Then he gazed at Anne, drinking in her beauty as most men did. "I've heard a lot about you, Darcy. I think I would have guessed that you're a model even if Tom hadn't mentioned it."

"It's a living," Anne said, still smiling up at Tom.

An awkward silence might have overwhelmed them except the maître d' caught Darcy's eye and signaled their table was ready.

Despite the cutesy name, The Mealy Mouth was an upscale restaurant catering to young professionals. A subdued maroon-and-charcoal decor enhanced an ambience vaguely reminiscent of corporate dining rooms. Since the purpose of this lunch was to end the relationship with Tom, Darcy had deliberately selected a restaurant light on romantic atmosphere.

Tom held out Anne's chair, and Bruce extended hers. When everyone was seated, they im-

mediately hid behind large, oversize menus.
Darcy felt a kick under the table and looked at
Anne.

Hidden by the menu, Anne mouthed the
words, "He's fantastic!"

Darcy lowered the menu to peek at Tom. He
was gorgeous, no question about it. Like his
brother Bruce, Tom had dark hair and dark eyes,
but a shade lighter. His was the classic perfect
profile. He had broad shoulders, a tapered waist.
Curious, she continued to stare at him after the
waiter had taken their orders. Tom Arden was
film-star handsome.

But surprisingly he did nothing whatsoever to
stir Darcy's libido. She had hoped he would be
handsome, but handsome like a real person, like
his brother, instead of film-star handsome. She
had never been drawn to men who were prettier
than she was. She just couldn't take them seriously.

Now that she'd met him, Darcy sadly decided
this lunch was not the tragedy she had been anticipating. She and Tom really didn't mesh in
person. He was too pretty, too smooth, and he
was a hand kisser. Yuck.

Tom raised his wineglass. "Here's to a meeting I've looked forward to for almost a year."

"And here's to your promotion," Anne said
brightly.

Tom and Anne touched glasses, then he remembered to include Darcy and Bruce before he returned his attention to Anne. "I sent you my latest chess move last night. Did you receive my post?"

Anne slid a quick glance toward Darcy. "Sorry," she hedged, "I didn't check my E-mail this morning." At least Anne recalled that Darcy and Bruce were also present.

When Darcy realized she was sitting like a lump sweating out the conversation between Anne and Tom, she swallowed hard then dredged up a smile for Bruce, who sat on her right.

"How long have you been in television?" she inquired politely. To her embarrassment, this man *did* do shivery things to her nervous system. Which flustered her. For a year she'd been half in love with Tom. Finally, after dreaming about it for months, she'd finally met him and what happened? He didn't do a thing for her, but she was strongly attracted to his brother. Talk about fickle. And confusing.

"Twelve years," Tom answered, interrupting his conversation with Anne.

They all looked at him. He cleared his throat and patted his brother's shoulder. "Old Bruce here interned at a local station in Denver while he was in college. Worked up from there."

"I can speak for myself," Bruce said, narrowing his eyes.

In Darcy's opinion, Tom looked more like a television producer than Bruce did. She could swear that Tom had added gold highlights to his hair, and his clothing had a hint of the avantgarde that she didn't usually associate with stockbrokers.

"What TV show do you produce?" she asked Bruce.

"At the moment, I'm developing a couple of new programs." He summoned a smile. "What do you do?"

"Me?" She glanced at Tom and Anne who had leaned close to each other and were chatting like old friends. She hoped Anne wasn't making any mistakes. "I'm just a computer programmer. Nothing exciting."

Bruce seemed as interested in Anne and Tom as she was, but he managed to send her another smile that made her stomach tighten and her cheeks warm. "Today's world would collapse without computer programmers. Look how quickly we've come to depend on computers for information, entertainment and even relationships." He glanced at Anne then back at Darcy. "Thanks to bright people like you, the industry will continue to expand."

She looked at him with new interest. "Do you own a personal computer?"

"Absolutely. I started out borrowing Tom's PC, then when he—" Bruce stopped talking, frowned, then shrugged. "Couldn't get along without it."

They both paused when Anne and Tom burst into laughter. "Darcy and your brother seem to be hitting it off," Darcy said finally. Her voice was tight.

Even though she wasn't attracted to him, it wounded her that Tom appeared so instantly infatuated with Anne. She knew it was unreasonable, but she'd half expected him to somehow sense that his E-mail soul mate was her, not Anne. And Anne sure as hell was not behaving like a woman who intended to dump the man gazing into her eyes.

Bruce nodded, a slight frown tugging his forehead.

Darcy thought a minute, then placed her napkin on the table. The only reason her napkin wasn't torn to shreds was that it was linen, not paper. "I need to powder my nose," she said lightly. She gave Anne a long meaningful look. "Would you care to join me?"

"Hurry back," Tom ordered, looking disappointed.

Darcy stared at him. She hated guys who were

so possessive that they urged a woman to rush back from the ladies' room. This was the kind of annoying trait you just couldn't pick up from an E-mail post.

The instant she was away from the table, she clasped Anne's arm. "You're *flirting* with him! Damn it, Anne. You're supposed to dump him, remember? Adios? Goodbye forever?"

Anne cast her a guilty look then entered the ladies' room and patted her hair in front of the mirror. "I forgot, okay? He's everything you said he was. Interesting, handsome, funny…"

Darcy ground her teeth and glared at her reflection. "He's not at all like I thought he was. He kissed your hand." She made a face. "Geez. How phony can you get?"

"I thought the gesture was charming."

"Oh, come on. And he's ignoring me and his brother. That is so rude! What a disappointment."

Anne's eyebrows rose. "Well, Tom thinks he's meeting someone he's been captivated by for a year. Of course he's focused." Leaning to the mirror, she applied fresh lipstick, then eyed herself critically. "Actually, this is going better than I thought it would. He suggested that we pretend we don't know anything about each other and talk as if we've just met." She rolled her eyes toward Darcy. "What a relief! So far, he hasn't made any reference to anything in your postings. At least not that I know of.''

"Well, that's pretty dumb." Darcy shoved at the springy curls around her face. They bounced back. She liked the new warm brown, but otherwise it was the same old hopeless hair. "Why pretend? I know everything about him, and he knows everything about me.''

"Pretending otherwise is making this lunch a whole lot easier for me." Anne spritzed some perfume behind her ears "God, he's good-looking. I can't believe he's a stockbroker. I could get him a job modeling in a minute. And his hands...did you notice the way he holds his glass?''

She hadn't. But she'd noticed the way Bruce held a taste of wine on his tongue before he swallowed. She did the same thing.

"You know what's crazy?" Darcy said, scowling at herself in the mirror. "I don't care much for Tom in person, but I like Bruce. I mean I *really* like him. I like the way he tries to include everyone in his conversation. I like his looks. I like his smile..." She closed her eyes. "God, I'll be glad when this is over! You can't imagine how confused I feel right now.''

Before they rejoined Tom and Bruce, Darcy held Anne back for a minute. "Look. Regardless of how lukewarm I feel about Tom, I spent a year baring my soul to him and he meant a lot to me. Dump him as gently as you can.''

Both men stood when they returned to the table, Bruce a fraction ahead of Tom. Everyone smiled at everyone. To Darcy's relief, Anne tried to stop flirting and Tom made an effort to include her and Bruce in the conversation, which was a bit stilted, but that was to be expected.

When a silence opened after the salad was served, Bruce gazed at Anne and said, ''I understand you like mystery novels, Darcy.''

''I do,'' Darcy answered promptly. Immediately she caught her mistake. ''Oh. I'm sorry, I thought you said Anne.'' Heat flooded her cheeks, and she felt foolish. The names didn't sound remotely alike.

''You're a mystery fan, too?'' Bruce asked her. His smile covered a moment of embarrassment and curled inside her like warm smoke. ''Do you like Tony Hillerman?''

''One of my favorites. A friend suggested him,'' she glanced at Tom who was staring at Anne. ''I've been a fan ever since. How about Elmore Leonard? Do you like his books?''

Bruce leaned back as the waiter served his entree. ''Yes, but I think Leonard is more mainstream.''

''Really? I don't agree.''

They argued the point over lunch and then into

coffee afterward. Darcy was so absorbed by the stimulating discussion with Bruce that she forgot to worry about Anne and Tom. When she remembered them, it shocked her that she could have so totally spaced out a man she'd been fantasizing about for nearly a year.

Falling silent, she shifted her gaze to Tom Arden, remembering the daily postings they had exchanged, and the deepening intimacy, listening as he and Anne shared their enthusiasm for a recent Jim Carrey film. Both of them were laughing.

Yesterday, Darcy would have bet the earth that her Tom wouldn't particularly enjoy a Jim Carrey film. It bewildered her that she could have been so wrong, and that he was so different from what she had expected and hoped he would be.

Turning back to Bruce, she studied the craggy lines that gave his face such interest and character. "Do you like Jim Carrey films?" she asked impulsively.

He grinned and exaggerated a shudder. "Not on your life."

"Me, neither."

Bruce and Tom seemed as different as, well, as Darcy and Anne. Guiltily, Darcy found herself wishing that she knew Bruce better. The thought made her feel weird and disloyal.

And she was being unrealistic. Bruce seemed almost as fascinated by Anne as Tom was. When

Darcy caught him studying Anne for the hundredth time, he gave her an apologetic smile and a small shrug. "Your friend Darcy is very beautiful."

"Really? Personally I've always thought she was plain as a post. I feel sorry for the poor girl."

Bruce stared at her, then laughed. "I like a woman with a sense of humor." He gazed at her. "You have lovely eyes. I can't decide if they're gray or blue."

"Hey, you don't have to compliment me. I know I'm not a babe like...Darcy."

He looked surprised. "Darcy is a model, and she looks like one," he said slowly. "You're beautiful in a more accessible way." Instantly he seemed uncomfortable, as if he were startled by what he had said.

Darcy squirmed beneath his scrutiny. It pleased her—a lot—that Bruce seemed to genuinely think she was attractive. For a brief instant, her gaze dropped to his lips and she wondered if he was a good kisser. The thought rattled her badly. Tom—*Tom*—was sitting an arm's length away, and here she was fantasizing about his brother. How low could she sink?

"So," she said, seeking a change of subject. "Do you think they're hitting it off?" They both glanced at Anne and Tom who were head-to-head again.

"The odds are against them," Bruce replied, frowning. "Cyberspace romances don't usually work out."

"I've heard the same thing," Darcy agreed, also frowning. She wanted to kick Anne under the table, but Anne had moved her chair closer to Tom and Darcy couldn't reach her.

"They're trying hard," Bruce added, his frown deepening. "But..."

"Probably they're being polite. Trying to ease out of a sticky situation gradually."

"Wouldn't surprise me," Bruce said.

Darcy brightened. Surely Bruce knew his own brother. His comments indicated that Tom was putting on a front. He wasn't as infatuated with Anne as it appeared. Good. Then it wouldn't hurt too badly when Anne dumped him.

Relaxing a little, Darcy smiled at Bruce. "I hope this doesn't offend you, but Darcy," she continued to stumble over calling Anne by her own name, "told me the hysterical story about you waking up married to a Las Vegas show-girl."

Frankly, she couldn't even imagine it. Bruce Arden was not the glib type that Darcy had discovered Tom was. Sincerity warmed Bruce's dark eyes, and intuition suggested that he was not an impulsive type. It was difficult to reconcile her impression with the party-boy image she'd received from Tom's postings.

For an instant Bruce's eyes were blank as if he didn't know what she was talking about, then he waved a hand and an embarrassed flush tinted his cheeks.

"Oh that," he said finally, frowning into his coffee cup. "It was…well, I'd rather forget it." Glancing up, he gave her a lopsided smile. "Marrying a showgirl was very out of character."

She agreed. She glanced at Tom and Anne, still head-to-head, talking and laughing. "Do you have children?" she asked Bruce.

"I beg your pardon?"

"I thought Darcy mentioned that you'd been married twice. Once to the showgirl and another time to…I don't know. Someone else."

"Oh." He glanced at Tom then touched his tie. "My first marriage was right out of college. We were too young. It didn't work out. And no, there were no children." He seemed so uncomfortable that Darcy wished she hadn't pried. "Have you been married?"

"Me?" She laughed. "I had a close call a couple of years ago, but…no. Mr. Right is taking his time putting in an appearance."

"Would you like to be married?"

"Is that a proposal?"

They grinned at each other.

"You're easy to talk to," Bruce commented, still smiling.

"So are you." Darcy finished her coffee, then shook her head when the waiter appeared with a fresh pot. "I didn't know what you and I would talk about, frankly." She tilted her mop of curls toward Anne and Tom. "We're sort of third wheels here. But it's been a pleasure."

His dark eyes traveled to her mouth and lingered for a long moment. Then he straightened abruptly and made a show of consulting his watch. "I didn't realize it was getting so late. Did you know it's almost four o'clock?"

"Really?" Darcy resisted lifting a hand to her lips to see if his steady gaze had left an imprint. The corner of her mouth trembled. *Stop this,* she told herself. Bruce probably had a date for the evening. She couldn't imagine that he spent many Saturday nights alone. Scooting down in her chair, she stretched out a leg and nudged Anne. "It's four o'clock."

Anne moved back from Tom and blinked. "My, how time flies." She and Tom both laughed although Darcy didn't see anything amusing in the comment.

Leaning to one side, Darcy lifted her purse from the floor. "Heavy," she remarked. "I need to *dump* this out and dispose of half of whatever I'm carrying." She narrowed her eyes on Anne, hoping she'd picked up on the word *dump*. Now was the time.

When the four of them stood, Darcy planned to draw Bruce ahead, giving Anne a moment of privacy to tell Tom that they wouldn't be seeing each other again.

Tom held Anne's chair and Darcy heard him inquire, "Are you free for dinner tomorrow night?"

Anne smiled up at him. "Yes."

Darcy froze in shock.

"There's a wonderful place in Chinatown that I've been meaning to try. Do you like Hunan?"

"Love it," Anne said.

Darcy and Bruce stared at them.

Then Bruce turned to her. "What time shall we pick you up?" His smile was grim.

Immediately Darcy understood that he was merely being polite. But there was no way she was going to risk having Anne and Tom be alone together. She looked Bruce in the eye.

"Seven o'clock would be fine."

"Good," he said shortly. Dimly she registered that he seemed as irritated as she was. "If it's all right with you, we'll pick you both up at Darcy's apartment."

"Fine," Darcy said between her teeth.

Once outside, Bruce flagged a taxi and opened the door for Darcy and Anne. Both men mur-

mured parting comments, but Darcy was too angry to hear whatever they said.

The instant the taxi door slammed, she whirled
to Anne. "What in the hell are you doing? You
were supposed to dump him! Not make another
date with him!"

"I know, I know." Anne wrung her hands in
her lap. "I'm sorry, all right?" She focused her
large green eyes on Darcy. "I feel terrible about
this. I'm really attracted to him, and I feel just
awful about it! You and I never liked the same
guys before. I just...I just forgot that he was your
Tom. I'm really sorry, Darcy. I apologize."

Darcy leaned back in the seat and folded her
arms over her chest. "What did the two of you
talk about?" she asked after she had calmed
down a little.

"For a stockbroker he knows a lot about show
business. He said he picked it up from his
brother. We talked about that, and..." Anne
spread her hands. "I don't remember everything
we talked about. Shoots, vacation spots, films..."

"Not chess or video poker or books?"

"No, thank God. I would have been in trouble.
I don't know a royal flush from a royal pain."
She looked at Darcy. "If he wants to talk about
that stuff tomorrow night, I'm going to need
help."

"I couldn't believe it when he didn't say

something when Bruce and I were discussing Tony Hillerman's books. Tony Hillerman is Tom's favorite author.''

Darcy sighed. What man would want to talk about books when he could look at Anne instead? Maybe because she and Anne truly were not attracted to the same kind of men, she had never before felt even a twinge of jealousy toward Anne. But she was out-and-out green with jealousy now.

Which flustered her because Darcy had to admit that she wasn't attracted to Tom in person. Still, after a year of daily postings, of baring her inner thoughts, she felt an emotional attachment to him. How could she still feel emotionally involved with a man she didn't particularly like in person?

Lowering her head, she rubbed her temples. This had been the most disconcerting afternoon she'd spent in a decade.

She dreaded the thought of going through the same thing tomorrow night.

And the strangest thing of all: She couldn't stop thinking about Bruce Arden, remembering the shape of his lips and the sound of his deep voice. The way he gestured with his hands, the warmth of his smile.

She sighed. What a mess!

CHAPTER THREE

SUNDAYS WERE FOR sleeping late and doing battle with the *New York Times* crossword puzzle. But this morning, Darcy couldn't concentrate. Her mind wandered from the puzzle and she kept glancing at the window, hoping for signs of a blizzard that would force Tom and Bruce to cancel dinner. Although the temperature hovered just above freezing, the skies, unfortunately, were clear.

Sighing, she slid out of bed and went to the kitchen for another cup of coffee, passing her computer in the living room. On her way back, she paused. Had Tom posted today?

Curious, she sat down and signed on to America Online, wincing when her computer sang out, "You have mail!" It had to be Tom. Reluctantly, she opened the mail file.

To: Darcy Connors
From: Tom Arden
Subject: Us
Darcy:

She noticed at once that he didn't begin by even saying hi.

I'm glad we finally met. But I owe you an apology. I put you on the spot by inviting you to dinner tonight in front of my brother and your friend. I suspect you accepted merely out of politeness rather than cause an embarrassing or awkward moment. If you prefer to cancel, I'll certainly understand.

You're as wonderful as I thought you would be, but not quite what I expected. I hope you'll understand what I'm trying to say. I think you will, as I suspect you're having similar thoughts about me. Odd, isn't it, how people can seem so different in person?

You bet she was thinking he was different from what she had expected. How could she have anticipated that he would turn out to be a glib-tongued hand kisser? Or that he would appear self-absorbed to the point of rudeness? Or that he'd be vain enough to add gold highlights to his hair. She couldn't get over it. And naturally Tom thought she was different from her E-mail persona; Anne hadn't addressed any of the topics he knew Darcy felt passionately about.

Did you get fifteen across?

She smiled at his last comment. That at least, sounded like the old Tom she knew and had been crazy about. Not the phony, hand-kissing, hurry back from the ladies' room, self-involved Tom that she'd met in person. It wouldn't have surprised her if *that* Tom had inquired about her astrological sign. Geez.

Leaning back in her chair and sipping coffee, Darcy considered his almost-suggestion about canceling tonight. But canceling wouldn't solve the problem. Now that she had met Tom, she conceded there was no sense continuing their E-mail relationship. Besides, their posts wouldn't be the same now that they'd met. No, they needed to have dinner tonight so Anne could dump him and make a clean break. If Anne remembered to do it, she thought crankily.

To: Tom Arden
From: Darcy Connors
Subject: Us
I have to admit that you aren't exactly what I expected, either. I'm glad we can be honest about this. And isn't it odd that we avoided the subjects we usually talk about? Maybe we've said all there is to say?
  You're right. Your invitation for dinner

tonight was a bit awkward. Since Anne and Bruce were listening, I felt I really couldn't refuse without embarrassing everyone.

She hoped her response made it clear that she would have said no if he'd offered the invitation privately.

But since we're committed anyway, I think we should give this one more try. Then, if it doesn't work out, well, we knew the odds were against us. If you agree, we'll make a decision tonight and talk about it after dinner.

The answer to fifteen across is: Montaillou. Can't believe you didn't get that one.

She reread what she'd written, fine-tuned it a little, then pressed the Send button. She'd done what she could to prepare him. Anne's rejection wouldn't arrive out of the blue. After Darcy's reply, Tom should be half expecting that they wouldn't see each other again. And in fact, there was a tiny suggestion in his post that he might be a bit relieved when Anne dumped him.

Twenty-four hours ago, that realization would have upset her and made her feel sad and bereft. Now it didn't. There was nothing like discovering a man was a turn-off in person to throw ice water on a budding romance.

Again, it was Bruce Arden who occupied Darcy's thoughts throughout the day and later as she dressed for dinner. Now this was a man who rang her chimes. Thick-lashed dark eyes, a firm wide mouth. Sure hands, an air of easy confidence. She felt as if she could talk to him forever. And although she tried to push away such thoughts, she kept wondering how his kiss would taste and feel.

Slumping on the side of the bed, Darcy closed her eyes and shook her head. She had never been the frivolous type who jumped from one man or one relationship to another. Loyalty and tenacity were two of her strongest qualities.

Yet, in less than a day she had gone from thinking she could easily fall in love with Tom Arden to daydreaming about his handsome, sexy brother.

She was shameless. There were flighty aspects to her character that she hadn't suspected. She had proudly pictured herself as a grown-up Girl Scout, while all the time she had the makings of a bimbo. Damn.

ANNE ARRIVED AT Darcy's apartment mere minutes before Tom and Bruce appeared. She threw off her coat, revealing a bold patterned silk suit with a mandarin collar, then flung herself into a chair and looked over at Darcy.

"I wish I'd never agreed to this," she said sullenly. "Tom is a very nice guy. I just hate to hurt his feelings!"

"You have to dump him, Anne. Otherwise, how do we get out of this?" Darcy looked around her apartment, plumped a sofa cushion, adjusted the ottoman.

"Giving me one of your kidneys isn't good enough! I just hate this!"

"Do you think I like it?" Darcy raked her fingers through her curls. "The way we get out of this mess is for you to dump him. Tom and I exchanged E-mails this morning, and I've prepared him. All you have to remember is *do* it. I think he'll be relieved, actually."

Anne sat up straight and looked stung. "He didn't like me?"

"How could he not like you? It's just that you weren't what he expected." Darcy threw out her hands. "He expected nail-biting, hyperactive, book-loving, exercising-loathing me!"

Anne made a face. "How on earth could you pretend to be a model and hate exercise? That doesn't even make sense, Darcy!"

They both glanced toward the door when the bell rang, and they did some hasty hair patting and dress smoothing. Darcy started toward the door then stopped and waved Anne forward. "It's supposed to be your apartment," she whispered.

"Hi," Anne said, opening the door with a quick smile. "Come in. Can I take your coats?"

Darcy skimmed over Tom's smile and feasted her eyes on Bruce. Tonight he wore a gorgeous charcoal three-piece suit and a black-and-red tie. When he shook her hand the sexy scent of Tuscany, her absolute favorite male cologne, reeled through her senses.

Tom was dressed more casually, wearing a trendy sports coat that would appeal to Anne, she knew, but which seemed affected to Darcy's more conservative eye.

After she nudged Anne, Anne said brightly. "What would you like to drink?" Both men decided on Scotch and water.

Darcy smiled sweetly and said she'd like a glass of wine. "White, if you have it," she added.

Anne headed toward the kitchen. After a minute, she leaned out and frowned at Darcy. "Would you mind giving me a hand?" When Darcy followed, Anne glared at her. "So, have you moved the damned glasses?"

"Up here."

When they emerged, Tom was sitting on the sofa. Bruce stood near the window, studying Darcy's chess board. He smiled at Anne. "Is this the game you're playing with Tom?"

Anne's eyebrows soared. "Yes," she said slowly, drawing the word out and looking toward Darcy for confirmation. Anxiety filled her eyes when she turned to Tom. "You don't want to play now, do you?"

"Not unless you do."

"I don't think so," she said, looking relieved. "I assume you've made reservations, we don't want to be late."

Darcy handed Bruce a Scotch and water. "Do you play chess?"

"Occasionally." He touched his tie then tasted his drink. "Tom and I grew up with many of the same interests. Do you play?"

"Occasionally. Darcy and I have many of the same interests, too."

Bruce nodded, his warm dark eyes admiring the black cocktail suit she wore. "I hope you didn't have to make a long trip to meet us here. Do you live nearby?"

For a minute the question didn't make sense. "Oh yes," she said finally. "My apartment is a lot like this one, in fact." She drew a breath. "How long have you lived in New Jersey?"

"Only a few...ah, years. Where are you from originally?"

"Denver."

"Really? Tom and I are from Denver, too. Where did you go to school?"

"Lakewood High. Darcy's folks moved when we were in the eighth grade and we didn't resume our friendship until college, so she... Never mind that. Where did you go to school?"

"Wheatridge High."

Green flecks sparkled in his dark eyes, reflecting an intriguing hazel color. They stood close enough that Darcy's perfume mingled with his cologne. His body heat radiated like a magnet drawing her toward him. Suddenly Darcy wondered how long they had been standing toe-to-toe, gazing into each other's eyes.

"I wish I'd met you under different circumstances," Bruce said in a husky voice, dropping his gaze to her lips. Immediately, a dark color infused his cheeks and he hastily moved backward a step. "What I mean is," he said awkwardly, searching for words, "we've been sort of thrown together without any choice."

"I know what you mean," Darcy murmured. She didn't have a clue what he meant, but she agreed with him. God, she wished she had met him under different circumstances. She wished he wasn't Tom Arden's brother, wished there was no deception between them. She wished she could see him again after tonight, but of course that wasn't possible. He didn't even know her real name.

Without thinking, he reached down and moved the knight on her chess set, taking one of her pawns. "Are you seeing anyone?"

"Not exactly. Are you?"

"Not exactly."

After studying the board, she took his knight with her bishop. "Bad move," she crowed.

Instantly, his eyes sharpened and he leaned over the board. "I didn't notice your bishop. Overs?"

"Not a chance!" Darcy said, grinning.

Abruptly she realized they were moving pieces on a board that presumably belonged to Anne. "We're messing up their game," she commented with a glance toward the sofa. Anne and Tom were sitting very close together, flirting outrageously. Darcy frowned and replaced the pieces she and Bruce had moved. This was going to be a long, nerve-racking evening.

"You have an excellent memory," Bruce commented, when she replaced the pieces without thought.

That she did. She remembered almost all the postings she and his brother had exchanged. They had shared jokes and quotes and memories and dreams. They had talked about family and philosophy, work and play.

And even though Darcy was looking at Tom right now, she felt no sense of connection or communication. Feeling as if she were studying a complete stranger instead of her Tom made her feel disoriented. She didn't understand how he could be so different from the person she had expected.

"You seem more like Tom than Tom does," she said to Bruce. Instantly, she wished she could retrieve the words. They wouldn't make sense to him. A rush of color warmed her cheeks. "What I mean is, Darcy told me a lot about Tom. I guess I expected a stockbroker to be more like..." Lord. She was only making things worse.

"Like me?" A tight smile thinned Bruce's lips.

"Never mind, I was just..." She drew a deep breath and pasted a bright smile on her lips. "We should probably be going, don't you think? I'm starving!"

When Bruce helped her on with her coat, his warm fingers brushed the nape of her neck and a lightning bolt shot toward Darcy's toes. For a moment she stood as if rooted to the floor trying to recall if any man had ever elicited such an immediate physical response. Helplessly, she decided none had. When she turned her head, she noticed that Bruce wore a strange expression, as if he, too, were struggling with perplexing thoughts.

A few minutes later, she watched Bruce maneuver the seating so that Tom sat in front of the taxi with the driver, and Bruce sat in back with Darcy and Anne. Even through the layers of his topcoat and her coat, she felt the hard heat and the muscles of his thigh pressed against hers.

Lord. When was the last time she had been this physically aware of a man? His heat, his scent, the way he moved and spoke affected her on a level that seemed woven into her very fiber. She responded to Bruce Arden as if every cell were yearning in his direction.

That wasn't all. She felt as if she *knew* this man. She could almost predict what he would say before he said it, would have sworn that she knew his personal philosophy and could foretell how he would respond to events or situations.

Part of this strange feeling was undoubtedly explained by the fact that Bruce was Tom's brother. Naturally there would be strong similarities. But it went beyond that. When she looked at Tom, she felt no sense of knowing him at all, and that was strange because she should have. She could list his favorite foods, places, books and so on. Yet, when she looked at him, she saw a stranger.

"I know this restaurant," she said when the

taxi drew to the curb in front of Destiny House. "I was here two months ago. The food is wonderful!"

Unfortunately the fortune she had received inside her fortune cookie had turned out to be prophetic. Deception brings heartache.

At the time, the warning had seemed meaningless, a disappointment in fact. But now, Darcy stepped out of the taxi and gazed at Bruce and her heart ached exactly as her fortune cookie had predicted. If only she hadn't deceived Tom and gotten herself into this mess.

On the other hand, if she hadn't deceived Tom, she might never have met Bruce. It was all so mixed up and heartbreaking.

Drawing a deep breath of frosty air, Darcy walked toward the door of Destiny House, noticing that Tom had his arm around Anne's waist. A frown of alarm tugged her brow when she saw Anne's starry-eyed expression. This was not a good sign.

Inside the restaurant, Darcy gave both men a weak smile. "If you'll excuse us, we'll just freshen up a bit." She sent Anne a stern glance, then headed toward the ladies' room.

"Don't even say it," Anne warned the minute the door closed behind them. She sat in a chair in the lounge and stared at her toes. "Darcy, I'm sorry. I don't know what's happening to me. It's just that I've never met a man like Tom. I could fall for him like that.'' She snapped her fingers, then gave Darcy a look of misery. "I can't believe I'm falling for my best friend's man. I hate myself!''

Darcy dropped into the chair next to her. A huge sigh collapsed her shoulders. "The thing is, I was crazy about Tom until I met him.'' Bewilderment filled her eyes. "He's just so different from what I expected. So don't hate yourself on my account. It would never have worked between Tom and me.''

"How can you say that? He's the most gorgeous man I ever laid eyes on! And charming, and…he's just wonderful!''

"So is Bruce," Darcy said in a low voice. "Now there's a man. Have you noticed how sexy his eyes are? And his voice!'' A tiny shiver raced down her spine. "He can say 'How are you?' and I feel orgasmic!''

"When Tom looks at me, it's like I'm the only woman in the world.''

"I could talk to Bruce forever. We're on the same wavelength.''

"The problem is, Tom thinks I'm you. I keep worrying that he's going to talk about the postings you two exchange, or want to discuss poker strategy or chess.'' Standing, Anne walked to the mirror and shoved at her hair. "I can't stand it.

I finally met a fabulous man and he thinks I'm someone else.''

"I know the feeling," Darcy said sourly. "I'm sorry I got us into this mess, Anne. And there's only one way out of it."

"I know, I know," Anne said unhappily. "And I'm going to take care of it. Right after dinner."

"WHAT THE HELL are you doing?" Bruce said angrily. He slid into a red leather booth and stared at his brother. "You're supposed to break off the relationship. Instead, you keep stroking her hands and gazing into her eyes!"

"She's the most beautiful woman I've ever met," Tom said, frowning. "She's everything you said she was. Bright, funny, charming. She's wonderful, damn it."

The waiter brought a pot of tea to the table, and set out four cups. Bruce turned one of the cups between his hands. Darcy Connors was even more beautiful than he had imagined she would be. But the depth of personality and the interests that had captivated him in her E-mail postings seemed curiously lacking in person. He didn't understand it. He had expected someone more like, well, more like her friend Anne.

Anne could discuss chess and books, subjects Darcy had yet to mention, to his surprise. Anne had a quick bright mind that darted like quick-silver around topics deeper than fashion and the hot vacation spots. He could talk to her about anything.

And physically, Anne affected him like dynamite. Her small voluptuous figure reminded him of a Rubens painting, lush and full, wrapped in glowing skin. He wanted to touch her and it was an effort not to. An effort not to speculate about her smiling mouth and shapely legs. An effort to recall that it was Darcy whom he'd believed he knew, not Anne, even though he almost felt he could read Anne's mind and anticipate the direction of her thoughts.

Tom stared at him. "What would happen if I just told Darcy that when I visited you in Denver last year I opened an account on America Online, and you continued to use it after I returned to Jersey?"

"Then she'd feel foolish as hell. She thinks she's talking to someone she knows very well, someone to whom she's been talking for a year." Glumly, he poured a cup of tea, looked at it a minute, then pushed it aside. "I should have told her that I was using my brother's account, that my name wasn't Tom. Damn it. But I didn't know we'd develop a relationship. And after a while it was too late. If I'd admitted Tom wasn't my name, she would have wondered if I'd deceived her about other things."

"Did you?"

A flush heated Bruce's throat. "A few minor things. She thinks I love Mexican food. That kind of thing. I can't even explain why I did it. It's just that we had so much in common, I guess I wanted even more."

"You could have straightened this out."

"How? By telling Darcy that I lied about Mexican food? And by the way, my name isn't Tom either, but everything else is the truth? Right. That's certainly a good way to enhance a relationship." He shook his head. "It just...happened."

"We've got a problem here. Years ago we agreed not to poach in each other's territory...but I'm wild about your Darcy." Tom gave him a troubled defensive stare. "I never thought I could fall for a woman who likes chess or who's brighter than I am from what you've said about her. But the truth is, I could fall hard for her. Except she thinks I'm you."

"That's why you've got to stop screwing around and end the relationship tonight. Tom, I mean it. You got away with that line about pretending that you were strangers meeting for the first time, but we've just been lucky that she hasn't sensed something strange is going on."

After a minute of silence, Tom gave him a knowing look. "You don't fool me, little brother. If we were meeting these two women for the first time tonight…it's Anne you'd be wild about, not Darcy. Anne is your type. Short, curvy, energetic, and didn't she say she was a computer whiz of some sort? You like those brainy types."

"You're right," Bruce said reluctantly. "That's what makes this so crazy. I keep thinking I've met Anne before, but I know I haven't." He sighed. "I have a feeling she and I could really have hit it off."

What he felt was that he'd met the woman he'd been waiting for all of his life. In fact, earlier this evening he'd asked if Anne was seeing anyone. For one lunatic moment he'd convinced himself that possibly he could continue seeing her. Then he'd remembered that she thought he'd been married a couple of times, once to a Las Vegas showgirl for God's sake. Darcy had told Anne about Tom's history and she thought it was his.

He couldn't imagine starting an important relationship by having to debunk a string of lies. No, he couldn't continue to see her. He didn't trust his attraction for her anyway. Hadn't he been fantasizing about Darcy mere days ago? Tom was the brother who had chased women most of his life, not Bruce. Now, here he was, no longer interested in Darcy and wishing like hell that he could pursue Anne.

"Living with you is a bad influence," he said with a lopsided grin. "I'll be glad when I find an apartment of my own. What a mess."

"Here they come," Tom said, sliding out of the booth, his eyes on Darcy's flaming red hair and beautiful face.

Bruce followed, looking past Darcy at the springy brown curls that framed Anne's lovely face. "Remember," he said in a low voice. "Break off the relationship! I mean it, Tom. This craziness has to end."

DARCY WATCHED THEM like a hawk. She didn't relax until the entrees were served. Then, since Anne and Tom were still acting cool toward each other, thanks to her talk with Anne in the ladies' room, she let herself focus on Bruce. As she had wanted to do since he walked in her door earlier this evening.

As she warmed her heart by looking at him, it occurred to her that Bruce seemed a little tense tonight, too. But, like her, he had finally begun to relax a bit.

They gazed into each other's eyes and it was like making a connection that discharged a sizzle of electricity. Darcy felt as if she were happily drowning in a warm dark pool. A charge zipped through her nervous system and her legs went weak. She was glad she was sitting down.

"Wow," she said softly. This was the stuff of storybooks. Then they both laughed, releasing some of the tension crackling between them. They laughed for no particular reason, laughed because they were nervous about the powerful sexual chemistry fizzing between them while at the same time feeling as if they had known each other forever. They laughed because nothing made sense, yet it felt as if it did.

"I don't know what caused that," Darcy said, wiping tears of laughter from her eyes. "But it felt good."

Bruce grinned at her. "I don't have a clue what we were laughing about, but you wouldn't believe how much I needed to laugh at something."

Darcy shifted in the booth until they were comfortably facing each other. "Really? That sounds rather ominous. Are you having some kind of problem?"

"Oh yes." He glanced at Tom who had leaned his ear near Anne's lips to hear whatever she was saying. A happy goofy smile curved his lips.

Darcy nodded. "I suppose it's difficult having a houseguest, even when it's your brother. Especially if you're used to living alone. How long will Tom be staying with you? Has he found an apartment yet?''

The one thing she didn't understand about Bruce, Darcy decided, was his occasional blank looks. This one didn't last long, but she noticed and was puzzled.

"Tom's looking for a place, but he's welcome to stay as long as he likes. I enjoy his company." Bruce touched his collar as if it pinched his throat. "Tell me more about your job."

"You're kidding! Computer programming is about as exciting as waiting for bread to toast. I'd rather hear about the wonderful world of TV. What exactly does a TV producer do?"

"Seriously, I'm really interested in computers. I took some classes last year. Nothing as sophisticated as what you do, but it was interesting."

Actually, there were few people who really understood what Darcy did for a living, and she seldom talked shop outside of the office. But Bruce followed what she was saying and asked pertinent questions, made relevant comments. To her delight, his interest appeared genuine and she discovered that he was more knowledgeable than he'd indicated.

She was about to ask his opinion concerning a problem she was having on the Halberson account when Madame Wu appeared and set a plate of fortune cookies on the table. Darcy stared at them as if they were little bombs about to explode.

"Fear of fortune cookies?" Bruce asked, laughing at her expression.

She gave him a sheepish smile. "I wouldn't believe I'd ever say something like this, but those fortunes have a way of coming true. I'll pass, thanks, but you go ahead." She watched him take the cookie Madame Wu indicated for him, break it and withdraw a strip of paper. "I can't stand it. What does it say?"

"The truth shall set you free." He frowned and crumpled the paper in his hand.

Shifting uncomfortably, Darcy turned to look at Anne and Tom, intending to offer them a fortune cookie, too. But they were standing up and moving away from the cherry wood table.

Tom tossed some bills on the table at the same moment that Darcy noticed he and Anne were holding hands. The starry-eyed look had returned to Anne's expression and she seemed to have forgotten Darcy and Bruce. Darcy's heart sank in alarm.

"We're going somewhere for a nightcap," Tom announced, gruffly smiling down at Anne.

"Wait!" Darcy and Bruce said in unison.

Before the word was out of their mouths, Tom and Anne had dashed for the door, holding hands and laughing at each other. In another instant, they vanished through the restaurant door.

Stunned, Darcy fell back in the booth and stared at nothing. Beside her, she heard Bruce mutter something then fall silent.

After a moment she picked up one of the fortune cookies and turned it between her fingers. If she opened it, she knew what the prediction would read: "Anne is not going to dump Tom tonight."

Sighing heavily, she put the cookie back on the plate. The problem was getting worse, not better.

CHAPTER FOUR

BRUCE GLANCED AT the line of taxis waiting at the corner, then frowned down at Darcy. "Do you mind if we walk a bit? I'm wound tighter than a drum."

"Sounds good." Thrusting her hands into her coat pockets, Darcy fell into step beside him, listening to the angry sound of her high heels tapping against the sidewalk. She was furious, anxious and feeling utterly helpless. How could Anne do this? Didn't she realize that she was only making everything worse?

She and Bruce walked along Canal Street in silence, turning at the next corner and then the next until they reached Broadway. "I can't believe they left like that," Darcy blurted. She bit her tongue, but it didn't help. "I just can't believe it!"

"Me, either," Bruce said. He sounded angry, too. "May I speak to you in confidence?" he asked after a moment.

"Please do."

"I'm not sure how to say this." He kicked a

small rock toward the curb. "Despite what you may think, or how it appears, Tom has confided that the relationship between him and Darcy isn't working out as Tom had hoped it would."

"You could have fooled me," Darcy snapped. She sighed. "But, the truth is, Darcy feels the same way. She told me that Tom is very different from the way he seemed on AOL."

Bruce nodded. "Tom said the same thing about Darcy."

"She said she doubted they would see each other again after tonight." They stepped aside to avoid a couple strolling toward them.

"If this question is out of line, I apologize...but, did Darcy ask you to tell me that she doesn't want to continue seeing Tom? Hoping I'd pass along the information?"

"Not exactly... Did Tom ask you to—"

"Not exactly. But I know he's having difficulty finding a tactful way to tell Darcy that it isn't working out."

"Darcy's having the same problem!"

"Really? Then why does she start flirting the instant she sees him?"

"Listen. If you ask me, it's your brother who's the problem! He can't keep his hands off of her!" Even though Darcy didn't want Tom, didn't think she even liked him much, it felt like a betrayal that he appeared so hot for Anne. Sorting it out emotionally was harder every time she saw him.

She and Bruce stared at each other, sparks of anger flashing in their eyes.

Darcy was the first to say what they both were thinking. "Why are you and I fighting about this?"

"Hell, I don't know." Bruce took her arm and they started walking again. "I care about my brother and you care about your friend."

"I don't want to see Darcy get hurt. I know she had high hopes for this relationship, but computer romances just don't pan out. At least that's what I've heard."

"That's what I've been telling Tom." They paused to wait for a streetlight to change color. "Tom wanted the relationship to work, too."

"It's too bad that it didn't," Darcy said with a sigh. She burned with curiosity to ask why Tom was disappointed, wondered what he sensed about Anne that was different from Darcy's AOL postings.

She opened her mouth, then closed it. No, she'd have to be a glutton for punishment to ask why Tom wanted to break off seeing her—Anne. A depressing silence descended. "Maybe they're saying goodbye right now."

"I sure hope so," Bruce said with a fervor that surprised her.

"Me, too!"

Up ahead, on Prince Street, they spotted a lighted sign for a tavern, and Bruce pressed her arm close to his side. "Would you like a nightcap?"

There was nothing Darcy would have liked better than to sit in a cozy dark corner close to Bruce Arden and talk about everything and nothing. But she was no masochist. Earlier in the evening she had recognized that it was torture being with him, wondering about kissing him, knowing their relationship would end when Tom and Anne's did. It could not be otherwise.

Although she wanted to accept his invitation, she recognized that spending more time with him would only make it harder to let him go.

"Actually, I'm tired and think I'd better head for home. Plus, I'm worried about..." she waved a hand and gave him an apologetic look "...everything. I don't think I'd be good company."

He nodded, looking disappointed. "Darcy's lucky to have a good friend like you." Stepping into the street, he waved down a taxi. "I'll take you home."

Automatically, Darcy gave the driver her address. When she realized what she'd done, she turned a stricken look to Bruce. "I'm, uh, staying over with Darcy tonight," she explained hastily. Damn, she hated this. One lie led to another and then to another. Bruce was a nice man. He didn't deserve the lies, but she didn't know what else to do.

He took her hand. "Look, when I said I hoped Tom and Darcy were saying goodbye, I only meant that's what they both want and I hope they're finally getting free of a relationship that isn't working for them." He looked into Darcy's eyes. "I don't want you to think that I haven't enjoyed meeting you or getting to know you."

"Well, you were sort of stuck with me," Darcy said, gazing at his lips. He had wonderful kissable lips. Lips made for husky whispers and daring explorations.

"Stuck with you? Hardly! Meeting you has been wonderful," he said softly. His gaze lingered on her mouth, dropped briefly to her breasts then returned to her eyes.

They sat on the taxi seat, thigh pressed to thigh, slightly facing each other. Bruce's proximity made Darcy's head reel. His eyes seemed almost black in the shadows. When he spoke, warm breath flowed across her lips and a tiny excited shiver raced down her spine, making her body tingle.

"I wish…" she murmured, lost in the intensity of his eyes.

"What do you wish?" he asked hoarsely. Lifting a hand, he trailed a finger down her jawline.

"I wish we could continue seeing each other, but that isn't possible." Her gaze settled on his kissable lips. His teeth were as white as eggshell. The scent of his cologne was driving her wild.

"I wish we could, too," he whispered, tilting her face up to his. "But..."

If he hadn't kissed her then, Darcy would have grabbed him and kissed him. His mouth touched hers and it was like setting a match to dry kindling.

A wild fire raced through her body, made her blood boil to the surface of her skin. A tremble began in her fingertips and shivered toward her toes. Never in her life had Darcy experienced such an explosive or instant reaction to a kiss.

Bruce drew back and stared into her wide eyes. "Anne," he breathed. He hesitated a minute, then pulled her close and kissed her again and again.

Neither of them noticed when the taxi drew up in front of Darcy's apartment house. "Hey, you two. You're steaming up the windows." The driver hooked an arm over the seat and grinned back at them.

They pulled apart and gave each other embarrassed glances. Then they both laughed.

"Wait here," Bruce told the driver. He walked Darcy to the door, glanced at the doorman just inside, then turned her to face his troubled frown.

"Anne…" he smoothed back the curls springing around her face. "This is awkward, but…"

"I know," Darcy said mindlessly, staring at his mouth. Her own lips felt swollen and thoroughly kissed. Her heart was still racing in her chest. She couldn't stand it that they had to say goodbye.

"I'd like to see you again, but I can't." Anger, sadness, something like helplessness flickered in his dark eyes. "I wish I could explain, but I can't do that, either."

Darcy closed her eyes on an expression of hopelessness. How had she gotten into such a mess? "I can't see you again, either," she whispered. She hardly knew this man, yet she felt as if her heart were breaking. Leaning forward, she rested her forehead on his chest. "Oh, Bruce. I don't know you, yet I feel as if I do. I wish I'd met you at a different time and place, in other circumstances."

His arms closed around her, holding her close to his body. "I've really made a mess of things," he murmured.

"Me, too," she said, her voice muffled against the front of his coat. "Kiss me goodbye?" she asked in a tremulous voice, lifting her lips.

"I'd love to," he said gruffly. "But I wish I was kissing you hello."

No, she hadn't imagined it. His kiss left her shaken to her toes. Left her wanting him as she had wanted no man before. For one wild fiery moment, she considered taking him by the hand and pulling him inside. They would hurry to her apartment, shedding clothing the instant they opened the door, and then they would make mad passionate love until they were both sated and exhausted. She had a strong feeling that Bruce would do things to her that no man had ever done before. And she would surrender herself totally as she had never before been able to do.

Trembling, she stepped out of his arms. What on earth was she thinking? When it was all over and they lay naked and damp in each other's arms, what would she say? "Oh, by the way, my name's not Anne. I'm Darcy. Anne and I were playing a little game with you and your brother. I'm sure you understand."

Like hell he would understand. He'd be furious. He'd feel as if she'd been playing him for a fool.

"Goodbye, Bruce." Aching inside, she whispered the words, gazing into his eyes.

"Goodbye, Anne."

Anne. Whirling, she ran into the apartment house before he saw the tears filling her eyes.

WHEN THE PHONE RANG as Darcy was getting dressed for work, she snatched it up on the second ring, hoping it might be Bruce.

"Well, I hope you're happy. I did it," Anne said. She sounded as if she'd been crying. "We broke up."

Darcy sank to the edge of her bed and propped her forehead in her hand. "Good," she said in a dulled voice. "I'm glad it's over."

"We went to the Plaza for a nightcap," Anne said. She began weeping softly. "Afterward, we bought cups of hot chocolate and rode in one of the horse-drawn carriages. It was cold and we snuggled under the lap robe. Oh, Darcy."

"I know." Tom must have forgotten that she didn't like chocolate. Darcy wouldn't have liked riding in a horse-drawn carriage, either. She always felt sorry for the horses.

"Then we walked along Fifth and sat on the steps of the Metropolitan Museum. That's where I told him we couldn't see each other anymore."

"How did he take it?"

Anne fell silent a minute. "It was strange, Darcy. Heartbreaking. Tom agreed to everything I was saying. He told me it wasn't working for him, either. And yet…his eyes said something different." Her voice caught on a sob. "He was only saying those things because he thought it would make it easier for me. I know that's what he was doing!"

"I don't know what to say."

"This could have worked, Darcy. I'm sorry he was your boyfriend first, but it could have worked for Tom and me. We have so much in common. I guess it's because his brother is in TV, but you wouldn't believe how much Tom knows about every aspect of show business and advertising. And he knows the New York area as if he'd lived here for years instead of having only just arrived. We like the same restaurants, laugh at the same things...." Her voice trailed into misery. "I'm just sick about this."

"So am I, Anne. I'm sorry."

"You should be! I don't know when I'll meet another man like Tom. If I ever do. I was really falling for him! And you know what? He was falling for me!" Her voice became defensive. "And not just because he thought I was you. He really liked *me*. I could tell. And we clicked together. Damn it, Darcy, I'm so mad at you!"

"I don't blame you," Darcy said miserably, rubbing her temples.

After Anne hung up, she continued to sit on the side of the bed, feeling awful. Thinking about Tom and Anne, herself and Bruce. She felt sorry for everyone.

In the clear light of day, without Bruce's kisses still sweet on her lips, it occurred to her that she and Bruce had said some strange things to each other. He'd mentioned that he had made a mess of things, which Darcy didn't understand. And she had answered, "Me, too," which wouldn't have made any sense to him. They had been speaking to themselves more than to each other. In the throes of desire, neither had really questioned what the other was saying.

Well, it didn't matter now. She wouldn't see Bruce again.

"It's better that way," she said firmly, wishing she could believe it.

Bruce Arden was absolutely the wrong man for her, she told herself, trying to sound convincing. He'd been married twice, for heaven's sake. Once to a Las Vegas showgirl. Darcy was enough of a gambler to know the risk was high with that kind of guy. The odds for a successful relationship with a man who had two failed marriages behind him were very low. She should have felt glad that she wouldn't be seeing him again.

But she didn't. She felt miserable.

AT MIDMORNING, DARCY telephoned Molly Stevens, a friend she had known almost as long as she had known Anne. She needed to talk to someone and right now she couldn't talk to Anne. "Hi," she said when Molly answered the phone. "How are things in Colorado?"

"I've returned to the old homestead," Molly said, yawning in Darcy's ear and reminding her of the time difference. "The remodeling is going to be more extensive than I first thought. But guess who I hired as the contractor? Joe Townsend. Remember him?"

"Eighth grade. History class. Great looking." Molly laughed in her ear and confirmed her memory. "How are you doing, that's the question?"

Instantly Molly's voice sobered. "I'm angry about Apple Cosmetics firing me as the Apple Girl. I haven't come to terms with it, Darcy. I know the scars show up on film and in the stills. I understand the company's position. But it isn't fair!"

Molly's problems put her own in perspective. After a year of incredible success as the Apple Girl, Molly had suffered a skiing accident that left a couple of small scars on her face which could not be repaired by surgery. Now Molly was trying to come to terms with the end of a successful modeling career, trying to make sense of her life.

They talked awhile about the changes Molly was coping with, then Molly said, "Now tell me about you. I've known you for most of my life, and I know when you're upset."

"Oh, Molly. I've done the stupidest thing."

She talked for twenty minutes, then sighed. "There's no way out of this, is there?"

"Sure there is," Molly said in her crisp, no-nonsense way. "Bite the bullet and confess the truth. Anne's miserable, you're miserable, maybe the two guys are miserable, too. Get everyone together and explain what happened."

"Oh, geez. I just can't," Darcy whispered, pushing pencils around her desk blotter. "It's pride, I know, but I don't want Tom to learn that I lied to him."

"It isn't Tom that you're interested in, so it doesn't matter what he thinks."

"But I care a lot what Bruce thinks. I don't want him to know that I'm a liar, either."

"Darcy, you're not a liar," Molly insisted. "Anyone might have done what you did."

"Maybe. But I doubt that's how Bruce would see it."

"Take my advice. Suck it up and tell the truth."

"Thanks for listening and thanks for the advice. But I'll probably suck it up and *not* tell the truth."

After hanging up, she realized that Molly had pointed out something that was bothering her.

The circle had widened. Protecting her pride meant hurting Anne and Tom. Maybe they really did have a chance at happiness together. Perhaps

Anne was right and Tom had genuinely been falling for her. Maybe he'd only gone along with saying goodbye because he thought that was what Anne wanted.

Frowning, Darcy tapped a pencil on the surface of her desk and gazed out of her midtown office window.

If that's how it was... If two people were missing a chance at something good only because Darcy was too proud to admit that she had fudged the truth...

Anne had been a good friend for fifteen years. And Tom was someone she had cared deeply about.

She owed them both better than this.

"Damn."

Molly was right. She was going to have to tell everyone the truth. It was going to be the most mortifying, the most embarrassing moment in her whole life.

THE FIRST THING SHE DID after arriving home and fixing herself a light supper was switch on her computer and click to American Online. She had mail, but nothing from Tom.

After sighing deeply, something she'd been doing a lot lately, Darcy leaned back in her chair and watched the snow accumulating on the windowsill. Losing Tom had already created a hole in her life. She didn't miss the Tom she had met in person, but she longed for the Tom she used to speak to every evening on AOL. She missed him with an ache that spread through her body.

Eventually her gaze settled on the chessboard and their unfinished game. But she didn't see the pieces. She looked into the future and imagined an endless string of dull lonely evenings.

Tom had been the reason she hurried home after work. She'd been eager to read his postings, eager to share little tidbits that she'd been composing in her mind off and on throughout her day.

Usually when she signed off for the evening, she'd been surprised that it was time to prepare for bed. Reading Tom's posts and drafting her replies made the hours fly by.

Tonight, the hands on the clock seemed to drag, hardly moving at all.

"Come on," she chided herself, watching the snowflakes. "It isn't like Tom is the only man in the world. Somewhere out there is a wonderful man and he's looking for you just like you're looking for him."

This wonderful man would play chess and like to read. He'd enjoy crossword puzzles and an occasional trip to the casinos in Atlantic City. He'd be curious enough to explore the Internet

and try other new things. He would be a man she
could talk to, really talk to about any subject.
And when he gazed into her eyes she would feel
like fireworks were exploding inside.

He'd be a blend between Tom on AOL, and
Bruce in person.

A sigh eased past her lips. It wasn't likely that
she'd ever find such a paragon. Maybe she was
destined to spend her life alone. Maybe there was
no Mr. Right for Darcy Connors. What a depressing thought.

The temptation to sink into a pit of self-pity
was great, but she fought it. That would come
later. First, she had to do the right thing for Anne.
And Tom. She'd been putting it off long enough.

Drawing a breath, she thought a minute then
typed:

To: Tom Arden
From: Darcy Connors
Subject: Need to talk
Dear Tom, You'll probably be surprised to
hear from me after I told you we wouldn't
see each other again.

No, she couldn't tell him the truth in writing.
He deserved a face-to-face confession. As much
as she wanted to, she couldn't be cowardly about
this. She had to take her medicine like an adult.

There's something I have to tell you, and I
need to tell you in person. I know you're
putting in some long hours getting settled in
your new job, so I think we can wait for the
weekend.

It was going to be a very long, very dreadful
week.

Could you meet me at my apartment Saturday night? About seven-thirty?

Darcy

Before she sent the post, she phoned Anne and
told her what she was about to do. "So," she
finished, "can you come over here Saturday
night?"

Anne's voice was teary. "You'd do that for
me? You'd tell him that you lied, and that you
asked me to pretend to be you, and—"

"I'm not promising anything, Anne. Maybe
we're misreading the situation. I guess we'll find
out. But at least I can clear the way so you and
Tom can continue to see each other if that's what
you want to do."

"Oh, Darcy. I've been crying all day. Thank
you for doing this. I know it's going to be hard
but...thank you. I just know Tom didn't want to

break it off! Once he knows the truth, he and I
can—''

Anne's happiness was difficult to listen to.
Darcy was genuinely happy that Anne and Tom
would be able to continue seeing each other. But
part of her experienced a pang of envy. And part
of her mourned for the Tom she had lost. She
had been falling in love with her E-mail Tom, a
man that didn't really exist. The fantasy Tom was
the man she missed so badly.

When it came to real men, men in the flesh, it
was Bruce she regretted. Bruce, who was absolutely wrong for her. Bruce with two ex-wives.
Bruce, who was a TV producer and probably met
fabulous women every day of his life. Bruce,
whose kisses had touched something inside of
her that had never been touched before.

After hanging up from Anne, Darcy leaned
forward and dropped her head in her hands,
blinking rapidly.

She didn't remember ever being this emotionally confused and upset.

IN THE MORNING, before she dressed for work,
she checked her mail on AOL. To her astonish-
ment, she had a posting from Bruce Arden.
Bruce? Bruce was sending a post to her? She'd
half expected a reply from Tom. But...Bruce?
Frowning, she wrapped her terry robe around her

body and opened the post, reminding herself that Bruce would think he was posting to Anne, not her.

To: Darcy Connors
From: Bruce Arden
Subject: Good idea
Dear Darcy, I know this will puzzle you, but we need to talk. Tom and I will meet you at your apartment Saturday night at seven-thirty as you suggested. I'll explain everything then.

Bruce

Frowning, Darcy skimmed the rest of her mail. There was nothing from Tom. Scrolling backward, she read the post from Bruce again. Why on earth would Bruce need to talk to Tom's friend? What did Bruce feel he had to explain?

Her eyes widened suddenly as a stunning suspicion occurred to her.

"No," she said aloud, trying to think it through. "That's too ludicrous. It couldn't be."

Could it?

Surely not.

CHAPTER FIVE

BRUCE ARDEN STARED at his Quotron but he didn't see the information on the screen. What he saw was Anne Clancy's brown curls and sparkling blue-gray eyes. It disturbed him that once he cleared up this god-awful mess, Anne would learn that it was he who had been exchanging intimate postings with her friend Darcy for a year, and that he had arranged the recent deception with Tom. As close as Anne and Darcy were, Darcy would certainly tell Anne that he was a louse.

Anne would remember the kisses in the taxi and conclude that he was disloyal and fickle, a game player and about as sincere as a con artist.

Ignoring the chaotic noise of ringing phones and shouted conversations, he leaned back in his desk chair, frowned and tried to imagine how tomorrow night would turn out. He dreaded it.

Tom was utterly convinced that once Darcy knew the truth she wouldn't care. She would shrug off the truth and want to continue seeing

Tom. But Bruce wasn't as sure of this as his brother was.

He thought it was equally possible that Darcy would be furious. She might understand why he hadn't revealed on-line that his name was Bruce, not Tom, but he doubted she would forgive him for asking Tom to pretend to be the person who had sent the posts.

It certainly appeared that she was attracted to Tom even though she hadn't put up any resistance when Tom said goodbye. But she might feel very differently when she learned that Tom wasn't the person to whom she had poured out her heart. Tom wasn't the brother who shared her interests. And Tom had a couple of ex-wives.

Bruce muttered a curse between his teeth.

When he had caved in to Tom's urging and finally agreed to tell Darcy the truth, he'd had a moment of fantasy that maybe the fortune he'd received in the fortune cookie might come true. The truth would free him to pursue Anne.

This fantasy lasted about three seconds before reality squashed it. He'd deceived Anne, too. He'd let her think that he was a television producer for God's sake. Almost everything she thought she knew about him was wrong.

That is, except the effect she had on him. That was devastating and true. No woman had ever made him feel as alive as Anne Clancy did.

When she smiled, he vibrated inside. When she took his arm, he became a giant among men. She was lovely and smart and funny and interested in every subject under the sun. She sparkled. And there was just a hint of vulnerability about her that made him want to hold her in his arms and protect her.

Actually, Anne was everything he had hoped Darcy would be. But the only thing about Darcy that equaled his expectations was her beauty. He could see why her modeling career was successful.

In person, however, she seemed somewhat wispy and insubstantial. He didn't understand how a personality that had seemed so crisp and well-defined on-line became so amorphous in person. At dinner the other night, Darcy's opinions about books, chess—everything—had seemed vague and indifferent.

It saddened him that after he'd met her, a woman he had adored on-line became a woman he preferred to admire from a distance. And, God, how he missed the person he had believed she was.

He would have liked to tell that person about settling into his new position, about his impressions of the East. He would have enjoyed sharing the small details of his life with the wonderful woman he had known on-line.

Now that he had met Darcy, he suspected the life of a stockbroker would bore her silly. Maybe it always had and she had merely been polite. He didn't know anymore.

"I miss you, Darcy Connors," he said quietly, still staring at his Quotron. He missed Anne Clancy, too. He suspected he would wonder for the rest of his life what might have happened between him and Anne if they had met honestly.

His phone rang and he reached for it automatically then hesitated. He hoped to hell that he handled his new career opportunity better than he'd handled his personal life recently.

He was going to feel both better and worse after tomorrow night's confrontation was behind him.

DARCY'S HANDS trembled as she straightened her apartment, then set out a tray of nibble food that she suspected no one would sample. After glancing at the clock, she ran into her bedroom and changed her sweater for the third time. This time she chose a soft blue cashmere that she hoped would make her look sincere and forgivable.

That was asking a lot from a mere sweater, she decided with a sigh. And her hair wasn't cooperating. Tonight, her curls were especially unruly. Bouncing curls looked too happy for someone as miserable as she felt.

When the doorbell rang, she jumped and dropped the hairbrush. Then she froze, staring at her reflection in the mirror and wishing she'd worn the green sweater. She'd read somewhere that green inspired trust. Well, it was too late now, she'd have to go with sincere.

"It's you," she said, placing a shaking hand over her heart as Anne stepped past her and hung her coat in the hall closet. "I'm a wreck. Can a person die of mortification and embarrassment?"

Anne hugged her. "Thank you so much for doing this."

"There's no way to predict what Tom is going to think. But maybe you shouldn't get your hopes up too high," she said, biting her lower lip. "Men hate it when women play games, and this was a doozy. He might be really ticked when he finds out what we did."

Anne arched an eyebrow. "What who did?"

"Okay, sorry. What *I* did." She wrung her hands together. "The thing is, Anne, this might not turn out the way you want it to. Tom might turn around and walk right out the door."

"I don't think he will," Anne stated confidently. But her hands were trembling, too. "We clicked. I know I didn't imagine that."

"It clicked for you. But Bruce told me that Tom didn't want to continue the relationship. I'm sorry to be blunt, but you need to remember that.

And you yourself said he didn't put up much resistance when you dumped him. I'm sorry, but..."

Anne's face fell. "That's true," she said uncertainly. "Maybe I should have stayed home. In fact, maybe I should leave." Spinning on her high heels, she took a step toward the closet then halted when the doorbell rang.

"Too late," Darcy whispered. "You might as well sit down and eat a cheese puff." Anne suddenly looked as miserable as Darcy felt. "Look. Good luck, I hope this works out the way you want it to. Maybe it will."

She drew a deep breath, flexed her fingers, and squared her shoulders then opened the door. Neither Tom nor Bruce were smiling. "Come in," she said in a voice husky with nerves. "Let me take your coats."

Bruce stared at her with such misery and yearning that Darcy suddenly felt like weeping. "I wish Darcy hadn't asked you to come over," he said in a low voice. "Having you here is going to make it harder to say what I have to say."

"Whatever you have to say is nothing compared to what I have to say." Darcy gave him a longing smile. For one crazy instant she thought about grabbing him and kissing him hard before everything exploded and the Arden brothers stormed out of her apartment.

When she turned around, she stopped short at the sight of Anne and Tom sitting together on the sofa. They were pressed thigh to thigh, holding hands, gazing at each other as if the world had fallen away and left them alone.

If Darcy had harbored any second thoughts about putting herself through this, the sight of Anne and Tom chased them away. Anne was right. She and Tom had found something together that deserved a chance.

Darcy wet her lips. "Does anyone want a drink?" No one did.

Bruce glanced at the chess set then he cleared his throat and touched his tie. He lifted his handsome head and looked at Anne. "Darcy, there's something I have to tell you."

"Wait." Darcy touched his sleeve with shaking fingers. "Whatever you have to say, could it wait a minute?" She gave him a pleading glance. "I have something to say, too. Something I've been rehearsing all week and if I don't say it now, I'm going to have a heart attack." She held out her hands then smoothed them down her sincere blue sweater. "I'm shaking like a leaf."

"I need to tell Darcy—"

"Please, Bruce?"

He hesitated, then sat down in the chair facing the sofa. Darcy stood with her knees against the narrow end of the coffee table, trying to steady her legs. She wished she had a napkin to tear apart and roll into little balls.

"Tom? Could I have your attention, please?" She doubted he would have heard her if Anne hadn't given him a playful poke and made him look at Darcy.

"This is so hard." Hot color flooded her cheeks and the floor seemed to shift beneath her feet. "Okay." She made herself look at Bruce, then she addressed the truth to Tom. "My name is not Anne Clancy. I'm Darcy Connors." Both men frowned, looking back and forth between her and Anne who was anxiously studying Tom's expression. "That's my friend, Anne Clancy. I asked her to impersonate me and she—very reluctantly—agreed.

"I'm the person you've been posting to on AOL," she said to Tom. Even her voice was shaking. "But I lied to you about how I look and what I did for a living."

It wasn't Tom who responded, it was Bruce. "Why?" he asked, leaning forward. He looked incredulous.

She made herself turn from Tom's blank expression and answer Bruce. "Tom is a stockbroker. He leads a glamorous exciting life. I...I wanted to seem glamorous, too. So I..." God, this was hard "So I borrowed Anne's description and part of her life. It was wrong and I regretted it the moment I did it.''

Bruce dropped back in his chair. ''You think being a stockbroker is…glamorous?'' He sounded amazed.

''Well, it is,'' Darcy said defensively. She turned back to Tom who was grinning broadly. The grin was like a slap in the face. She swallowed hard and stumbled on. ''Anyway, when I learned you were moving to the New York area, I didn't know what to do. I didn't want you to know that I'd…that I'd lied. So,'' she tilted her head and blinked at the ceiling, ''so I persuaded Anne to pretend to be me. Since I couldn't tell you the truth, I asked Anne to break off our relationship.''

Tom laughed out loud and Darcy cringed. Whatever she had expected, it hadn't been that he would laugh at her. His idiotic grin made her feel about two inches tall, and it hurt.

''The thing is, you and I just aren't… Well, it would never have worked out for us in person. But Anne really cares about you.'' She drew a long shaky breath. ''Once you get to know her, I think you'll care for her, too. That's why I'm telling you the truth, in the hope that you and Anne will start over.''

''You're Darcy,'' Bruce said in a marveling tone. It made her nervous knowing that he hadn't looked away from her since she'd begun speaking. "I should have guessed."

"I need another minute, then it's your turn," she said, too embarrassed to glance at him. "Tom?" She had to call his name twice before he looked away from Anne. His obvious infatuation with Anne made a mockery of what she wanted to say next, but she said it anyway, more for her sake than his.

"I want you to know that talking to you on AOL was the best part of last year for me." It just killed her that Tom looked as if he couldn't care less what she was saying. "You're a wonderful man," Darcy said between her teeth, wondering if she still believed that. "Your postings made me laugh, made me angry, made me think, tugged my heart.... I want you to know—"

But Tom wasn't listening. Jumping up, he pulled Anne to her feet, holding her loosely in his arms. "Let's get out of here," he said gruffly. Anne was so starry-eyed and happy that she'd forgotten Darcy and Bruce were even present. She nodded and they almost ran to the coat closet. In a moment the door slammed behind them.

Stunned, Darcy stood as if rooted to the carpet. Finally, she walked to the sofa and dropped on the cushions. Tears swam in her eyes. He hadn't even said goodbye to her. She didn't particularly like him anymore, and he was crazy about Anne, that was plain to see, but still... They had talked to each other several times a day for over a year. He should have said *something*.

"I know what you're thinking," Bruce said quietly.

"I don't see how you could." She covered her eyes with a shaking hand. "I wish I could fall through the floor right now. I'm so embarrassed that I asked Anne to pretend to be me. I can't believe I let her do it. I can't believe I lied in the first place." She gave him a damp-eyed look. "There's no reason for you to believe this, but I'm a stickler for the truth. I don't know what came over me."

Suddenly Bruce was on the sofa beside her, taking her hands in his. "I do know what came over you." He was quiet for a long moment, then he straightened his shoulders. "Darcy, it's me whom you've been talking to for a year, not Tom."

"I beg your pardon?" Her eyes widened and she stared at him.

He told her about using Tom's AOL account while Tom was in Denver, told her that after some time elapsed he didn't feel comfortable telling her that his name wasn't Tom, not after he'd been signing his posts that way. "It started because I didn't know if I wanted an AOL account.

I thought I'd use Tom's account, see if I liked AOL, then subscribe in my own name if I did. But by then I'd met you.... I thought if I told you that I'd signed on under someone else's name, you'd figure everything I told you was a lie.''

''Was it?'' she whispered.

His face darkened uncomfortably. ''Well, I don't like Mexican food.''

''Neither do I.''

''Why did you say that you did?''

''Why did *you* say that you did?''

They looked at each other. This was the moment when Darcy should have thrown herself into his arms with joy. Bruce was the man she had been falling in love with, both on-line and in person, not Tom. This was the man that turned her to hot mush inside, the man she couldn't stop thinking about.

But her mind was racing, trying to sort out a confusion of emotions and facts. Bruce had not been married twice—that was Tom. And Tom was the TV producer, not Bruce. Tom's laughter had not been cruel as she had supposed; he'd laughed because the situation struck him as ridiculous and he'd laughed with happiness because he was free to pursue Anne without thinking she was Darcy. He hadn't said goodbye to Darcy because he felt no connection to her; he hadn't read her postings as she had believed. That had been Bruce.

When she gazed into Bruce's dark eyes, she sensed that his mind was spinning, too.

"This is your apartment, not Anne's," he said slowly, looking around. "That's your computer and your chessboard. Your books."

"You asked Tom to impersonate you," Darcy said. "And you took on his persona. You let me think that you'd been married, that you produced TV shows."

"You would have let me meet Anne thinking it was you."

"You did the same thing."

They studied each other warily as Darcy eased her hands out of his grasp. Her thoughts had jumped past the on-line posts to the time they had spent together in person. What was true and what wasn't?

"I...I need to think about all this," she said finally. "I'm kind of mixed up right now...."

"Anne—" He stopped, shook his head. "Darcy." Bruce gazed at her lips then lifted his glance to meet her eyes. "Are we going to get past this?"

"I don't know," she whispered, turning her face away. She didn't want him to see the tears glistening in her eyes. "At least Anne and Tom are happy."

"I guess that's what tonight was about," he said after a lengthy pause. "I'm sorry, Darcy. Right now we're both surprised, and a little angry and embarrassed. I'm wondering what to believe and so are you. Maybe with some time..."

The next sound she heard was his footsteps, then the click of the coat closet. And after that, the final sound of the door closing behind him.

Moving like an automaton, Darcy rose, looked down at the tray of cheese puffs with blind eyes, then she stumbled toward the bedroom and threw herself across the bed in a storm of weeping.

She'd lied; he'd lied. Neither one of them could be sure of anything.

The only thing Darcy knew with any certainty was that she hurt inside. She was proof that hearts could really break.

THIS WAS ONE weekend that Darcy did not want to spend alone in her apartment with nothing but her thoughts for company. So where should she go? And was it nutty to go somewhere at nine o'clock on a Saturday night?

She was standing at the kitchen sink eating the cheese balls and thinking about it when the phone rang.

"Darcy? It's Anne."

"How are things going?" Darcy asked, looking at the clock.

"Wonderful! Fabulous! Listen, I can't talk long, we're in the middle of dinner. I just wanted to say thank you, thank you, thank you! And I want to ask if Bruce is still there."

"No."

"No?" She sounded surprised. "Tom told me that Bruce is crazy about you, and I know you're crazy about him. I thought for sure the two of you would fall on each other once you found out that Bruce was Tom." She laughed. "You know what I mean."

"I'm upset that he deceived me, and he's upset that I deceived him. I don't think we're going to work this out," she said in a dulled voice. "Oh, Anne. I'm as miserable as I've ever been in my life!"

Suddenly she knew where she was going to go.

"Look, maybe if you sleep on it..."

"What I need is a break from all this, a few days of putting my brain on hold and thinking about something besides how rotten I feel."

"You're going to Atlantic City," Anne guessed. They had had similar conversations.

"Lucky at cards, unlucky at love. That's me. I might as well capitalize on the lucky at cards part," Darcy said with a sigh. "I need people and noise right now. I've got a couple of vacation days coming.... Look, go back to your dinner with Tom. I'll call you next week, after I get

home and when I'm feeling halfway civil again.
Anne? I really am glad that it's working out for
you and Tom.''

"Darcy—"

"Don't say anything more or I'll cry." She
swallowed hard. "I...I'll talk to you soon."

She hung up and then, before she could change
her mind, she picked up the phone again and left
a message at work that she wouldn't be in until
Wednesday.

Aching inside, Darcy pulled off her sincere
sweater and put on her lucky shirt and vest. She
already knew she wouldn't sleep tonight. She
might as well go to Atlantic City and play some
video poker. It was better than sitting in bed and
crying.

AS IT TURNED OUT, she was tired enough that after she arrived in Atlantic City she did manage
to sleep for a few hours. In the morning she ordered breakfast and the *New York Times* from
room service, and worked on the puzzle while
she ate. But the puzzle reminded her of Tom. No,
Bruce.

And, she discovered, so did video poker. How
many times had they argued poker strategy over
the past year? A dozen times? A hundred times?

They were so much alike. Right now, Bruce

was undoubtedly struggling over the *Times* puzzle just as she was.

Eyes glistening, she pushed the puzzle away from her, then dressed hurriedly, blinking tears from her eyes. When she was clad in her lucky clothes, she rushed out of her room and downstairs to the casino floor.

The noise hit her like a wave. A person could be lonely in a casino, but not alone. That helped a little.

She found a seat at a bank of video poker machines and fed a twenty-dollar bill into the credit slot. It also helped to have something to think about besides her problems. When she was trying to decide which card to discard, she couldn't think about Bruce or how deeply she missed him. Or what a fabulous kisser he was.

An hour later someone slid into the seat before the poker machine next to her. Darcy sensed he was studying her screen. Because that annoyed her, she didn't look at him lest he interpret her glance as an invitation to chat.

"Don't hold a face card with a pair. That cuts your odds of pulling four of a kind."

Darcy spun on the seat. "Bruce!"

"Anne told me where to find you. Please listen a minute." He placed a finger over her lips when she started to speak. "When I got the promotion in the New York area, I knew we'd meet. I thought you were a model, a person who met great-looking guys every day.'' He gazed into her eyes. ''Tom was the good-looking brother, the one who always knew what to say to women. I couldn't figure how to get around the wrong name problem, so I figured our relationship would end. But I didn't want you to be disappointed when we met. So I asked Tom to pretend to be me. I was wrong, Darcy, and I apologize.''

''Oh, Bruce. You're a great-looking man!''

''You can't imagine how unsettling it was when we met for lunch and then for dinner and I was attracted to you instead of the person I thought I'd been writing to for a year.''

''Oh, yes I can.'' She gazed at him with shining eyes, amazed that he had tracked her down and come to find her.

''I've thought about this and I think I understand what happened. You and I are both about a quart low on confidence. You didn't think you'd be interesting as yourself. I didn't think I'd be attractive as myself.'' His fingers were shaking as badly as hers when he took her hands in his. ''We're so right in so many ways, Darcy. Can we forgive each other and start over? As ourselves?''

Darcy gazed into his warm dark eyes and remembered the postings about his childhood, growing up in the shadow of an older brother.

She remembered telling him how shy and unsure she had been in school. She recalled everything he had written to her. And she remembered the electric thrill of his kisses.

"Hi," she said in a husky voice, her eyes sparkling. "My name is Darcy Connors. I'm an idiot. Would you like to start over anyway?"

He laughed. "My name is Bruce Arden, and I'm an idiot, too. And I'd love to start over with you."

They sat facing each other, knees touching, holding hands and gazing into each other's eyes.

"The thing is," Bruce said slowly, "I don't know where we start. I know everything about you already."

"There's one thing you don't know...." Darcy said in a low voice, her shining gaze dropping to his kissable mouth.

A low groan issued from his throat and his hands tightened around hers. "I have a room upstairs...."

"We could order dinner from room service."

"And breakfast, too."

"You like your eggs sunny-side up."

"And you like yours scrambled."

They stood at the same moment, oblivious to the flashing lights about them, the noise and people. They held hands, their hips touching, teasing. And it was so right. So perfect.

"I feel I know everything about you," Bruce said, "except two things. One we're going to find out as soon as we can get to my room. The other...where do you want to celebrate our fiftieth anniversary?"

"Either in the Greek Islands," Darcy said, laughing into his smiling eyes, "or the same place we're going now." Hurrying, hardly able to keep their hands off each other, they dashed toward the elevators.

Once inside, Bruce caught her in his arms and kissed her passionately. Shaken, they broke apart when another couple stepped inside. Holding hands, they stood close together, grinning into each other's eyes.

"Son of a gun," Darcy murmured softly, melting as his gaze made love to her. "This really is my lucky vest."

Bruce laughed and pulled her into a tight embrace. He knew exactly what she was saying. Now that the deception and heartache were behind them, she suspected they would always understand each other.

When the elevator doors opened, they ran down the corridor, laughing and unbuttoning buttons, eager to explore each other and their future.

Occasionally, Darcy thought as Bruce fumbled with the room key, on-line romances do work out.

Then she was in his arms, returning his passionate kisses. There was nothing virtual about it...this was reality. And it was fabulous.

Author: Darcy Arden
To: ZaraH, LauraLac
Subject: Bliss!

I did it! Bruce and I eloped to
Las Vegas and were married in a
chapel here. (No, an Elvis
impersonator did not officiate).
Laura, will check in with you
later. Gotta run, Bruce is waiting.
Gambling isn't the only thing to do
here...LOL

**A showgirl, a minister—
and an unsolved murder.**

EASY VIRTUE

Eight years ago Mary Margaret's father was
convicted of a violent murder she knew he
didn't commit—and she vowed to clear his
name. With her father serving a life sentence,
Mary Margaret is working as a showgirl in Reno
when Reverend Dane Barrett shows up with
information about her father's case. Working to
expose the real killer, the unlikely pair also
proceed to expose themselves to an unknown
enemy who is intent on keeping the past buried.

**From the bestselling author of
LAST NIGHT IN RIO**

Available in December 1997
at your favorite retail outlet.

The Brightest Stars in Women's Fiction.™

WELCOME TO *Love Inspired* ™

A brand-new series of contemporary inspirational love stories.

Join men and women as they learn valuable lessons about facing the challenges of today's world and about life, love and faith.

Look for:

In Search of Her Own
by Carole Gift Page

Unanswered Prayers
by Penny Richards

Home for the Holidays
by Irene Hannon

Available in retail outlets
in September 1997.

LIFT YOUR SPIRITS AND GLADDEN YOUR HEART with *Love Inspired* ™!

Steeple
Hill™

LI1097

HARLEQUIN AND SILHOUETTE
ARE PLEASED TO PRESENT

Born in the USA

Love, marriage—and the pursuit of family!

Check your retail shelves for these upcoming titles:

July 1997
Last Chance Cafe by Curtiss Ann Matlock
The most determined bachelor in Oklahoma is in trouble! A
lovely widow with three daughters has moved next door—and
the girls want a dad! But he wants to know if their mom needs
a husband....

August 1997
Thorne's Wife by Joan Hohl
Pennsylvania. It was only to be a marriage of convenience—
until they fell in love! Now, three years later, tragedy
threatens to separate them forever and Valerie wants only to
be in the strength of her husband's arms. For she has some
very special news for the expectant father...

September 1997
Desperate Measures by Paula Detmer Riggs
New Mexico judge Amanda Wainwright's daughter has been
kidnapped, and the price of her freedom is a verdict in
favor of a notorious crime boss. So enters ex-FBI agent
Devlin Buchanan—ruthless, unstoppable—and soon there is
no risk he will not take for her.

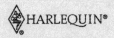 HARLEQUIN®    *Silhouette*®

**Harlequin's newest 12-book series
begins in September 1997!**

DELTA JUSTICE

**A family dynasty of law and order is shattered
by a mysterious crime of passion.**

Romance blossoms as the secrets of the
Delacroix family unfold amidst the drama
of their Louisiana law firm.

The story begins with:

Contract: Paternity
by Jasmine Cresswell
September 1997

Available wherever Harlequin books are sold.

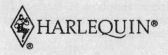

HARLEQUIN®

Coming in August 1997!

THE BETTY NEELS RUBY COLLECTION

August 1997—Stars Through the Mist
September 1997—The Doubtful Marriage
October 1997—The End of the Rainbow
November 1997—Three for a Wedding
December 1997—Roses for Christmas
January 1998—The Hasty Marriage

COLLECTOR'S EDITION

This August start assembling the
Betty Neels Ruby Collection. Six of the
most requested and best-loved titles have
been especially chosen for this collection.
From August 1997 until January 1998,
one title per month will be available to avid
fans. Spot the collection by the lush ruby red
cover with the gold Collector's Edition banner
and your favorite author's name—Betty Neels!

Available in August at your favorite retail outlet.

HARLEQUIN®

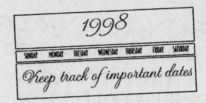

1998

SUNDAY · MONDAY · TUESDAY · WEDNESDAY · THURSDAY · FRIDAY · SATURDAY

Keep track of important dates

Three beautiful and colorful calendars that celebrate some of the most popular trends in America today.

Look for:

Just Babies—a 16 month calendar that features a full year of absolutely adorable babies!

1998 CALENDAR
Just Babies
16 months of adorable bundles of joy!

Hometown Quilts
1998 Calendar
A 16 month quilting extravaganza!

Hometown Quilts—a 16 month calendar featuring quilted art squares, plus a short history on twelve different quilt patterns.

Inspirations—a 16 month calendar with inspiring pictures and quotations.

Inspirations
A 16 month calendar that will lift your spirits and gladden your heart

Steeple Hill™

 HARLEQUIN®

Value priced at $9.99 U.S./$11.99 CAN., these calendars make a perfect gift!

Available in retail outlets in August 1997.　　CAL98

CHRISTMAS MIRACLES

**really can happen, and Christmas
dreams can come true!**

BETTY NEELS,
Carole Mortimer and Rebecca Winters

bring you the magic of Christmas in this wonderful
holiday collection of romantic stories intertwined
with Christmas dreams come true.

Join three of your favorite romance authors as they
celebrate the festive season in their own special style!

Available in November at your favorite retail store.

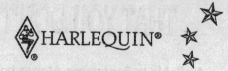

HARLEQUIN®

Look us up on-line at: http://www.romance.net

CMIR